Praise for Rogue Crusader

"With his third novel ROGUE CRUSADER, Qualified Submariner-turned-author John Monteith capstones a stunning literary hat trick of vividly cinematic technothriller suspense! Breathtaking combat and espionage action, across a canvas of continents and under the sea, in the air, and on land. Monteith's visionary tale rings as true as the U.S. Navy SEALs' hit on Osama Bin Laden!"

— **JOE BUFF,** Best-selling author of '*SEAS OF CRISIS*,' and '*TIDAL RIP*'

"Another page-turning thrill-ride from John Monteith. This man owns the submarine warfare genre."

— **JEFF EDWARDS,** Award-winning author of '*SEA OF SHADOWS*,' and '*THE SEVENTH ANGEL*'

Praise for Rogue Betrayer

"After reading John Monteith's extraordinary debut novel, ROGUE AVENGER, I had no idea how he was going to top his own performance. Now I know. ROGUE BETRAYER is a heady mix of suspense, steamy sensuality, and white-hot action. If you're a military thriller fan, or an adrenaline junkie of any stripe, BUY THIS BOOK NOW! You won't be disappointed."

— **JEFF EDWARDS,** Award-winning author of '*SEA OF SHADOWS*,' and '*THE SEVENTH ANGEL*'

"Easy to read, easy to understand, and easy to enjoy (even if you didn't read ROGUE AVENGER), ROGUE BETRAYER is definitely worth picking up, and definitely hard to put down."

— **ROB BALLISTER**, Lead Reviewer, Military Writers Society of America

Praise for Rogue Avenger

"*ROGUE AVENGER is such a stunning action thriller that I devoured it all in one gigantic and delicious bite! John Monteith is a rare talent indeed, with a commanding 'been there, done that' knowledge of high-stakes submarine warfare and brilliantly Byzantine world geopolitics.*"

> — **JOE BUFF,** Bestselling author of '*SEAS OF CRISIS,*' and '*TIDAL RIP*'

"*Former Trident submarine officer John Monteith combines technical and tactical expertise with seedy politics and heart-pumping action to create the hottest naval thriller I've read in years. I can sum up my opinion of ROGUE AVENGER in seven words: I wish I had written this book.*"

> — **JEFF EDWARDS,** Award-winning author of '*SEA OF SHADOWS,*' and '*THE SEVENTH ANGEL*'

"*ROGUE AVENGER is an action-packed narrative by a real sailor, not the arm-chair variety. For those who want to know what life is genuinely like on one of our atomic subs.*"

> — **BILL LINN,** Bestselling author of '*MISSING IN ACTION*'

"*ROGUE AVENGER mixes hard realism with great writing skills. The characterizations and dialog are done with gifted skill. The details about the workings inside a submarine are uncannily accurate and make the plot seem even more real. One can only wonder what the sequel will be like.*"

> — **BILL MCDONALD,** former President of Military Writers Society of America

ROGUE CRUSADER

ROGUE CRUSADER

John R. Monteith

STEALTH BOOKS

Rogue Crusader

Copyright © 2010-2012 by John R. Monteith

All rights reserved. No part of this book may be used or reproduced by any means, graphic, electronic, or mechanical, including photocopying, recording, taping or by any information storage retrieval system without the written permission of the publisher except in the case of brief quotations embodied in critical articles and reviews.

STEALTH BOOKS

THE NEXT GENERATION IN PUBLISHING
COMING IN BELOW THE RADAR...

www.stealthbooks.com

The tactics described in this book do not represent actual U.S. Navy or NATO tactics past or present. Also, many of the code words and some of the equipment have been altered to prevent unauthorized disclosure of classified material.

ISBN-13: 978-0-9850443-0-5

Printed in the United States of America

To Aida

My Chaldean Queen

CHAPTER 1

A bead of sweat dripped from Hana al-Salem's jaw as the sonar display counted down distance to the Israeli submarine overhead.

As the reading inched towards zero, a thud echoed throughout the submersible *Jammal*. Salem cringed.

"Careful!" he said.

Haitham al-Asad, the ex-naval officer seated before him, grabbed joysticks to level the tiny submarine.

"Leveling out," Asad said.

"Did we just announce ourselves to the *Leviathan*?"

"Doubtful," Asad said in a tone that impressed Salem with its calmness. "The rubberized tiles on our hull silence the impact."

Salem tried to straighten his six-foot frame within the control center, but his dark hair brushed the overhead piping. He crouched again over Asad's shoulder and watched the digital display.

"Bazzi reports that we have only thirty minutes of battery energy remaining at this speed," Asad said.

"I know," Salem said. "I heard him."

"Sorry, Hana. I'm nervous."

"I understand, Haitham. Work through your fear."

The display ticked with glacial lethargy while Asad and Mahmoud Latakia, the retired Syrian Navy warrant officer seated beside him, lifted the *Jammal* to the *Leviathan* again. As the sonar reading approached zero meters, Salem looked to monitors showing footage from external cameras. One showed a world eclipsed by the *Leviathan's* keel, and the other showed the dual-arced panels of suction units atop the *Jammal's* twin hull.

"Lower the after camera," he said.

"Right," Asad said.

Salem felt the *Jammal's* ascent stop against the *Leviathan's* underbelly. He held his breath as Asad flipped a trigger guard and pressed a button. Humming echoed from the *Jammal's* overhead superstructure as a pump drained water and created vacuums within the suction couplings.

"We're on, I think," Asad said. "The midsection suction units are holding."

"Up! Drive into them," Salem said. "Just to be sure."

Asad and Latakia exchanged a quick verbal volley and jostled joysticks. As the ship pressed against the *Leviathan*, Asad depressed buttons, and again Salem heard pumps whirring.

"Are we holding?" Salem asked.

"We've already cut back our thrusters," Asad said. "The *Leviathan* is pulling us."

The *Jammal* rocked, and Salem braced himself against one of the hull's circular metal ribs.

"What's wrong?" he asked.

"Nothing," Asad said. "We're rocking with the *Leviathan*. They must have passed into deeper water."

"We didn't rock like this in training."

"We trained on an old submarine that was being towed in calmer waters."

"Is this a problem?" Salem asked.

"There's flexibility—rocker arms—built into the suction panels," Asad said. "We can only trust the design."

Salem looked at a digital speed display.

"Ten knots," he said. "We're attached well enough to be towed faster than our top speed. This is good."

"Latakia is using minimal thrusters and stabilizers," Asad said. "Our battery is good for two hours now."

"Look," Salem said, nodding at analog gauges. "Number three starboard suction unit is losing vacuum. So is number ten port."

Asad leaned to Latakia.

"Line up to pump from starboard midline unit three."

Asad energized the pump. By Salem's left ear, from the *Jammal's* superstructure atop its parallel twin hulls, a whir rose and fell. Pressure in the suction unit dropped.

"Line up to pump from port midline unit ten," Asad said.

Again the pump whirred and ceased, but pressure in the suction unit steadied.

"Poor mating," Asad said. "Perhaps barnacles in the way. We'll let its pressure rise and try again after it equalizes. We don't need all of the suction units. We are well mated with the ones that are working."

Salem felt relief to be a limpet on the Israeli submarine, but doubt started to eat through his mind. Grabbing hold of a submarine was one thing. Breaking into it and taking control of it was another.

*   *   *

Fifteen months before Salem's mission, retired brigadier general Aaron Simon chuckled as he watched the missile leave the rail and begin its fifty mile trip to the White House.

"To the president, with love," he said.

After retiring from the United States Air Force, Simon had become a vice president of product development for Raytheon. With a lifetime of wise investments, Air Force retirement pay, and a severance package from Raytheon, the seventy-three year old multimillionaire found a life of leisure intolerable. To fill the void, he became politically active.

He had spoken out against defense policies, gained support among a small but powerful group of retired flag officers, and became the figurehead of a push to tighten security against air threats on America's coastlines. He demanded automated air batteries at sensitive locations, and an inroad to the Armed Services Committee caused the concept to reach the floor for a vote. But when the bill stalled in Congress, Simon took a stronger approach.

He gathered investors, created a company, and made his own land attack cruise missile. The first prototype traveled ten miles across a friend's ranch in New Mexico, and the second flew fifty. The third prototype had just traced a low-altitude contrail across the Virginia shoreline as Simon walked into the pilot house of his yacht.

He pulled plastic ear muffs over a full head of graying hair and yanked foam plugs out of his ears. He dialed an emergency channel and picked up a radio hand set.

"This is pleasure craft *Lord Simon*," he said. "Come in Coast Guard Station, Washington, over."

"This is Coast Guard Station, Washington. What is your emergency, *Lord Simon*, over."

"Coast Guard Station, Washington, this is the *Lord Simon*. I can't tell you what I just did, because you would warn someone, and that would be cheating. So just trust me that you need to apprehend me. I'll send you my location and wait for one of your crews to board me. Out."

He sat in his captain's chair and watched two monitors. One showed missile telemetry—the other Cable News Network from his satellite television.

Five minutes after launch, the tracking software showed the subsonic missile approaching Washington, DC on a photographic overlay of the city. CNN showed the floor of the New York Stock exchange as a heavy day of trading approached its finale.

Telemetry showed Simon that the missile dipped as it targeted the White House. Simon felt conflicted as his missile flew with flawless accuracy, seconds from mission accomplishment, and as the country he once served was revealing its weakness.

The missile zoomed over the White House, turned south, and continued over the Potomac River. It slowed, dipped, and crashed into the water.

He heard a Coast Guard vessel hailing him with orders to await their arrival. He swiveled his chair and silenced the radio, and when he turned back to the television, he saw breaking news on CNN about an unidentified object landing in the Potomac River.

"At least somebody knows how to react like they mean it," he said to himself. "Too bad it's not the people who count."

Three months after Simon's cruise missile display, the Trigger stood on the bridge of an Iranian supertanker.

Orphaned by the loss of a father to the Iran-Iraq War and by a mother's death during childbirth, the Trigger lived with an aunt who failed to conceal her resentment of having to raise him. Arriving in this world in abandoned isolation disconnected him from humanity. He considered his given name meaningless and called himself "the Trigger" because it described the one thing that soothed his pain of living—destroying things.

Small arms bird hunting grew into a hobby of taking down big horn sheep with game rifles. In his teens, he discovered nitrogen-based chemical mixtures and started blowing things up, including carcasses of his prey. A university education in chemistry and engineering completed his formation into a munitions expert.

The name of "the Trigger" became known within spheres of extremist influence as he orchestrated a series of high-altitude tests of ship-launched ballistic missiles in the Caspian Sea. His last demonstration had placed upgraded Shahab III missiles, variants of the Russian Scud, into low earth orbit.

As he worked on his newest and grandest project, the Trigger stood beside the captain of the supertanker—a mariner he trusted from the Caspian Sea tests. Disliking given names, he addressed his companion by title.

"This disappoints me more than it does you, Captain."

"I am certain of it. Are you sure that General Simon's missile demonstration necessitates this?"

The Trigger kept his gaze on the open tank below, watching the launchers being disassembled under moonlight and soft halogen lighting. Deckhands unfurled a canopy as a crane hook slipped into shadows to retrieve a section of a missile's launcher mounting.

"Yes, we must delay our attack," the Trigger said. "Although I have yet to decide if General Simon is a fool or a genius."

"He created a media circus courtroom trial that a nation of idiots is gobbling up with mindless gluttony," the Captain said.

"You are missing the more important outcome."

"I am aware that his missile demonstration stunt has driven up the value of his armament company. At least the speculation of western newspapers supports this."

"If it's true, it won't last," the Trigger said. "Making one prototype missile that can dive into a river is simple. Design and production of a fleet of missiles for sale in a highly competitive global armament market is an entirely different consideration."

"Then he sounds like a fool to me. Why might you consider him a genius?"

"If his true intent was to shift the American defense strategy, then he has walked a delicate path to success."

"I had suspected American military responses but was unsure. You have access to better sources of information than I do. Excuse me."

The Captain raised a bridge to bridge radio to his mouth and ordered his deckhands to stay the swaying of a swiveling crane. When satisfied the motion had stopped, he lowered the radio.

"You know of the American response to General Simon?"

"Since you will be risking your life in this," the Trigger said, "you deserve to know. They are tightening their coastal air defenses. Anti-air systems of naval vessels in port are on standby, Patriot missile batteries have been deployed, and it is probable that alert aircraft defenses have been expanded. The American sky is all but blanketed with missile defense coverage."

"This creates a difficulty for us, but surely there are gaps we can exploit."

"Indeed there are gaps which they will attempt to fill with warships armed with Aegis defense systems and Standard SM3 missiles designed for this very purpose."

"Where does that leave us in exploiting gaps?" the Captain asked.

"That is uncertain. What is certain, however, is that if we can find an Aegis warship patrolling off the American coast, we have then found a gap in the land and air based defense net, which is an ideal location from which to launch our attack."

"Ideal? I disagree. Aegis warships provide an impregnable defense."

"Not impregnable. Even an Aegis destroyer's missile defenses can be defeated."

"Dubious," the Captain said. "But if true, why wait? If we can somehow slip our missiles past the defenses, why not strike now?"

The Trigger felt a deep stab of sadness. He was unsure what caused the recurring stabs, but they hit when he thought of death. His words passed through a drying throat.

"Because defeating an Aegis destroyer's air defenses requires defeating the destroyer itself."

The Captain snorted.

"How do you plan to defeat the world's mightiest warship?"

"From below and from inside," the Trigger said.

"Inside? A mutineer?"

"Not quite, but just as useful. Better that you know no more about it."

"Fine," the Captain said. "But an attack from below? Our allies have very few submarines at our disposal, and they are constantly watched."

"You are correct. We cannot use the submarine of any ally."

"Then what are you planning?"

"We have allies who are planning to steal an Israeli submarine, and I have united with them in a coordinated purpose. They have already invested two years into their operation. The timing is perfect."

"I had heard rumor," the Captain said. "The purpose is to launch its cruise missiles at Tel Aviv with the appearance of a mutinous self-inflicted wound. An admirable goal."

"The rumor is true, and the launch against Tel Aviv was the purpose," the Trigger said. "It is no longer. The *Dolphin* class submarine *Leviathan* will instead be at our disposal."

"The rumor stated that no government is involved. This hijacking is led by inexperienced people. If it goes awry, we may never have a chance to launch our missiles."

"Nobody is experienced in stealing submarines," the Trigger said. "The task requires capable and intelligent men who can plan, execute, and adapt."

"You would trust a Syrian team?"

"We share a common purpose."

The Trigger felt an awkward and rare sensation that he would later tag as reverence.

"You've met the man who will lead them, haven't you?" the Captain asked.

"Once, outside the university in a planning meeting. He strikes me as insightful and driven. He is noted regionally as a rising leader in economic thought."

"Men of pontification are not men of action. Let him lead a capital ship through high seas before I consider him capable."

"I also doubted him until seeing him talk through a plan of his own design with a conviction and confidence of a man of action. Apparently, he has led underground resistance activities in Damascus for years while maintaining his status as a talented economist. If anyone can steal an Israeli submarine, he can."

"I had considered you the most interesting, although depressing, man I've known. But should this Syrian man and I survive long enough to make each other's acquaintance, I will reassess my opinion."

"Do you care to know his name?"

"I would be impressed if you, the Trigger, who considers given names meaningless, would say it."

"This man's name is worthy of hearing. It is Hana al-Salem."

CHAPTER 2

Thirty minutes after Hana al-Salem had turned the *Jammal* into a limpet on the Israeli submarine, *Leviathan*, Haitham al-Asad and Mahmoud Latakia, the Syrian naval veterans, had redrawn vacuum in half of the suction units. The failing portside aft unit never held, and Salem had given up on it.

"Some of the outer units have caught," Asad said.

"Our upward buoyancy and their rocking pressed them together?" Salem asked.

"Yes, it appears so, at least for a few of them."

"May as well use them. Pump them dry."

As the pump whirred once more, Salem noticed a speed display trickling down from ten knots.

"They're slowing," he said.

"Preparing to dive, perhaps" Asad said. "We're in deep enough water."

Salem felt the deck plates angle downward, and he watched the depth display count downward.

"Apparently so."

He turned and crept aft to a motley team of soldiers, technicians, and linguists who were seated in cramped chairs in the starboard hull of the twin-hull submersible. He saw fear in their eyes. Metallic cracking popped from the ship's metal shell, startling them.

"It's okay," he said. "Submarine hulls do this during depth changes. The *Leviathan's* hull will make the same noise, and they can't tell our hull noise from theirs."

He walked to an older man seated by a panel of gages.

"Almost five hours left on the battery now. Asad and Latakia are doing well conserving energy."

"That's too little time, Bazzi" Salem said. "Get a new reading as we submerge with the *Leviathan*."

*   *   *

Ten minutes later, the *Jammal* hitched a ride underneath the *Leviathan* at eight knots. At one hundred meters, the seas grew calm, and the rocking ceased. The *Jammal* expended no energy except maintaining suction.

"Seven hours now," Bazzi said. "That will take us to nightfall."

"Perhaps," Salem said. "But check our atmosphere."

"Oxygen is low. I assume that toxins are high."

"Bleed in high pressure air from the tanks. I'll get you help pumping our air out with the hand pump."

Salem gestured to a soldier dressed in a wetsuit and sneakers who crept to him.

"This lever pumps air from our compartment into the port side hull," Salem said. "Be careful not to jerk or it will make too much noise. Deliberate and rhythmic. When you're tired, have a colleague relieve you."

Another soldier caught Salem's attention and pointed forward, and he noticed Asad working a joystick. He slinked forward.

"They're turning," Asad said. "We're turning with them to minimize torques on the suction units."

Asad worked the *Jammal's* thrusters through the turn.

"We're holding," Salem said. "It looks like we lost only four or five units."

"Right," Asad said. "But we can probably get them back. And we're steady on course."

Asad twisted and leaned over a paper navigation chart. He ran an eraser over penciled markings and redrew a line representing their new direction of travel.

"This is crude navigation, and our gyroscope is questionable, but it appears they're heading north."

Salem snorted.

"Ironic justice," he said. "I suspect they're beginning a patrol with cruise missiles ready to strike Beirut and Damascus. A deterrent. An insurance policy."

"We'll know soon enough, Hana," Asad said. "When we're on the inside."

Two hours later, Salem sat beside his friend and colleague, Ali Yousif, a professor of electrical engineering at Damascus University. He stretched his legs across the compartment.

"Your idea of incorporating motor generators into our design was a good one," Salem said.

He felt the heavyset engineer's shoulders bump him as he turned and smiled.

"I'm proud of it. Water spinning our thrusters backwards to charge the battery is hardly an efficient system, but it's free energy provided by the *Leviathan*."

"It's buying us an extra hour or two of operations. It could make a difference."

Yousif pointed to a slender man in a wetsuit, a mechanical engineer, who napped despite his body's contortions in the cramped space.

"You'll have to thank him when he awakes. His suction panel design is impressive."

"I'll thank him if his netting idea works," Salem said. "That will be our grandest trick."

An hour later, Salem awoke from dreams of a happy childhood. Stale air reoriented his awareness, and he realized that his neck hurt from sleeping sideways. His mouth had a foul taste of anxiety.

He crept forward to discover that the ex-naval sailors remained vigilant in monitoring and controlling the *Jammal*.

"We're at one hundred fifty meters now," Asad said. "There's no reason for the *Leviathan* to go deeper, but we're ready in case they do."

"Good," Salem said.

"I feel a turn to the left," Asad said.

He jostled his joystick to twist the *Jammal* to the left with its unsuspecting escort.

"Damn," he said. "They're heeling into the turn. We're losing suction units on the starboard side."

After a ninety degree course change, the *Jammal* settled underneath the *Leviathan*. Ten minutes later, the Israeli submarine repeated the maneuver in the other direction, steadying on its original course.

"We lost most of the outer suction units, both sides," Asad said. "The midsection units are holding us, but I don't know for how long. I'm attempting to raise us and reconnect to starboard units."

"My patience is wearing thin," Salem said.

"Me, too," Asad said. "One more turn, and we could fail. We can hasten our plans and attempt the ingress in daylight, but that increases the risk of being found. It's your call, Hana."

Salem's instinct selected action over caution.

"It's a large sea," he said, "and I'll take my chances of not being seen. We'll deploy the netting and accept our fate. Flood the port hull and compensate for ballast. I'll suit up and have Hamdan join me in the lockout chamber."

Closing a watertight door separating him from the *Jammal's* main compartment, Salem moved latches quietly. He sat, and the eldest of his Hamas-trained warriors, a man in his mid-twenties named Adad Hamdan, stared at him with eyes that had seen nothing but misery and disadvantage.

"Two atmospheres?" Hamdan asked.

"Yes, and remember to equalize before we go out."

"I remember the training."

Salem's ears popped and he grabbed his nose and blew. He then reached for the straps to a SCUBA tank that rested in his seat's webbing behind him. He pulled them tight and extended his hands overhead for his mask and mouthpiece.

Sealing the mask over his face, he breathed from the tank. He then let the mouthpiece fall to his chest and lifted the mask atop his head.

"Mine's good," he said.

"Mine, too," Hamdan said. "We're at two atmospheres."

Salem pulled a console to his lap and energized it.

"Who designed this?" Hamdan asked.

"Yousif."

Salem nodded to the bulkhead.

"The sound powered phone," he said.

Hamdan slipped a headset over his ears, lifted a microphone to his mouth, spoke, and nodded.

"Ask Asad to open the port hull's rear door."

Moments later, he heard a clink and creak.

"They'll hear that!" Hamdan said.

"That's acceptable. We want them to think they're running into a fishing net anyway."

The computer console in Salem's lap consumed his attention. He saw the world through the camera of the remotely operated vehicle drifting out the back of the uninhabited port hull of the *Jammal*.

Assisted by two spotlights, the ROV saw nothing in the deep blackness. But Salem knew where to drive it and tapped keys that commanded it upward.

"This will require some luck," he said.

The *Leviathan's* hull came into view, reflecting just enough light for discernment. The ROV hit it and bounced off. Salem drove it upward again.

"There's the rudder," he said. "Damn, I can't get it. We're moving too fast. Aiming for the stern plane…"

He heard the ROV crash against the *Leviathan's* stern plane. He kept maneuvering it, hoping to get it close to the propeller. The last image the ROV sent was a shot of a swishing blade.

"Perhaps we should pray," Hamdan said.

"I already am. Silently."

Salem waited for seconds that seemed an eternity.

Then, the cacophony began. He heard nylon netting abrading the *Jammal's* port hull rear door and thumping and bumping the *Leviathan's* stern.

"What's happening?" Hamdan asked.

"I sent the remote vehicle on a suicide mission with the harness of a trawling net attached to it. If all goes well, my brother, one hundred meters of netting is emptying from our starboard hull and wrapping itself around their propeller."

Hamdan's eyes opened wide.

"And then what? Will they try to shake loose?"

"We're trusting that they're humanitarians," Salem said. "A net may be attached to a trawler that would be pulled under if they drive away. A good submarine commander knows this and will stop and come shallow to evaluate."

Hamdan raised his sound-powered phone to his mouth.

"Thank you, Asad," he said.

"What did he say?" Salem asked.

"He said the *Leviathan* is slowing."

Thirty minutes later, Salem became anxious. The *Leviathan* had drifted to a dead stop, tried to free itself by running its screw in reverse, and had repeated the back and forth effort three times.

"When will they give up?" Hamdan asked.

"At least they've come shallower. We're at one hundred meters, right?"

"Yes. That was Asad's last report."

The world tilted and dumped Salem against the lockout chamber's rear door. Hamdan grabbed piping to steady himself and work the phone.

"Asad say's we're losing suction," he said. "Their maneuvering is too radical."

"Tell him to hold on as long as he can."

"He wants to talk to you."

Salem pushed his facemask behind his neck and slipped Hamdan's phone over his ears. Asad's voice seemed distant and electronic but anxious.

"They're driving up steeply," Asad said. "I'm not sure if we're holding. I've lost most suction readings."

Salem lifted the mouthpiece.

"What's their intent?" he asked.

"Apparently, breaking free of the net is more important than..."

"What's wrong?" Salem asked.

"We're slipping free. Damn! What do we do? We didn't plan for this!" Asad said.

"Steady us. Flood our ballast to control our ascent. And make use of our high-frequency sonar and short range cameras to watch for the *Leviathan*. Trust that the information you need is there."

Asad leveled the *Jammal* at twenty meters.

"We can see just enough light," he said. "We have both cameras, following the *Leviathan's* last course."

"They couldn't have gone far," Salem said into his mouthpiece.

"It depends on how effective our netting seized their screw. I suspect they'll be shallow or surfaced. Either way, we're searching at the right depth."

"How's our battery?"

"Ten percent," Asad said. "It will drop rapidly as we search and chase. We can catch them, but we won't have much battery to stay with them unless we reattach."

"If they're on the surface?" Salem asked.

"To remove the netting? Then we're in good shape and will find them soon."

"Do your best," Salem said.

He lowered the microphone and lowered his head.

"To come this far and fail..."

"Hana?" Hamdan asked.

"Nothing."

"You're afraid of failing?"

"We need divine intervention. Just a little."

Uncertainty caused Salem to feel his fatigue and anxiety. He slumped over in his wetsuit, consumed with rapid-fire thoughts paralyzing his mind until he heard Asad's excited voice.

"*Leviathan*, bearing zero two zero!"

"Get us in front of it," Salem said, reenergized. "Hamdan and I are going to swim out."

"I can put you in front of their conning tower, but we have to hurry," Asad said. "Our battery is nearly gone."

"We'll prepare our gear and leave on your mark."

Salem pulled the mask over his face and pushed the breather into his mouth. Hamdan handed him a sarin nerve agent canister, which he clipped to his belt. Three canisters later, Hamdan handed him a nine millimeter pistol with a silencer and extra ten round clips sealed in a waterproof bag that he slipped into a pouch on his waist.

He also strapped suction cups to his wrists and over the knees of his black wetsuit and clipped twenty feet of elastic cord between his belt and that of Hamdan.

Hamdan equalized air pressure to the depths above the *Leviathan*, and he opened and shut valves letting a calculated amount of seawater into their lockout chamber. Water rose to Salem's chest as he pressed the phone's ear muff to his ear and lifted the mouthpiece.

"We're ready," he said.

"Almost there," Asad said. "They're at periscope depth and dead in the water. We're at five meters."

"That's perfect. Let me know when we're…"

"Go!"

Salem hung the phone on its latch and twisted a valve, and seawater glided up his mask. Hamdan opened an overhead escape hatch and pulled himself into the Mediterranean Sea. Salem followed, stopped, and closed the hatch.

He kicked past the *Jammal's* thrusters and rode the beams of setting sunlight toward the *Leviathan's* bright green tower. The rope between himself and Hamdan slacked as the soldier reached the welded ladder rungs on the submarine's conning tower.

His breathing slowed when he saw Hamdan lock his belt to a rung, and he accompanied the soldier as a limpet on the *Leviathan*. The Israeli submarine remained motionless, testing his patience until he realized that its crew solved a problem for him by waiting until sunset to surface.

Two Hamas soldiers in wetsuits startled him as they landed on the tower's higher rungs. One held a bag of meter-long aluminum bars wrapped in cloth. He withdrew the bars and screwed one into another like a pool cue. He continued until he had a long pole, which Hamdan held from the hull while attaching one of his sarin canisters to a hook on its tip.

Salem checked his SCUBA gear and noted fifteen minutes of air. A final soldier who had passed through the *Jammal's* lockout chamber joined the team with a spare tank on his back, ready to buddy-breathe with those losing air.

The depths turned dark as the sun's rays reflected off the swells and the rising silhouette of the *Leviathan's* snorkel mast caught Salem's eye. He thought he felt the submarine vibrate with the perceptible sound of a diesel engine, but only the ship's gentle rise confirmed that the Israeli vessel was snorkeling and routing air into its ballast tanks to float to the surface.

He pushed off the ladder rungs to the submarine's deck and placed his sneakers on its anti-skid walking surface. Above, the tower rose into the darkening night. Then his head pushed through the surface. To conserve his tank, he turned it off and breathed the humid evening's air. Beside him, Hamdan did the same.

The sky turned indigo as the *Leviathan's* deck rose through the surface of the sea.

"The hatch will open slowly," he said. "When it does, turn your air tank back on, but keep your eyes on the hatch. Remember, you shoot. I drop."

"Yes," Hamdan said as he withdrew the silencer from its watertight bag and screwed it over the barrel of his pistol. Salem attached his silencer but returned his weapon in its pouch.

His world fixated on circular steel. Seconds ticked as lifetimes as he waited. He heard a clunk that stopped his heart, and the hatch cracked an inch.

"Air," he said in a hoarse voice.

He tasted stale air through his mouthpiece and watched the hatch rise. He tore the pin off his sarin canister, and it belched poison. Moving with speed and clarity, he raced to the hatch, knelt to his side, and jammed the canister toward the *Leviathan's* ingress.

The canister caught the hatch's machined metal, and he pushed the hatch up with his free hand. Whiffs of poison subdued the Israeli sailor under the hatch, and Salem wrestled the heavy but free metal upward and pushed the canister inside the submarine.

Hamdan appeared by his side, helped him lift the hatch over its hinges, and disappeared into the *Leviathan*. Looking up, Salem saw the soldier on the conning tower gawking back at him. Salem extended his thumb.

The soldier tore the pin off his canister and lifted it with his aluminum pole to the induction mast intake, and it sucked the poison through the *Leviathan's* diesel engines and pumped it throughout the ship.

Salem slid down the ladder into the *Leviathan* and found himself in the sleeping quarters. Stepping over the canister that spewed toxins, he stopped for a vicarious moment to watch a man on the deck shudder and die.

Tearing open another canister, he ran aft through a door into the control center. Hamdan's first canister had sent sailors toward their shipboard emergency air breathers, but the Hamas soldier stopped each Israeli's attempt to breathe with a silenced bullet. Salem tossed his canister to the deck to exacerbate the horror show of convulsing fatality.

He lifted his pistol toward a sailor clutching his throat near the control panel. His silenced round sent the man to the deck, and Salem darted to the panel.

He was relieved to find that neither mast capable of external communications had reached full extension, suggesting that no messages of a hijacking had been sent. He flipped two switches downward, returning every mast into the *Leviathan* except the induction mast that sucked poison into the ship from above.

The two soldiers who had been guarding the after hatch entered the control center. Salem pointed to a door leading to the technical control center and raised one finger. He then pointed to a ladder heading down into the electronic equipment space. A soldier raced into each chamber.

Sensing his improbable success taking shape, Salem swallowed back bile to keep from vomiting. He clenched his teeth and lips around his mouthpiece and inhaled, but he drew half a breath.

Salem heard Hamden's reloaded weapon chirping behind him as he retraced his steps to the hatch. His lungs burning, he climbed out of the *Leviathan*. He heaved his chest to the deck, spat his mouthpiece, and inhaled the night air. Scrambling from the poisoned submarine's innards, he crawled to the conning tower, gasped lungful after lungful, and then vomited.

The soldier from the conning tower descended to the lowest ladder rung and stepped in front of him. The smug, youthful look of bravado became fear as he stared back.

"Hana?" he asked.

Salem wiped his mouth.

"Half the crew is dead but some may still be resisting. Be swift, shoot straight, and get the spare tank to Hamdan."

"We're succeeding aren't we, Hana?"

Quivering with a pounding heart, Salem knew that sarin nerve agent played no part in his reaction. No training could prepare him for his reaction to mass killing.

"Yes, boy," he said. "We are succeeding all too well."

CHAPTER 3

When the sonar system aboard the USS *Annapolis*, a *Los Angeles* class attack submarine, heard the *Leviathan* run into netting, Commander Brad Flint grinned.

"Better them than us," he said. "Let's get some extra ears listening on sonar for trawlers. I don't want to join the *Leviathan* as the catch of the day."

Flint twisted by the periscope's cylindrical mass. At six feet, three inches tall, he had developed early warning instincts for avoiding protrusions in submarines, especially those that moved.

His executive officer, Alex Baines, a dark skinned African American with a solid, bulky build, had been a cheerleader at the University of Southern California. Flint, a reserved Oklahoman from the U.S. Naval Academy, spoke with a drawl in contrast to Baines' perkiness.

"Two off-watch sonar techs are on their way up, sir" Baines said. "At least now we know what the Israeli fishing net extraction procedure is."

"I would have done the same thing. Running only adds risk of dragging down the trawler that snagged you. I think coming shallow and trying to drive it loose was all they could do, and waiting until sunset was also prudent."

"We should draft a message and tell squadron."

"We'll wait until they're under again to transmit so they don't sniff out our transmission."

"There's no hurry, sir. We'll know soon enough if the *Leviathan* has been defeated by a fishing net."

"Right," Flint said. "Rig the control room for nighttime periscope operations and get our translators into the radio room in case the Israelis broadcast a message."

"Aye, aye, sir," Baines said.

"When your mission is to spy on an Israeli submarine," Flint said in response to the cheerful grin forming on Baines' face, "this is as good as it gets."

* * *

Flint positioned the *Annapolis* within two miles of the *Leviathan*, came shallow, and watched the Israeli submarine with night vision through the periscope.

"It's fuzzy," he said, "but I can make out people topside. It looks like they're grouping towards the stern."

He heard his sonar chief's voice in a loudspeaker.

"Control, Sonar," the chief said, "we heard some strange noises."

"Define strange," Flint said, his eye pressed against the periscope optics.

"Non-mechanical," the chief said. "Human generated, like banging, with possibly raised voices."

"You mean like a pissed off captain howling at his crew to get the net off his ship?"

"Could be, sir."

A silhouette of a man on the *Leviathan's* bow stood and attracted Flint's attention. He wondered if he had missed the sailor on the first scan of the submarine's deck, if he was a *Leviathan* diver returned from inspecting the submarine's netting conundrum, or if the man's sudden appearance was a riddle yet to be solved.

Wearing an Israeli officer's submarine jumpsuit, Hana al-Salem crawled from the sea onto the *Leviathan's* bow. He had sloshed in the water to cleanse traces of sarin from the garments.

Dripping, he felt lethargic as he stood, but he had taken comfort in watching the remainder of his team swim to the *Leviathan* while he waded.

The smallish image of Asad, dressed in a wetsuit, leaned over the hatch. Salem lumbered to him and noticed that his companion seemed in good spirits.

"The technical team is below," Asad said. "Yousif barely fit through the hatch getting out of the *Jammal*, and then we nearly lost him. He lost sight of the *Leviathan* and panicked, but I swam back and calmed him."

"I should have planned for that. Swimming on the surface at night without SCUBA gear—men can become disoriented."

"You planned this well, Hana," Asad said. "There was no room for added SCUBA gear, and shame on the able-bodied man that can't swim thirty meters in calm seas when his life is at stake."

Salem appreciated Asad's enthusiasm.

"Latakia and Bazzi have found cutting tools inside the *Leviathan*," Salem said. "They're already working on freeing us from the netting."

"It will take time to cut ourselves free."

"How's the *Jammal*?" Salem asked.

"I left it at five meters, with cells reversing in its battery. I equalized all starboard compartments, including the lockout chamber, and I left the drain valve open. It's only a matter of time."

"Three years of design and testing," Salem said, "and it ends so quickly."

"It served us well," Asad said. "It was a brilliant design. It should slip quietly to its death."

"*Leviathan* is our home now," Salem said.

"How's the atmosphere?"

"Open canisters are expended, and we've been ventilating clean air for fifteen minutes."

"That should be enough," Asad said.

"Men are breathing freely in the control center. Anyone who goes elsewhere is on forced air."

"What about the Israelis?"

"Our soldiers were skilled," Salem said. "They swept all compartments, and I doubt there are survivors, but be on your guard."

Brad Flint tapped the shoulder of his executive officer, who was crouched into the *Annapolis'* periscope.

"May I?" he asked.

Baines stepped aside, and Flint flipped his wire-rim glasses under his chin. Bending his tall frame, he reached for the periscope's control handles and pressed his eye into the optics.

"They've closed the hatch and secured snorkeling."

"Looks like they'll make it before sunrise," Baines said. "They've been working all night on that netting."

"Yeah. And we've been working all night, too. Stooping over a periscope gets tough after a few hours."

"Can't wait until they submerge again," Baines said.

"And there it is," Flint said. "Ballast tanks are venting. They're heading under. Get a message queued up telling squadron what happened. And get as much audio and video footage to them as the satellite can take."

Salem stood on an elevated conning platform in the aft end of the *Leviathan's* control center. He saw crimson pools and smeared footprints tracing lines the Hamas soldiers had taken dragging corpses to the forward hatch.

Lifting his gaze from the blood, he saw Yousif sitting next to the other three academics in beige leather chairs, facing four pairs of stacked monitors. They were scribbling hand-written notes onto loose leaf paper, translating operations manuals into Arabic.

Those with technical backgrounds made guesses at which information was worth summarizing, playing with the systems to guide them. Yousif turned toward Asad to ask a question, but Salem hushed him.

"We're submerging," he said.

To Salem's right, Asad and Latakia sat at a ship control station, as they had in the *Jammal*. A clunk and whir above Salem startled him.

"That's our induction mast," Asad said. "I control all masts and antennae from here, except the periscopes, which you control with the hydraulic rings around them."

"Here?" Salem asked, wrapping his fingers around the steel tube encircling a silvery cylinder.

"Yes. But first raise the handles. Then give the hydraulic ring a yank to counterclockwise and stand back."

Salem twisted the ring, watched the periscope glide into the well at his feet, and walked to a monitor showing a video image of the world as seen through the periscope. The outside world turned dark.

When he looked over Asad's head, the digital readout read fifteen meters. Latakia wore the earmuffs of a sound powered phone and held a mouth piece to his lips. He exchanged words with Asad that Salem found inaudible but optimistic.

"Bazzi has control of our propulsion," Asad said.

Salem realized his lungs were burning from having been clenched shut during the dive. He exhaled as the digital readout crawled to thirty meters.

"Steady at thirty meters," Asad said. "Speed is four knots."

Sighing, Salem sat in the chair behind him.

"I believe we've accomplished the most ambitious phase of our task," he said.

He reflected upon his deeds, found them unsettling, and chose instead to assess his next moves. A flaw in his plan surfaced to his mind.

"Damn!" he said.

"Yes, Hana? What is it?" Asad asked.

"Food and water. Contamination. I was so preoccupied with winning the ship that I didn't think of it."

"I took care of it," Asad said. "Some dry stores may be wasted, but I verified positive pressure in the cold stores."

"Meaning?"

"The refrigerated food was airtight during your assault. The food is good. There might even be some sealed dry goods. With our small crew, we'll have plenty to eat."

"And water?"

"I pumped the potable water tanks overboard and ran the distilling unit. But it didn't make much. Two hundred liters. We'll need to snorkel again to catch up."

"Now is a good time to drain all standing water and to mark all potentially contaminated food," Salem said.

"A saltwater washing of dry food stores, followed by extensive laundering of linens and clothing and a full ship cleaning," Asad said.

Salem curled forward and rested his head in his hands.

"Hana?" Asad asked.

Salem raised his head.

"Yes?"

"Shall we head west now?"

Standing, Salem felt stiffness in his weary frame, and his mind kicked into gear.

"Not yet," he said. "This submarine was heading toward Lebanon and Syria, and we just spent an evening on the surface. Somebody may be watching, or listening. We need to continue the charade—act like Israelis."

Asad sighed and hunched his shoulders.

"I hadn't thought that far yet," he said. "But clues to their agenda may be in the torpedo room with their weapons load."

"Latakia, can you manage up here?" Salem asked.

The retired warrant officer nodded.

"Follow me below, Asad," Salem said.

Salem found the weapons arrangement to be simpler than he expected. Six racks, three per side, cradled reloads while ten breach doors lined the forward bulkhead. Piping for water, air, and hydraulics ran between the tubes and in unobtrusive recesses that struck Salem with its design elegance.

Asad, short in stature, rolled to the balls of his feet and lifted his nose over the highest rack to inspect weapons. He checked all six.

"I'll need translations of markings to be sure," he said, "but I believe we have two heavyweight torpedoes and four Harpoon anti-ship missiles as reloads."

"Let's see what's loaded," Salem said.

Stacked in five pairs, ten tubes pointed forward. The inner six spanned the common five hundred and thirty three millimeters while the outer stacked pairs were the larger six hundred and fifty millimeter variety.

Asad grabbed a flashlight from a bulkhead frame and opened breach doors one by one. After inspecting all ten tubes, the loaded weapon tally included four heavyweight torpedoes, two Harpoon anti-ship missiles, and, in the larger tubes, four Popeye land attack cruise missiles.

"I'll need translations to verify," Asad said. "But I think we can assume that the outer tubes hold land attack cruise missiles. The inner tubes hold a basic anti-shipping load out."

"How far are we from launch range of Damascus?"

"If these are indeed Popeyes," Asad said. "Then we may already be in range. We're not launching anything, are we?"

The concept intrigued Salem. An Israeli submarine conducting an unprovoked launch of cruise missiles on his homeland could create positive outcomes, but the endgame variables were too unpredictable and the immediate lives lost too great, he determined.

"No, but we can familiarize ourselves with the system and continue the charade of behaving like an Israeli submarine. We'll get the team down here to…"

"Look!" Asad said.

He slid his thin frame between breach doors and reload racks and reached for a rectangular block of equipment that was perched under a red and yellow radiation symbol.

"It's heavy," he said as he snapped it from a cradle.

"What is it?"

"I believe it's a radiation monitoring device."

"Nuclear weapons," Salem said. "The cruise missiles?"

"Yousif has a lot of instruction manuals to pour through. We'd better get him down here."

Flint woke from a brief nap and felt freshened, but he knew that he'd need deeper sleep to recharge.

"Captain," a sailor said after opening the door to his stateroom. "The executive officer says the *Leviathan* just opened an outer door."

"On my way," Flint said.

He wiggled his arm into his jumpsuit as he climbed to the control room. Baines sat in front of a sonar monitor.

"Thought you'd want to see this, sir," Baines said.

"We're recording?"

"They surprised us with the opening of the door, but we're recording now. If this is a launch exercise, they'll probably open more."

Minutes later, the *Annapolis'* sonar system recorded the *Leviathan* opening the outer door to a second torpedo tube. Then it recorded the closing of both.

"What do you think, XO? Did the Israelis just conduct a cruise missile launch rehearsal?"

"Yes, sir. Damascus, Beirut, or maybe one missile each. Not very effective if you have alerted air defenses, but a big deal if you don't know the missile's coming. This can count as a deterrent patrol for the Israelis."

"This is an important discovery," Flint said. "Let's draft a message and get to periscope depth."

"Aye, aye, sir. You may want to add that they're done, and off to their next big thing, too."

"What?"

"They just sped up and turned."

Flint studied the frequency data of the *Leviathan's* propeller blades.

"Okay, XO, hold on. Let's figure out their new course. They may just be repositioning for another exercise volley."

Thirty minutes of tracking the *Leviathan* led to a new discovery.

"Holy cow, XO," Flint said. "They're heading almost due west."

"Not repositioning for another exercise volley," Baines said. "They're pushing into new territory for Israeli patrols."

"Okay, we know what direction they're going," Flint said. "Let's go shallow and share the news with squadron."

CHAPTER 4

Jake Slate scratched his beard as a CIA intern who appeared too eager to impress led him down a hallway into the organization's headquarters building in Langley, Virginia.

The intern stopped at a door with a keypad that he made no attempt to decipher. He knocked.

The door opened, and Jake saw a thin smile spread across the fair skinned face of CIA officer, Olivia McDonald. A dark suit muted her athletic curves, but Jake noticed that office policy permitted her straightened auburn hair to caress to her collar.

"Thank you, Mister Johnson. I'll escort Mister Jones from here," she said.

The intern mumbled something nervous and nearly tripped as he excused himself. Unsure of protocol, Jake awaited Olivia's guidance. She extended her hand.

"Olivia McDonald," she said.

Jake recalled the name he would forever use on American soil as he shook hands with the woman who had seduced him years earlier.

"Jacob Jones," he said. "Pleased to meet you."

She led him into a room that smelled stale and reflected bright, sterile lighting. As Olivia closed the door with a click, Jake glanced at absorbent, egg carton foam-like walls.

"This reminds me of the rooms we had in the navy for reading special…"

Olivia appeared in his face, and he felt her lips against his. Tasting of mint, her warm tongue probed his mouth, and her deceptively strong arms drew him in.

"Hi," she said as she stepped back and released an honest smile. "I missed you."

"I missed you, too," he said.

"These soundproofed rooms are secure. You can tell the truth about anything, as long as doors are closed and everyone in the room is cleared for it."

"I realized that when you just tried to swallow me."

"It's been four months," she said. "I'm just excited. I mean, this is your first time back on American soil, and you must be excited to see your brothers, too."

"It's all a lot to deal with. I wasn't exactly tight with those screwballs, you know."

"I know. I just thought it would be nice to give you back a piece of your life."

Jake shrugged. He had been struggling for an identity since he was a naval officer derailed by foul play during a blood transfusion. Unstable and lost, he still carried the anger from the malicious HIV infection and its ensuing cover up, the anger that had compelled him to steal a Trident missile submarine.

Eking out a transatlantic relationship with the CIA officer who had operated against him before befriending him felt awkward. To invigorate him, Olivia earned permission for him to return to America, provided he followed basic identity concealing protocols.

After months of growth, his bushy hair touched his collar, and his beard grew thick. He wore contact lenses that changed his blue eyes to brown, and he had already purchased a new, thinner nose before meeting Olivia.

"I appreciate the effort," he said. "You've been great, and I love you as much as I always have. You just have to give me time to adapt to being home—if that's where I am. Plus I want to get this reunion with the chumps done before we focus on us."

"Sure. Follow me."

She led him through another door into an equally sterile but larger room. Behind a desk sat two men. The first wore a leather jacket and sunglasses and appeared dehydrated, irritated, and hung over. His features were smooth but pronounced—less rugged than Jake's—and his skin was olive.

"Holy shit," he said.

"Joe?" Jake asked. "It's good to see you're alive."

"Really? You care?" Joe Slate asked.

The second man looked older, thinner, and wiser than Joe Slate. He wore loose fitting garments of hemp.

"We all care about each other," he said.

Jake snorted.

"Shit, Nick," he said. "You're always the peacemaker. I'll never get you, but at least I know you mean well."

"What the fuck's that supposed to mean?" Joe asked, pushing his chair back as he stood.

"It means you've never done a damned thing for this family except suck up mom's attention and energy from the day you were born until the day she died," Jake said.

"Fuck you," Joe said. "I'm out of here."

The youngest Slate passed through a door on the room's far end and slammed it shut with a sound-isolated thump.

"We'll give him a chance to cool off," Olivia said.

"Shit," Jake said. "I don't know what it is about him, but he always sets me off."

"He's grateful," Nick said. "He's grateful that you're alive. He just doesn't know how to show it."

"Crap, Nick. Come give your little brother a hug."

Jake walked around the table and embraced the eldest of the three Slate boys. Nick felt lithe but strong.

"You've hardly changed," Jake said.

"Older and wiser," Nick said. "I didn't recognize you with the hair and beard. And you've beefed up."

"Being rich leaves a lot of time for working out."

"I always knew you were alive. I didn't believe that you scuttled the *Colorado*. They made you out to be a dead hero, but I never felt your death."

"Well, okay. Thanks, I guess."

"The truth is far more impressive," Nick said. "Olivia explained it to Joe and me an hour ago, and it's still sinking in. But I think I understand why you stole your submarine. It makes sense with your pain. You thought you had no other choice."

"I don't know, Nick."

"And then to risk your life on another submarine to stop a nuclear attack against an aircraft carrier—you saved tens if not hundreds of thousands of lives. You are a hero. It's too bad that so few will ever know."

"She told you everything?"

"Even the part where you stopped to repay your debt to Taiwan by facing Chinese submarines."

"Well, I try not to think about it."

"But you have to. These are life events. Perhaps now that I know the truth I can help you talk through it."

Jake's innards curdled.

"No, thanks, Nick."

"Whenever you're ready."

Jake felt Nick clasp his palms over his hand as he bowed his head.

"He does this weird stuff sometimes."

Olivia shrugged.

"Quiet, please," Nick said.

After several moments, Nick raised his gaze.

"You're still in danger," he said.

"What?" Jake asked.

"I sense danger. I'm sorry."

Jake yanked his hand back.

"That's a shitty way to greet your brother."

"These feelings are never one hundred percent."

"I hope not."

"There is something good I sense, though."

"Oh?" Jake asked.

"I believe that you and Olivia are going to have a great time on vacation—wherever she's taking you."

During an elevator ride to a hotel penthouse, Jake reflected that he had never enjoyed his freedom. He lived as a free man in the south of France with minimal probation oversight, and returning to America exposed a void of identity. Remaining anonymous and officially dead was part of the equation of enjoying America, and he trusted Olivia to teach him. He had let her select Charlotte as a vacation destination since he had never been there and had little chance of being recognized. The intelligence agency that once hunted him now offered him his best protection of anonymity with an alias, a fake passport, and an escort in the form of an officer-turned-girlfriend.

After receiving a windfall in payment from his role in stealing the Trident missile submarine, USS *Colorado*, Jake patronized Europe's finest luxury hotels. But this was the first American five star room he expected to enjoy. He entered a suite of the Westin Charlotte Hotel and, behind him, Olivia tipped the porter.

He leapt onto the plush king sized bed's satin sheets.

"It feels good to be in an American room," he said.

She joined him on the bed and kissed his neck.

"You seem tense," she said. "I brought you here to relax. Plenty of people are living in secrecy like this. I've studied tons of cases and even seen a few. It will take getting used to, but everything will be fine."

"Sure," Jake said. "Let's tear this city up."

"Tear me up first," she said.

Jake embraced her.

*   *   *

After showering away the scent of sex, Jake realized that the lovemaking seemed mechanical and distant as he followed Olivia to the street. A chill from the sidewalk lifted spring's early warmth into the night. Olivia strolled ahead, the belt of her thigh-length black leather jacket slapping her jeans. She bowed her head, cinched her strap, and stopped.

"You okay?" Jake asked.

"Just concerned."

"About what?"

"You. Us," she said.

"Right."

"We knew this wasn't going to be easy."

"Well, we didn't exactly find each other as perfect matches on a dating site," he said. "Can you imagine? HIV positive fugitive seeks HIV positive CIA seductress and rape victim for deception, fleeing countries, teargas parties, and combat deployments on submarines."

She grinned.

"Maybe I'm just being paranoid," she said.

"That's your job."

"I don't know, Jake. Your disguise is perfect. Nobody on earth who knew you back then would recognize you, and I'm not even a field operative anymore. But ever since your brother said you were heading into danger, I've had the chills."

Jake sighed.

"You mean a feeling like we shouldn't be together."

They walked in silence to a pizza parlor. Feeling at home in America, Jake ate thick, dripping pizza washed down with a midgrade macro-brew while overhearing conversations in slight southern-style English. He wanted to enjoy the surroundings, but trying to drift incognito in the mainstream highlighted the widening rift between himself and any sense of normalcy.

It also opened the distance he felt with Olivia. Unable to talk about their lives in public, their conversation centered on current events, which were like goings on in an alternative reality.

Back at the hotel, Jake tossed in bed. Jetlag released him to sleep at two in the morning, and the sun was tracing a rhomboid across the floor when he awoke. He glanced at the night stand and scanned a scribbled note from Olivia telling him to take his time prior to joining her at Starbucks.

Jake's mind buzzed with the excitation of being back in America, and he placed his bare feet on the carpet to orient himself. He debated lifting weights before showering when a feeble knock and inquisitive voice startled him.

"Housekeeping," a woman said.

"Just one second," he said.

Wearing boxers and a tee-shirt, Jake slid into his crumpled jeans.

"Okay, come on in."

A woman wearing a black uniform dress entered, and at first glance Jake thought she was Hispanic. Her curves were voluptuous and pronounced, and he imagined that her hair, tied in a bun, would reach shoulder length if freed. Her dark, swarthy skin suggested a woman in her late twenties, and she caught him staring at her.

"Where are you from?" he asked.

"I can come back," she said.

Jake discerned no accent.

"I've visited many places and have met people from different cultures, but there's something special about you," he said.

She stood motionless.

"I'm sorry," he said. "I've been traveling a lot. I just woke up, and I didn't expect to have a beautiful and exotic looking woman walk into my room. Well, exotic to me. I'm sure you're quite used to yourself by now."

She smiled.

"I'm Iraqi American, second generation."

"Wow," he said. "That's the coolest thing I've ever heard—and now that's the dumbest thing I've ever said."

"No," she said. "Awkward, but not dumb. Not rude either. But I need to get to work or come back later."

"Yeah, sorry. I'll just keep my comments to myself and clean up. You can clean while I shower, right?"

"No," she said. "I'm afraid that's against policy."

"Dang. It's just that you seem like the most interesting person I've met in a while, and I've met a lot. First instincts at least."

"I get that from a lot of male guests."

"No, I'm not hitting on you. Well, maybe silly flirting a bit, but I'm here with my girlfriend."

"That's good," she said. "Because you'd be doing a horrible job if you were."

He squinted at her name tag.

"I'm sorry to slow you down, Linda. I should let you get back on schedule. Hopefully I'll be cleaner and more eloquent next time we meet."

"Well, if you don't mind, can I be honest?"

"Of course," he said. "I've been forward enough."

"My weekend job is a hairstylist. I've got to tell you, your mountain man thing is a disaster. You'd be much better looking with a clean cut."

"Maybe I should find you on the weekend."

"I'm not allowed to solicit business on company time."

"I'm asking."

"I have a card," she said. "Oh no, wait. Shoot. My twelve year old took lunch money out of my wallet and forgot to give it back."

"Wait, what?" Jake asked. "You don't look old enough to have a twelve year old."

"I had him when I was seventeen. I've got three more. I'd show you pictures, but they're in the wallet."

His cell phone rang.

"Crap," he said. "That's Olivia."

"I should go," she said.

He reached for her hand.

"I'm Jake. Jake Jones, and it's a pleasure meeting you, Linda."

"Linda Hindy," she said.

Her smile would protect anyone from harm, Jake thought, and the fear his brother had placed in his heart vanished for the moment. Linda closed the door on her way out, and Jake lifted the cell phone to his ear on its final ring.

"Did I wake you sleepyhead?" Olivia asked.

"Yeah," he said. "Well, kind of. I was awake but hardly up to speed with the world yet."

"You going to join me sometime today?"

"Sure. And I'm really looking forward to that heart to heart talk about 'us'."

CHAPTER 5

Six months prior to taking the *Leviathan*, Hana al-Salem had passed through customs on an academic visa at Dulles International Airport and continued to Norfolk, Virginia.

He carried a duffel bag on his shoulder as he swam in a sea of native Virginians, college students, and military personnel towards ground transportation.

Summer had been drawing to an end and Salem shivered while zipping a windbreaker. Spying an attractive woman in her mid-thirties with swarthy skin on the sidewalk, he matched her face and physique against memorized images of the Iranian accomplice he sought.

"Professor Ghaffari?" he asked in English.

"You must be Professor Salem," Farah Ghaffari said, her voice hoarse from cigarettes and alcohol.

"Yes," he said.

She extended her hand. He hesitated, reminded himself to follow local customs, and grasped her soft fingers.

"Call me Farah," she said.

Her pupils dilated as she slid the cigarette between her lips, and Salem suppressed the lust her aura invoked. She slinked like a cat toward the parking lot.

Harlot, Salem thought as he caught up to her.

"You're here because you don't trust women," she said. "Or is it that you don't trust Persians? Or Sunnis? Or any label, accurate or not, that you wish to place on me."

"With the responsibility that I bear, I trust no one. It's a wise precaution that someone verifies your work."

"Once you've verified it, you still won't trust me, except for having no choice. So why torment yourself?

"I could delay the operation," he said. "There is no hurry."

"Delay for what purpose?" she asked. "So that I may seduce another sailor? I've already spent a year sifting through these men. There is no doubt that I have found our best opportunity. Or would you ask another woman to take my place and try again? I think not."

Ghaffari reached for the door of a red convertible mustang. Salem stopped short.

"I will judge that for myself," he said.

"I have ensnared the commanding officer of the *Bainbridge*," she said. "I'm certain you'll be impressed."

"Perhaps," he said.

"What's wrong? You're sprouting roots in the concrete. Is it that you don't want to be driven in a racy vehicle by a sexy woman?"

"I think you've taken your American liberation too far. It's commendable that you overcame a difficult upbringing to educate yourself, but transforming yourself into a well-polished whore is degrading."

He reminded himself to stop insulting her, recognizing that he needed her.

"I like an honest man," she said.

She lobbed the keys at his chest and slid over the hood. A shrewd look displaced her sultriness.

"Don't think about it," she said. "I don't give a damn about your opinion, and you'll overanalyze it like every other left-brained economist. Just drive my fucking car."

Unwilling to yell above the wind whipping over the convertible, Salem said little on the fifteen-minute drive west on Norview Avenue and I-64 West toward Ghaffari's apartment near Old Dominion University.

After turning into her complex, Salem heard the wind subside.

"Turn left," she said. "It's the next street."

Salem nodded and drove the Mustang westward.

"You thought about it during the entire trip, didn't you?" she asked. "About how you feel about me. You couldn't help but analyze it. You have so much conflict within you that you try to think your way out of."

"Conflict is unavoidable," he said.

"For a man like you it is. You have your beliefs as a Muslim, as an Arab, and as an economist. That combination alone is difficult. Add to that the handicap of a penis, and I wonder how you don't go mad."

Dim lights cast weak shadows into parking lots surrounded by a mini-forest of transplanted firs. Stopping in front of a three-bedroom unit, he asked about the sleeping arrangements.

"You need not worry," she said. "The university pays me well, and the apartment is large. You will have the entire ground floor to yourself."

"We should discuss tomorrow's agenda."

"You're tired," she said. "You should rest."

"Honestly, I am exhausted. The flights were long and uncomfortable. Perhaps you are correct. I don't need fatigue skewing my judgment."

"You look hungry, too," she said. "I'll order a pizza while you settle in."

Salem dropped his duffel bag on his bed and inhaled his stench. He needed a shower. Popping his head through the doorway, he caught Ghaffari talking on a cell phone and staring at him with eyes that seemed sensual. Even with her mind elsewhere, she reminded him of a succubus.

"Mushrooms and pepperoni?" she asked.

"Towels."

"No, on your pizza."

"I don't care. Towels?"

"I've laid everything out in your bathroom."

Salem closed the door and enjoyed the privacy. He worked the knobs and waited for steam to rise. As he slipped under the water, he felt the grime of transcontinental flight wash away.

He reflected upon the western pleasures he noticed in Ghaffari's life. A large screen television, a sports car, reliable utilities, and decadent food delivered on a whim. With their lives being so easy, he understood how Americans could become ignorant about the plight of the human condition. He liked the thought of remedying that.

After donning clean slacks and a dress shirt, he combed back his dark hair and slid through the door. Ghaffari was staring at him while chewing a piece of pizza, and her gaze captivated him.

"Don't worry," she said after swallowing. "Yes, you are a gorgeous man, but I won't seduce you. From what little I understand about your mission, you have no time to be distracted by thinking that you're falling in love with me."

"Your seductive skills have become too automatic. Fortunately, one of us has self control."

He ducked into his bedroom and draped his dirty clothes over a chair. When he returned to the living room, she was pouring a two-liter bottle of cola into a glass.

"That shows what you know," she said.

"Excuse me?"

"I can help myself from tempting a man. I only do so for my agendas. What I might enjoy, actually, would be a man tempting me with his mind."

"That wouldn't happen tonight, even if I had the energy or interest."

"Unfortunately," she said as she stared at her half-eaten pizza, "no man ever does."

*   *   *

Salem awoke feeling refreshed but numb. Glancing at his watch, he noticed it was late morning. He put on his clothes and walked into the room where Ghaffari sipped coffee while reading a newspaper.

"Good morning," she said.

"You should have woken me."

"You needed rest. There's coffee in the kitchen."

Salem didn't move. She looked up at him.

"Never mind," she said. "I'll get it for you."

"I didn't mean…"

"Don't," she said as she stood. "I'm just being a good hostess. You can crack a stick over my head later for having gone outdoors without a male escort."

He gestured to protest but bit his tongue as she turned the corner. When she returned with his coffee, she preempted his retort.

"I'm sorry," she said. "I still carry old wounds. Your reputation and publications prove that you're a better man than those who destroyed my childhood."

"I'm trying to understand you."

"It's not important that you do," she said. "But then again, I imagine you need to understand everything. It's the curse of a critical mind."

"You're quite the psychologist," he said.

She sat, and he joined her at the table. His coffee tasted weak, and he squinted at the cup.

"American coffee is an acquired taste," she said. "We'll have some stronger brew at lunch."

"Have you confirmed our meeting with your fiancé?"

"Yes," she said. "I called him while you were asleep. We'll be meeting him for lunch."

He let her drive the Mustang and grew concerned as she maneuvered it past a sign for Naval Station Norfolk.

"We're meeting him at a restaurant near the base?"

"Of course not," she said. "I'm his fiancée. When I dine with his majesty, it's in the captain's mess."

"Captain's mess?" he asked.

"His personal dining room adjacent to his quarters on the ship. It's a pompous concept that fits his personality perfectly."

Salem cringed.

"You didn't mention we'd be visiting the ship."

"I assure you," she said, "it's completely safe. He summons me aboard for lunch every day and whines if I tell him I have to give a lecture. It's become ritualistic."

"And me? A Syrian national? I can just waltz aboard the *Bainbridge* at my whim?"

"You're the personal guest of the captain and a colleague of his fiancée. You're also a noted economist guest lecturing at a local university. You assured me you'd pass any background check."

"It's not the background check that bothers me."

"Then what is it?" she asked.

"I refuse to set foot on the ship."

He braced himself against the console as she whipped the Mustang to the side of the road. His chest chafed under the taut seatbelt.

"You're paying me to manipulate a man on an American destroyer, and any idiot could deduce that there's violence in your agenda. If you lack the spine to visit the ship and look its crew in the eyes, then you'd be better off going home."

Her words stung, and he decided at that moment that he would demonstrate the courage necessary to take the *Leviathan* to its final destiny.

"Drive," he said.

The USS *Bainbridge* appeared unimposing in its simple elegance. The muted grays and soft edges that enabled visual and radar camouflage subdued the ship's profile, but the metallic world of the *Burke* class destroyer swelled as Salem crossed its brow, approached its cliff-like bulkhead, and craned his neck to the bridge.

His heart raced as a sailor in a dress blue uniform snapped a salute.

"What do I do?" Salem asked.

"Nothing," Ghaffari said. "Just wait."

Seconds later, a young, slim man in a blue-gray digitized camouflage work uniform stepped through a door.

"Good afternoon, Doctor Ghaffari," he said.

"Hello, Ralph," she said. "This is my cousin, Doctor Hana Salem, Professor of Economics at Damascus University."

"Lieutenant Ralph Dotsen," he said. "Pleased to meet you, sir."

Salem shook hands with a man he expected to kill.

"Likewise," he said, forcing a smile.

"Please, follow me. The captain is waiting for you."

Salem hoped to meet few sailors, but each corner he turned or ladder he climbed produced a new face, no older than twenty-five years. Each young man smiled and stepped aside, treating him, Ghaffari, and their officer escort like honored guests.

Two flights up, a teenager with a rich skin tone and dark Mediterranean hair reminded Salem of his sister's oldest son. As the youngster pushed his back to the bulkhead to allow passage, the crate of lettuce he carried shifted and revealed his nametag—Barakat—the surname of his second cousin's husband.

Wondering how many family tree levels separated him from the sailor, he swallowed and labored up the next ladder. As he approached the highest decks, the lieutenant knocked on a door. It opened, and a mess specialist stepped aside.

"Your guests are here, sir," Lieutenant Dotsen said.

"Very well," Commander Richard Pastor said.

Salem followed Ghaffari into the room. A man of average stature wearing silver oak leafs on the lapels of his camouflage uniform sat behind a small dining table. Ghaffari moved to him and shifted into a subservient persona.

"Kiss me," Pastor said.

She leaned over and obeyed.

"This must be your cousin," he said.

Pastor pushed his chair back and stood, awaiting Salem to approach. Salem walked to him and extended his hand.

"Welcome to my ship," Pastor said.

As he looked into the eyes of arrogance in the captain of the *Bainbridge*, Salem regained confidence that destroying him would be acceptable collateral damage.

"I am Doctor Hana Salem," he said. "Your ship is impressive."

"Indeed it is," Pastor said.

Ghaffari sat to the captain's left, and Pastor spent most of the first course doting over his fiancée while making every effort of gesture and tone to appear masculine. But Salem could see that he was a lonely, insecure man for whom Ghaffari played puppet master.

Salem nibbled his three bean salad and admired the ease with which she transformed the commander of a warship into a child.

She smiled, tilted her head, and said something inaudible. Pastor nodded, touched her shoulder, and turned to Salem. His carriage reverted from child to top dog.

"So, what is it exactly that you're a doctor of?"

"Economics."

Pastor's brow furrowed and his nostrils flared.

"This downturn," Pastor said, "will be enduring."

"That's a strong possibility," Salem said, "at least for Japan, America, and Western Europe, but there are signs of growth in other regions."

Pastor's face furrowed deeper, disliking the argument, the challenge to his authority, or both, Salem thought.

"So, you're Farah's cousin," Pastor said. "Tell me about that."

"We're not blood related," Salem said. "My mother's sister and her father's brother—their son and daughter, respectively, married a few years ago. Farah and I met at the wedding and grew close ever since. There aren't that many post-doctoral professionals in the family, and it was a natural bond for us."

He feared that Pastor would probe for details of the fictitious wedding, but the captain proved self-absorbed.

"Weddings sure are nice," he said. "We'll be married soon after I get back from my next major deployment."

The mess specialist cleared salad plates and returned with plates of lamb chops, mashed potatoes, and broccoli.

"Where are you taking me for our honeymoon?" Ghaffari asked, appearing sheepish.

"Hmmm… Antigua," he said. "Now that's a good place for a honeymoon."

"Oh," Ghaffari said. "I hear it's unclean."

Pastor glared at her. Salem disliked his demeanor but watched Ghaffari work her head tilting and childlike tone.

"Does it matter where we go, as long as we're together?" she asked.

"Yes," he said and snorted. "This is my second marriage, and I'd like to start it off right. I don't know how many chances I'll get."

"What if we went somewhere else in the Caribbean that we both like? You can reconsider for me, can't you? What about the Bahamas or the Virgin Islands?"

"Don't get your hopes up," he said, as his face softened, "but for you, maybe I'll consider it."

In the Mustang, Salem felt uncertain.

"That man is an arrogant idiot," he said. "Do they really entrust him with command?"

"He expects to give orders and be obeyed. It's a side-effect of military culture."

"I don't like it. Can you manipulate a man who believes he is the apex of humanity?"

"Weren't you watching? As long as he thinks he's in control, I am. He can't resist the urge to indulge me and feel magnanimous about it. This is trivial. He'll deliver what we need when we need it."

"Why does he want to marry you?" he asked.

"A careerist naval officer needs a wife."

"Does it matter that you're Persian?"

"I asked him, of course, playing the dutiful would-be wife concerned about her husband's career. He said it was advantageous because it showed tolerance and cultural breadth, neither of which he's known for."

"I'm not surprised," he said.

"Or it could be that no American woman tolerates him. You're lucky that I do."

"It's only temporary."

"That's correct, and no matter what, I have no intention of marrying that jackass. So whatever you're doing, it had better be decisive."

Salem lectured that afternoon at Old Dominion University about economic trends in several of the countries known in the western world as the Middle East.

With a knack for simplifying the complex and infusing the right words with emotion for a given audience, he enthralled an auditorium full of students. For the hour, several faculty members also shared his passion for the subject. One female Persian psychology professor caught his eye as paying deep, earnest, attention from the front row.

During the post-discourse networking, he received the usual pandering and sympathizing that his guest lecturing often earned, but nobody asked the hard questions about how to improve the global macro-economy.

Ghaffari, who had given him space with the students and other faculty members, joined the circle around him.

"I believe Professor Salem has had a long day," she said. "Perhaps we can let him return to his hotel."

The sun cast long shadows in front of the Mustang.

"Hotel?" he asked. "I could have stayed in a hotel?"

"No, you came here to assess me," she said. "You can't do that from across town. I mentioned the hotel for appearances."

They said nothing for the rest of the drive. When they arrived in her apartment, she dropped her purse on a table and turned to him.

"Perhaps for dinner tonight we can do better than pizza," she said.

"You were impressed with me during my lecture."

"Yes, I was. Your mind is sharp. Whatever your master plan is, I'm sure it is inspiring."

Her pupils widened as she stared into his eyes. He grabbed her and kissed her deeply. Then he carried her upstairs to her bedroom and ravaged her.

CHAPTER 6

Commander Brad Flint scratched his head.

"What's that, Sonar?" he asked.

The voice of his sonar room supervisor belched from a loudspeaker overhead.

"We lost the *Leviathan* again. Can we get a thousand yards closer?"

"That's pushing counter-detection range," Flint said. "Why'd we lose them?"

"It's just a quiet ship," sir. "It's a bitch to hear."

"Let's be patient and keep an eye out. If they drive fast we'll hear them. If they don't we'll pick them up again soon. We always do."

Aboard the *Leviathan*, Salem realized he hadn't slept in a day and a half. Static and fuzz filled his head as he ducked through a hatch into the propulsion spaces and saw pock marks on a reddened scalp.

"How are you, Bazzi," he asked.

The retired Syrian naval submarine mechanic, seated before battery indications, looked up with concern.

"The distillate unit is consuming battery power. I'm calculating how long we have until we need to snorkel."

"How long?"

"If we move at six knots, then at best twenty hours."

"We're moving at four knots," Salem said. "For safety, since we hardly understand the portions of this ship that we've managed to turn on."

"Can we move that slowly?"

"There's no hurry. The Iranian tanker isn't due through the Suez Canal for another three days, and it will overtake us whenever it overtakes us."

"The slower the better," Bazzi said. "But if you ever go fast, remember to ask me what's leaking, smoking, and shaking at the end of the run. I don't trust a ship until it's proven itself at speed and depth."

*   *   *

Salem worked his way to the control center, disheartened to see smeared blood and lingering corpses during his walk.

Asad and Latakia slouched over the ship's controls while the four academic experts reminded him of mannequins in various stages of sleep and daydreaming. The four soldiers were absent.

"Gentlemen!" Salem said.

The mannequins stirred.

"We've reached the point where rest is both deserved and necessary," Salem said.

"We can staff three people throughout the ship and let the others rest," Asad said, "as long as we're doing little more than drifting."

"Then that's what we'll do," Salem said. "Who do you need awake?"

"Myself, Bazzi, and one man roaming between us."

"Then I will be the roaming man."

The rotund professor of electrical engineering stood.

"Hana, no," Yousif said. "You're exhausted."

"As we all are."

"I managed a couple hours of sleep on the *Jammal*," Yousif said. "Let me walk the spaces while you sleep."

"Then who will relieve Asad and Bazzi?"

"Latakia will manage the control center while I sleep," Asad said. "Yousif, I'm afraid you're the most qualified to understand the propulsion spaces in Bazzi's place. You should sleep now and let one of our soldiers march the open spaces."

"Where are they?" Salem asked.

"Probably sleeping," Asad said. "They were in the crews berthing last I knew."

Salem drifted in a haze of fatigue to the crew's berthing area. The compartment was dark except for a reading light in one bunk. Hearing a man snoring, he thought that his Hamas-trained operatives had demonstrated wisdom beyond their youth by resting at first chance.

The curtain in the illuminated top bunk slid open, revealing that at least one man remained awake. He moved to it and saw Hamdan holding a Qur'an.

"You're a warrior like the Prophet," Hamdan said.

"There is none exactly like him."

"But there are many who honor him through action," Hamdan said. "As you have and must continue to do."

"He was a unifying leader in a fragmented, agrarian society," Salem said. "Comparison between the Prophet and men of today and is difficult."

Hamdan closed his holy book.

"I was warned you overanalyze things."

"Thought is what drives us."

"I disagree," Hamdan said. "Passion drives us."

"Okay then. What passion drives you? What drove you to Hamas?"

"Purpose," he said. "I sold meats—beef and lamb—on the Euphrates riverfront in Ar Raqqah, and I ran my business profitably. But to what end? To start a family and seek a life of comfort, hoping and waiting for others to shape the world for me?"

"I doubt that would ever be your fate."

"I knew that younger men," Hamdan said while nodding at the other bunks, "would need men to lead them. I felt the calling, and I have been rewarded by being selected to join you."

"You look tired, Hamdan."

The soldier slid the book in a cubby hole by his head.

"I'm stronger than my fatigue."

"I appreciate that," Salem said. "But you have systems and processes to learn. A fresh mind will be necessary."

"Then you want me to sleep?"

"Soon. I first want you to walk the ship for a three-hour duty session. We're going to take turns watching the ship and sleeping."

"I'm ready for duty," he said.

"Thank you."

"And what of you, Professor Salem?" Hamdan asked. "You gave up a life of education and privilege."

"Privilege? Hardly. I consider education to be every man's birthright, and I have found that the academic field is intriguing and rewarding."

Hamdan slid his bunk curtain aside and slid his feet out of the bunk.

"But I will share with you," Salem said, "that I found leaving my life easy. I lost my wife and son to a drunk driver—a fat, wealthy, lazy waste of humanity that had inherited his life of leisure and sloth. He was drunk on American whiskey driving a western-made luxury automobile. I intend to inspire people to cast away the sense of entitlement that allowed that wretched waste of human flesh to take my life from me."

"I'm sorry."

"Don't be," Salem said. "It's not your fault. I blame the state of the world. And that's what I intend to fix."

Six hours later, Salem awoke, alone in the captain's stateroom. He urinated and watched his toilet drain dry after flushing it.

He slipped into the jumpsuit of the deceased Israeli commanding officer, climbed to the control center, and saw its lone occupant, Asad, pacing.

Haitham al-Asad had transferred from a tour as executive officer on an ex-Russian Osa II missile craft to Russian-sponsored submarine training in preparation for Syria's purchase of *Amir* submarines. A generous sum of money to his relatives and to the Syrian Navy had purchased his discharge and his loyalty to the mission taking place aboard the *Leviathan*.

Unsure of Asad's abilities, Salem trusted his instincts that Asad would prove competent in submarine operations and tactics. His instincts seemed on target.

"Did you sleep?" Salem asked.

"A few hours. And you?"

"Enough, but there's a problem with my toilet. I flushed it and it didn't refill."

"There's probably a problem with flowing water."

"How so?"

"Based upon what you just said, there is none."

"But we can make more, right?" Salem asked.

"In theory, we can do anything we want," Asad said. "In reality, we have too few people and too much to learn. It took four of us to start the distillate unit the first time, and we did it with all diesels running on the surface. I expect a surprise or two when trying it at snorkel depth."

Salem stepped to the conning platform and sat.

"Then we put all our effort into it," he said.

"Oh yes? And what about starting a diesel at snorkel depth? We have yet to attempt that trick."

"The ship was built for that to be routine."

"It may all become routine in a short time," Asad said. "But we have contaminated food to discard, bodies to stow, blood to wipe, sealed dry stores to clean, and—as you just enlightened me—drinking water to make."

"One thing at a time," Salem said. "First we snorkel. Is Bazzi ready?"

"Yes. We're as ready as we can be," the ex-naval officer said. "Everyone is awake and has at least three hours of sleep. Hopefully, we are an alert crew."

"Good."

"We checked the ventilation lineup to the diesel, but I'll feel better once I see it working."

"Go to six knots and twenty meters," Salem said.

"Yes, Hana, but you have to raise the periscope. It's best that you look through the optics instead of the monitor. There's better focus."

Salem twisted the metal hydraulic ring clockwise, heard hydraulic valves clunk overhead, and watched the silvery tube rise. He pressed his eye to the optics but his field of view remained dark.

"I don't see anything through the periscope," he said.

"That's because we're too shallow," Asad said. "I'll take us up to fifteen meters."

The blackness on Salem's monitor turned gray.

"I still don't see anything," he said.

Asad jumped from his control station and gazed at the monitor showing a video of the periscope's view.

"Damn. We didn't darken the control center to prepare your eyes for the night," he said as he returned to the control station.

Salem withdrew his eye from the optics and became disoriented as the control center's lighting inundated his dilating pupil. Then the room turned dark, backlight by panels and red ground lighting.

"You'll need fifteen minutes to get used to the darkness," Asad said. "Thirty to be completely comfortable. But there's no harm in looking now and seeing what you can see. I'll raise the snorkel mast."

Groping for the handles, Salem palpated their rubber grips with his fingertips to orient himself in the dark.

"Snorkel mast is up," Asad said.

"Are we going to run the diesel?" Salem asked as he reconnected his eye socket to the optics.

"Bazzi just started it. Listen, behind you, to the air flow through the mast."

"So we're charging the battery?"

"Yes," Asad said. "And starting the distillate unit."

"All on one diesel?"

"He just started a second."

"The ship is well engineered and practically automatic, don't you think?"

"So far," Asad said.

Salem swiveled the periscope optics in a lazy circle around the *Leviathan* while his eye grew sensitive to the moonlit, starry night.

An alarm whined.

"What is it?" Salem asked.

"I'm not sure," Asad said. "Help!"

One of the linguists darted to Asad's side from his seat at the tactical displays. Asad, Latakia, and their translator held a rapid conversation.

"Hydrogen level in the after battery compartment," Asad said. "Bazzi has a similar alarm and has asked Yousif to look in the compartment."

"Look for what?" Salem asked. "Hydrogen atoms?"

"Local gages, ventilation levers…"

"This is a danger, right?"

"Yes."

A second hydrogen alarm whined. Salem reached for a cubby that held emergency air breathing masks and pulled one out.

"Should we be wearing these?" he asked.

"I don't know. I think not. It's more of an explosive hazard than anything, I believe."

"This is a crisis. Think clearly," Salem said.

"Bazzi doesn't know what the alarms mean for propulsion space levels. He's quite concerned."

Darkness enshrouded the room except for emergency lighting and panels. New alarms howled in protest.

"Obviously," Salem said.

"Bazzi just shut down our AC power," Asad said. "He believes the gas is an explosive risk."

"Can't we use just the forward battery compartment for power?" Salem asked.

"The cells are in series. If you take half of them out, you have half voltage and can't run anything."

"This is a deepening concern."

"I'll have Latakia head back to help him," Asad said.

"Right. Is there anything we should do up here?"

"Keep the ship at depth. Perhaps you should keep looking out of the periscope to make sure no ships are coming to run over us."

Salem kept himself occupied by tracing circles around the conning platform. The world on the surface of the Mediterranean Sea was quiet. He pulled his face from the eyepiece and glanced at Asad, who wore the earmuffs of a sound powered phone set.

"Nothing new to report?" he asked.

"They still suspect that they forgot to position the louvers and valves for ventilating the battery room, but they haven't yet figured out the right positions."

"Does it really take this long?"

"With emergency lighting, piecemeal translations of whatever manuals we've found, and valves hidden in recesses, nooks, and corners, yes."

Salem returned his eye to the periscope optics and recommenced his circular dance around the conning platform. The sea was desolate.

Then, something caught his eye.

"Asad?"

"What is it, Hana?"

"Take a look," Salem said while backing away from the periscope. "It looks too bright to be a star."

"That's a starboard running light! And above, mast head lights. What's our magnification?"

"I don't know," Salem said.

"Then we don't know how close it is. We're going back down to avoid collision. Latakia, take us down."

Asad darted to the ship's control station.

"We have no propulsion," he said. "Bazzi cut the engines from the battery. No pumps to draw in water."

"Get us down!" Salem said.

"We still have momentum and hydraulic power to drive down," Asad said. "I'm opening valves to flood tanks."

Numbers on the depth meter indicated that the *Leviathan* slid below the approaching surface vessel.

Asad's backlit silhouette appeared before him.

"We need to ventilate the ship," he said.

"I know," Salem said. "But it appears that doing so without being struck by traffic is a challenge."

"We can't use the diesels," Asad said. "The explosive risk is too great."

"Then how?"

"There's a low pressure blower for pushing air out of the ballast tanks. But I'm unsure if we can route the exhaust elsewhere. If we don't, we'll end up surfacing."

"Is there a problem with running electronic machinery because of the hydrogen?" Salem asked.

"There will be a risk. The less strain we place on the battery, the better."

"Is there no other way to ventilate the ship?"

"Fans," Asad said. "But we must be surfaced to use them. They aren't strong enough to push air out against the backpressure of seawater."

Salem pinched his forehead.

"Work with Bazzi, come up with a plan, and get it right," he said. "Head back there and return when you're confident we can at least ventilate the battery cells."

*   *   *

Asad returned with a plastic-laminated diagram in his hand. In the red lighting, Salem glanced at its dark spaghetti-like traces.

"Hana, we believe we've solved the battery compartment air flow issue. Here, I'll show you."

"Have you decided if the blower or fan is better?"

"No, not yet."

"But either will work, right?" Salem asked. "And either way, we must surface?"

"Yes, Hana."

"When we reach the surface, you'll remember to have the men grab the contaminated dry stores and throw them overboard. We may as well make use of this time surfaced."

"Are you sure we want people topside?"

"No," Salem said. "You'll have men pass the stores up through the hatch with the last man tossing them down the side. And make sure the stores are cut open so they sink."

"A wise choice."

Salem thought through risks and consequences of having the *Leviathan* attract attention through noise, detectable visual presence on the water's surface, and time spent in its compromised status.

"Are we ready to ventilate?" he asked.

"Just awaiting Bazzi's recommendation on the best option between the blower and the fans. It's a tradeoff between noise, ventilation rates, strain on the battery, how we choose to surface…"

"I'll make this easy," Salem said.

He walked to the control station and pinched two knobs between his index fingers and thumbs. He extended them and rotated them upward, surprised by their ease of motion.

High pressure air hissed, echoed, and knocked open valves that enabled a dissonance of air shrieking through pipes. Pulling Salem's stomach to the deck plates, the *Leviathan* shot to the surface, bobbed, and rocked.

"Decision made," Salem said. "Use the fans."

Commander Flint listened to the voice from his sonar room over the loudspeaker and raised his eyebrow.

"You're kidding," he said.

"No sir, they're no shit on the surface again. They did an emergency blow, and we didn't hear a damned thing to suggest why they did it."

Baines, the executive officer, stepped into the control room.

"The *Leviathan* blew to the surface, sir?"

"We lost them but then regained them while they were snorkeling. Then they quit snorkeling abruptly, went deep, and then about fifteen minutes later, they blew."

"That's bizarre, sir."

"Based on our best solution, they weren't really close enough to that freighter we were tracking to warrant an emergency deep maneuver, but then again, they had no business trying to snorkel that close to it."

"You think they screwed up, did an emergency deep, and maybe had to blow to the surface because the induction mast head valve stuck open, or something unlucky like that?"

"Maybe, XO. The Israelis and this crew especially are supposed to be darn good, but they ain't acting like it. If I had red flashing lights, I'd pull them over to the curb and take their submarining license."

Baines chuckled.

"Nice, sir, but seriously. We're watching some of the worst submarine behavior I've seen."

"It's time to draft a message," Flint said.

"Another situation report?"

"Yes, but with a little added flair. Add that I urge our brass to put pressure on the Israelis to tell us a bit about what this patrol is about."

"Sounds good to me sir. But if the Israelis know that we're tracking the *Leviathan*, they'll tell the *Leviathan* the next time it pops up an antenna, and then the fun's over."

"That's not for us to decide," Flint said. "When a skilled submarine crew takes their submarine into new waters and starts making a bunch of rookie mistakes, you have to wonder what's going on inside the hull—and wonder who's calling the shots."

CHAPTER 7

Hours earlier, after the limousine had picked him up and driven him through the coffee plantation, past armed guards, and by checkpoints to the villa, Jake Slate had thought that the sprawling estate reflected his old friend Grant Mercer less than it stank of black market money.

Fiddling with an Internet terminal in the sitting room was losing its allure. As he folded a hand of online Texas Hold'em, Jake wondered if he were waiting for an old wealthy friend or if he had been duped into visiting the lair of a dangerous stranger.

He scratched a cheek turned hypersensitive from a fresh shave while he watched his mentor, Pierre Renard, lower a copy of <u>The Economist</u> and wave a gold plated Zippo lighter under a Marlboro. Gray wisps rolled over the Frenchman's sharp features.

"What's that now?" Jake asked. "Half a pack? I thought you were trying to quit."

"The rules are different in Chile," Renard said. "When in Rome, do as the Romans, you know."

"You must have loved it in Taiwan," Jake said.

"The freedom to smoke, yes. The waiting, no, although your friend is challenging my patience as badly as did the Taiwanese Defense Minister. I had expected him to give higher priority to old colleagues."

"That's why I'm getting nervous," Jake said. "Maybe someone stumbled into our chat room and was pretending to be Mercer when he invited us here."

"Unlikely. My experts evaluated your online security scheme," Renard said. "The only way it was breached is if someone coerced data out of him, in which case Mercer is already dead."

"That's what I'm afraid of."

Renard picked up his magazine.

"Don't be," he said. "I can smell a negotiation from across the ocean. Mercer is in this very building wondering what I intend to propose. I can sense his anticipation through the walls."

"But if you're wrong," Jake said, "we've just walked into trap."

"Two hours ago you were as giddy as a school girl with hopes of reuniting with him," Renard said. "And now you would let a delay frighten you away?"

"Maybe."

Renard flicked ashes into a tray.

"You can blame me for the delay," he said. "Mercer never trusted me except when he had no choice. He will only accept my proposal if he believes that your trust in me is absolute, which is why he's likely observing us through that camera to judge how we interact."

His patience worn, Jake walked to Renard.

"Stand up," he said.

"Why?"

"Just humor me."

"Very well," Renard said. "If you insist."

Jake felt the Frenchman's body tense as he snatched him into a one-armed hug.

"Jake, you know I loathe this."

"Shut up and turn to the camera."

Jake twisted Renard's squirming torso, pressed his lips against his cheek, and waved to the camera. He then lowered his hand, patted the Frenchman's silvery hair, and released him.

"That was uncalled for," Renard said while tugging at the lapels of his blazer.

"Got the message across," Jake said.

Five minutes later a door opened, and a Chilean man with high cheekbones dressed in a pinstriped suit swept his arm into the next room.

"Senior Martinez will see you now."

"Martinez," Renard said in Jake's ear. "Mercer trusted me enough to keep the alias I gave him four years ago. That is encouraging."

Jake passed the door attendant and entered a chamber that could have been a drug lord's lair.

A flat screen television stretched over a cherry wood wall between a marble vase and the edge of a well-stocked wet bar. Leather stools formed a walkway through potted evergreens between what Jake assumed to be a door to Mercer's private kitchen and a Jacuzzi in the center of the room. Brass rails led from the water towards a recreation area replete with a pool table, dart board, and a two-lane bowling alley.

"If we accomplish nothing else on this trip," Renard said, "your friend can at least let us borrow his interior designer. This is exquisite."

"Senior Martinez is in the office at the room's far end," the door attendant said. "Follow me."

Jake followed the attendant over a teakwood catwalk that encircled the room. He traced his fingers over the brass banister bordering the sunken Jacuzzi as he decided that the room's recreational flair exceeded his remembrance of Mercer's hedonism.

Then again, Jake realized, Mercer had hinted in an online chat that in the four years since their attempt to deliver Trident missile warheads to Taiwan that he had multiplied his twenty-million dollar take many times over. Jake sensed that he had underestimated Mercer's wealth.

Any doubt Jake retained that he walked through his old friend's property evaporated as he reached the room's corner. Behind protective glass hung a portrayal of eighteenth century patrons in exodus from a southern European church. The image seemed caught between a Renaissance painter's attempt at replicating reality and an Impressionist's exploration of interpretation.

Jake nearly bumped the cigarette from Renard's mouth as he pointed.

"That painting?" he asked. "Is it Spanish?"

The door attendant stopped, turned, and admired the artwork.

"Indeed," he said. "Goya's *Village Procession*—dated to seventeen eighty seven. There are few paintings by Goya in private collections, and Senior Martinez had to make three offers before the prior owner would part with it."

"Oil on canvas," Renard said. "As he deviates from the sharpness of reality, you can see that he portrays the villagers with just a slight hint of buffoonery. He was exploring satire as he bordered on impressionism."

"You're an art connoisseur?" Jake asked.

"Culture separates us from the beasts," Renard said. "You would do well to immerse yourself in art. Over there, across the room. Is that not a Velázquez?"

"Most experts agree that it is, although it was once thought to be painted by Murillo," the attendant said. "*Sainte Rufina*. It went for nearly nine million dollars at auction ten years ago. Senior Martinez paid an even higher price for it."

Jake's anxiety subsided.

"When we were in high school," he said, "he studied Spanish while I studied French. We argued about whose art was better. He said that if he ever struck it rich he'd buy up every Spanish painting he could find."

Renard smiled.

"Shame on you for doubting my snout."

When they reached the enclosed office at the room's far end, the attendant raised a wireless phone to his ear and spoke in Spanish. He lowered the phone and depressed a large oaken door's brass latch.

He pulled open the door, let the visitors pass, and closed the door behind them.

Four flat screen televisions covered an entire wall and showed international news and market data. In front of the screens, a conference table rose from the floor, and leather chairs faced multimedia stations. Next to the table, an oak desk filled a quarter of the room, and Jake saw Grant Mercer standing behind it.

Mercer had always been a tall combination of fat over muscle, but Jake guessed that he had grown forty pounds in all directions since their last meeting. Mercer studied Jake, who had beefed up and slimmed down during years of studying martial arts.

"Well," Renard said. "You molest me in the waiting room, but now you just stare at your long lost friend?"

Jake kept his gaze on Mercer.

"From the looks of this place," Jake said, "I don't know you anymore—Senior Martinez."

"I'm the same guy, just richer. And you can drop the Martinez crap. The room is secure."

Mercer stepped across the room and hugged Jake.

"I missed you buddy," he said.

Jake felt that the embrace and salutation seemed standoffish.

"Me too," he said. "You remember Pierre, of course."

"Of course," Mercer said as he drew Renard into a half-handshake, half-hug.

"I apologize for making you wait," Mercer said. "I was closing a deal to sell sugar cane land for ethanol production. I love the business of South America. Sit down, guys. We have catching up to do."

Jake sank into leather and heard Renard do the same.

"These seats are magnificent," the Frenchman said. "I must know who your designer is."

"Not yet," Mercer said. "I know you have a lot of questions, but I've taken a huge risk in letting you find me. You guys have a lot of explaining to do."

"Where to begin?" Renard asked.

"How about with—what the hell made you think it was safe to sprinkle a trail of breadcrumbs from France to this secret paradise I've taken great pains to create?"

Renard stirred but Jake cut him off.

"A lot has happened in four years."

"True," Mercer said. "And people and priorities change. Perhaps you've decided to side with the feds?"

"I'd never…"

"I wouldn't blame you buddy," Mercer said. "Just in case you're trying to get out of a death sentence by helping the feds bring me in, you should know that I have a lot of well-armed and well-paid men to assist me."

"Indeed," Renard said. "We witnessed a sampling of your thugs on the way in. Other than the gentleman who brought us to this room, your men are brutish."

Jake scowled.

"Go on," Renard said. "I didn't mean to interrupt."

"But you always do," Jake said.

He turned back to Mercer.

"Forget about it. We're the ones the feds wanted," Jake said. "You were just icing on the cake."

"Wanted?" Mercer asked. "Past tense?"

"No one is hunting us anymore," Renard said. "It's a complex matter."

"I'm all ears," Mercer said.

Jake lay back in his chair and sighed.

"Go ahead, Pierre," he said. "You tell better stories."

"Very well."

Renard lit a fresh Marlboro.

"After you left for Spain," he said, "Jake and I started our new lives in Avignon. I was relieved when Jake mentioned that he had established a secure chat room with you and that you had continued to South America. At that time, the more distance between us, the better."

"Then why did you let Jake stay in Avignon?"

"We did more than steal and destroy an American Trident missile submarine," Renard said. "We took one hundred and twenty million dollars from Taipei before scuttling the *Colorado* with its warheads. Scrutiny from those in the Taiwanese Defense Ministry was tighter than any net your country's feds could throw over us. I had to keep Jake close to protect him."

"Great," Mercer said. "Two nations out for our hides."

"I fought to a détente with the Taiwanese for about two years," Renard said, "but then they forced my hand. They purchased a Pakistani *Agosta* submarine and made me staff and command it."

Mercer's face became flushed.

"I read about a Taiwanese submarine purchased from Pakistan that single-handedly pushed back the Chinese blockade," he said. "Was that you?"

"Indeed it was me," Renard said.

Jake cleared his throat.

"Excuse me," Renard said. "It was us. We were officially advisors augmenting a Taiwanese crew, but we were responsible for sinking a Chinese *Kilo* and forcing another to surface for capture."

"I should've guessed you guys were involved. I assume that settled the score with the Taiwanese?"

"Of course," Renard said. "But we also discovered that a Pakistani submarine had gone rogue with the intent of attacking the carrier *Stennis* in Pearl Harbor."

Renard tapped his Marlboro against an ashtray while he let Mercer digest the story.

"I read about that too," Mercer said, "and I saw the footage. That Pakistani submarine succeeded. I remember seeing smoke from the back of a crippled aircraft carrier."

"Succeeded?" Renard asked. "I think not. The popular version of the story is that an American submarine intervened just in time to prevent the Pakistani rogue from sinking the *Stennis* with conventional torpedoes, but the truth is that we prevented a nuclear torpedo attack and spared Honolulu from a radioactive fallout storm."

Mercer's jaw dropped and he looked at Jake, who shrugged his shoulders.

"That earned us favor with American officials," Renard said, "and the CIA has made a deal. We are essentially on glorified parole. We are free."

"I can go back to America," Jake said, "as long as it's a prearranged trip, specified location where nobody is likely to know me, and for limited duration."

"This is a lot to swallow," Mercer said.

"It gets better," Jake said. "The CIA knows exactly who you are and where you are, and they have for years."

"Then why haven't they brought the hammer down on me?"

Jake watched a sly smile curl over Renard's face.

"Apparently, Director Gerald Rickets of the CIA has secretly been considering you an asset. Now he wishes to cash in."

"So on top of your quasi freedom, I learn that I'm now supposedly the victim of constant surveillance…"

"Oh no, it's not constant," Renard said.

Mercer frowned.

"Sorry," Renard said. "Please. Continue."

"On top of my periodic surveillance, I'm a resource that a bigwig at the CIA is waiting to what? Blackmail?"

"I wouldn't call it that," Renard said. "I see it as an opportunity whose time has come."

"Okay," Mercer said. "Convince me. All details. From the beginning."

"From the beginning?" Renard asked. "Well, I have retained my contacts with DCN International, whose *Scorpène* class submarine is selling well. With design and fixed costs covered, I have a verbal agreement with the *Scorpène* program director, an old colleague of mine, to lease the unit that was just recently declared ready for sea trials prior to delivery to Malaysia."

"Lease?"

"Thirty million dollars for two months of use. Fifty million for three months."

"That's an inverted volume discount," Mercer said.

"It's not about usage," Renard said. "It's about keeping the Malaysians waiting for their submarine."

"I'm surprised they're willing to wait at all."

"It will be no more than a month from their perspective," Renard said. "DCN is actually ahead of schedule on the submarine's delivery."

"I can't wait to hear what you're going to do with it while they wait. I assume, of course, that whatever it is, it's in total secrecy to the Malaysians?"

"Indeed," Renard said. "And an insurance policy must be underwritten for the full value of the submarine. Plus damages of delivery delay. Director Rickets can't move the funds without leaving evidence he would prefer to not to leave, and he is inviting you to underwrite the operation."

Renard jabbed his cigarette into an ashtray.

"What operation?"

"It's possible that an Israeli *Dolphin* class submarine, the INS *Leviathan*, has fallen under the control of a hostile force, through mutiny, hijacking, or other nefarious means."

"Holy shit! What is it with you guys and crazed submarines?"

"Director Rickets would like for Jake and me to lead the pre-commissioning *Scorpène* unit in a clandestine effort to sink the *Leviathan*, if it can be verified to be outside the control of the Israeli government."

"Why not just have an American submarine do it?"

"One reason is plausible denial," Renard said. "If the Israelis fall short of admitting that they've lost control of their submarine, the Americans would like to have acoustic evidence of a non-American torpedo delivering the final blow, and a joint Spanish-French built *Scorpène* under the dominion of a shipyard makes for an unlikely suspect."

"You make it sound like it's easy. A done deal."

"The submarine is being tracked now and showing evidence of substandard management," Renard said. "Acting alone as it is, the outcome is hardly in question should its demise be deemed necessary. Jake and I also developed an excellent rapport with my team of veteran French submariners on an *Agosta* submarine during our operations in Taiwan and Hawaii. A *Scorpène* is essentially an updated version of an *Agosta*."

"What's another reason for pulling you guys into it? You said one reason was plausible denial. Is there more?"

"I believe Jake had a term for it. What was it?"

Jake remembered his brother's omen and felt a knot tighten in his belly.

"A puncher's chance," he said.

"You mean…"

"I mean any dumbass operating a submarine as capable as the *Leviathan* could press one button and get lucky with a counter-fire," Jake said. "The political fallout is too huge to risk an American submarine getting into a one for one exchange in this, no matter the odds."

"What do you need me for?"

"We need you to fund a mission," Renard said, "and we also need you to assure it in the event that we lose, damage, or destroy the *Scorpène*. The total cost is four hundred million, held in escrow under contract with a reputable Zurich bank, of which at least three hundred fifty million will be returned upon success of our duty."

"So I put almost half my fortune at risk?"

"Almost half?" Jake asked. "Dang, you have done well."

"And in return, what's my upside?"

"Ironically," Renard said, "your assurance of the *Scorpène* earns Director Rickets' assurance that you may continue your life unfettered in South America, and, since you escaped any official list of suspects, free access to return to the United States."

"Come on," Mercer said. "I put four hundred million at risk, say goodbye to at least thirty million, and all I get is the status quo."

Renard reached into his blazer and tossed photographs onto Mercer's desk.

Mercer's eyes tightened as he lifted the photos. Jake had already seen them and knew that his friend felt uncomfortable seeing himself in photographs taken from cameras over customs stations at five different American airports.

"Some of your disguises were excellent," Renard said, "especially the long hair, pony tail, and sunglasses. But you have been watched for some time, facial detection software is powerful, and you have never returned to your homeland with the freedom you thought you enjoyed."

"If I go through with this, I can put the Colorado Incident in my past? Never have to hide or look over my shoulder again?"

"Director Rickets assures it, and he's proven himself trustworthy," Renard said. "Of course, we've arranged for you to speak with him this evening to verify for yourself, but we need your verbal commitment now."

Mercer dropped the photographs.

"I'm in."

Renard reclined in his chair and lit a fresh cigarette. A sense of calm overcame his features that Jake recognized as confidence in a successful negotiation.

"Some negotiations are trivial enough that they manage themselves," Renard said. "But there is one little detail we've left out."

"What's that?" Mercer asked.

"Our *Scorpène* needs a name, at least an unofficial one while our team uses it," Renard said. "I figured that since you're the financier, we'd call it the *Mercer*."

"Oh, and what do I receive for lending my name?"

"On the contrary," Renard said as he caressed the arm of his leather chair. "For us paying you the honor of being our submarine's namesake, you owe us."

Mercer snorted.

"Sure. How else can I offer to help you?"

"You must give me the name of your interior designer. His taste is absolutely exquisite."

CHAPTER 8

Salem sat beside Asad in front of stacked monitors.

"How accurate is it?" he asked.

"During our last period at periscope depth," Asad said, "it was a GPS fix within ten meters. It degrades with uncertainty of currents and gyroscope errors while submerged. It's approximately accurate to within two nautical miles now."

"That's not good enough for our rendezvous."

"We'll ascend for GPS fixes as needed to be sure," Asad said. "We'd be fools otherwise."

His brow furrowed in militaristic focus, Hamdan marched into the *Leviathan's* control center.

"We stacked as many bodies as possible in cold storage," he said. "Four didn't fit. We wrapped them in garbage bags to contain the stench of their decay."

"Didn't fit?" Salem asked as he turned in his seat.

"We could move only so many cold stores into dry storage. Otherwise, food would spoil."

"We may receive dry goods from the *Zafar*," Salem said. "But we may not. You made a good judgment call."

The appreciation Salem hoped to see on the soldier's face proved elusive. His sullen eyes showed suspicion.

"I don't trust the Iranians," Hamdan said.

Asad stood and walked to the ships control station, distancing himself from the soldier's challenge.

"We have no choice," Salem said. "Without their participation, we'd be mindlessly meandering the seas with inadequate fuel to reach our destination, and we'd certainly be heard by hydrophones as we pass the Strait of Gibraltar."

"But we have weapons," Hamdan said. "Why not use them against enemies within reach?"

Salem stood, trying to display authority over a man trained to kill with his bare hands.

"We've invested far too much to take sporadic jabs," he said. "This mission—trust me on its greatness—requires patience and trust in our outcome."

"How can you be sure?"

"A future is never certain," Salem said. "But it can be seen."

"Seen? Have you seen it?"

"Yes, I've seen it," he said. "In my dreams. And I feel it now, alive in me."

"God is speaking to you."

Salem risked placing his hand on the soldier's shoulder. Hamdan raised his chin to meet his glare.

"Indeed, he is, my brother. We need only keep our wills strong and our intent pure to see it through"

"My imam said you had a special blessing," Hamdan said. "I am now beginning to see it."

"Good," Salem said. "Now go. Bazzi needs your assistance in preparing for our high speed run."

The soldier nodded and marched off. Salem exhaled, and Asad turned to him.

"This isn't part of the plan," Asad said.

"What isn't?"

"Our brothers from Hamas. They're supposed to follow orders. Not question them. We were told we'd receive solders to support us, not challenge us."

"I'm afraid that Hamdan is intelligent and inquisitive," Salem said. "He may question my every move until the end."

"Then I pray that God stays on your side."

"He will," Salem said. "One way or another."

Salem ducked his head through a door into the propulsion spaces and saw reddened skin glistening through gray strands.

"How are you, Bazzi," he asked.

The retired sailor looked up with concern.

"I'm calculating how long we have until we need to snorkel again."

"Any idea yet?"

"If we move slowly, say at six knots, then at best fifty hours."

"That's plenty of time," Salem said. "This ship is built smartly, and it has endurance."

"I don't trust this modern automation," Bazzi said.

"This is solid German engineering," Salem said. "And you have a translator, the ship's technical documents, and an exceptional mechanical engineer at your disposal."

Bazzi looked to the propulsion motor and followed the form of the thin man, a mechanical engineering doctoral student in his young thirties, who held hand written translated notes about lubrication oil leakage rates and pressure ratings in hand while crouching by the shaft. Hamdan crouched by the student's side, learning.

"These men spent months studying and training," Salem said. "Have faith."

"I would like to," Bazzi said. "But there's so much we don't know."

Salem ignored the comment and stepped beside Yousif, who studied the controls and indications for the *Leviathan's* propulsion, electronics, and machinery.

"It's starting to make sense to me," the rotund professor of electrical engineering said.

"Good," Salem said. "I trust your skill."

"I'm ready," Yousif said.

"Then it's time."

Salem returned to the control center and found Asad pacing behind Latakia. A post-doctoral student linguist sat at the stacked monitors. All other educated minds joined able bodies in the propulsion space or scattered themselves throughout the *Leviathan*.

"I've stationed men throughout the ship at locations where leaks would most likely occur," Asad said, "but this is a guessing game on a new ship."

"Take the ship to two hundred meters," Salem said.

"Don't you want speed first?" Asad asked. "Speed to drive back shallow if needed."

Salem sensed that the submarine training provided to him and his crew from Russian vendors and remnants of the Syrian submarine fleet would be taxed.

"Sure," he said. "Do we just jump to top speed or move in increments?"

"Increments," Asad said. "Try ten knots."

"Ten knots then."

Asad maneuvered a joystick, and Salem thought that the *Leviathan's* metallic pulse quickened.

"We're at ten knots," Asad said."

"Okay. Two hundred meters, now, right?"

"Yes, Hana."

Shifting numbers on a digital gage, a creak, and a groan informed Salem of the *Leviathan's* new depth. Asad and Latakia, who wore a sound powered phone headset to speak with men throughout the submarine, exchanged words.

"All is well, Hana," Asad said.

"So what's next?" Salem asked. "Fifteen knots?"

"Yes. Why not?"

"Okay. Fifteen knots."

The vessel quivered. Salem's heartbeat quickened.

"Fifteen knots," Asad said. "All is well."

"Do we dare go all out?"

"Bazzi wants us to go all out, and I agree," Asad said. "We shake the ship to find its weaknesses before they find us."

"Okay. Full speed."

"You mean flank speed, right?"

"Yes, thank you. I had forgotten the term. That's what I mean. All the ship can do."

The *Leviathan* settled into a trembling cadence that Salem found ominous and graceful.

"Twenty-two knots," Asad said. "And it looks like we'll soon reach... yes... twenty-three knots."

"All is well?"

"So far. Bazzi wants to stay at this speed and watch the battery discharge."

"Fine."

The deck shot downward and, his heart in his throat, Salem reached for a railing.

"What's wrong?" he asked.

Asad ignored him, jostled a joystick, but the ship gave no apparent response.

"Asad!"

"I don't know, damn it."

The ship dived, and the door to berthing loomed at the bottom of the hill the *Leviathan's* angle created.

"Do something!" Salem said. "Do the opposite of everything we just did!"

"Bow planes are unresponsive," Asad said, one arm curled around the back of his chair. "We're applying the stern planes now."

"Should we slow the ship?" Salem asked. "We're driving ourselves too deep."

"Bazzi already took the liberty of slowing us. I recommend a backing bell."

"Do it!"

The *Leviathan* shuddered in protest as it slowed and leveled. When it returned balance to Salem he fixed his gaze to the depth meter. It read four hundred meters.

"That's too deep," he said.

A groan enveloped the control room and continued in ominous echoing along the length of the hull. Salem saw his life ending as water erupted through tearing metal.

The echo subsided, the *Leviathan* held, and Salem noticed that his jugular vein throbbed.

"I would like to go up now," he said.

"We have full rise on the bow plane and stern plane," Asad said. "Let Latakia move water from forward trim tanks to aft to assure an upward angle on the hull as well."

"I prefer not to wait."

"Neither do I, Hana, but we obviously don't fully understand the ship's hydrodynamic response."

Salem felt the deck angle upward a degree or two but no longer trusted his orientation.

"We're already rising," Asad said. "The denser water at this depth made us relatively lighter and…"

"Curse your analysis and get us up!"

"Yes, Hana. Five knots."

The ship climbed past three hundred meters. Salem stared at the digital depth meter, demanding silence by example, until it read one hundred meters.

"Steady us on a safe, shallow depth," he said.

Smelling the stench of fear wafting from his armpits, he turned and left the room.

"What happened, Hana?" Bazzi asked.

"As a veteran, I hoped you could tell me."

"Asad and Latakia could explain it better than I could, I'm sure."

"I don't want to talk to them now. They nearly killed us," Salem said.

"I share the blame for requesting the flank bell."

"No, we needed to do this to test the ship and our ability to operate it. They should have known better."

Yousif, scribbling readings at the electric control panel, looked away as Salem shook his head.

"Please, Hana," Bazzi said. "Speaking against our own men is dangerous."

"You're right, Bazzi. Perhaps I've judged too quickly. Tell me then, what do you think happened?"

Bazzi stiffened his palm, angled it downward, and pressed his other rigid palm against it.

"The bow planes must have turned down, like this, pushing the bow of the ship down, like this. At some point, if there's enough speed, the ship's angle becomes a powerful force in driving us up or down, and it can be overpowering. I believe that's what happened. At that point, you have to use the stern planes, but righting the angle takes time. I didn't mean to assume that you wanted to stop, but it was my only choice."

"You did well to slow us on your own initiative, Bazzi. I commend you."

The old man smiled, and sweat rolled around the corner of his mouth.

"And how about the systems that we meant to test?"

"We're checking sea water piping and lubrication oil for leaks, but everything seemed to hold."

"Like I said, this ship is solid. We must learn it and work with it."

Salem reentered the control center. Asad sprang to him, his eyes wide with eagerness.

"Hana, we know what happened and can explain."

"The bow planes forced the ship's angle down too far?"

"Yes. How did you…"

"Bazzi explained it to me."

"Hana, we had no way of knowing."

Ire rose within him and coursed through his limbs. He slapped his palm against a hand railing and felt it sting.

"Damn it, yes you did. The answer's somewhere in the ship's manuals, and we risked our lives and mission because we were too foolish to translate the book and read it."

Asad lowered his gaze.

"When's the last time you slept?" Salem asked.

"Eighteen, nineteen hours ago."

"But we've all endured chronic sleep deprivation," Salem said. "We now know beyond doubt that this ship is strong and solid and that we can crawl safely with just a few men awake. Where are we in relation to the rendezvous with the *Zafar*?"

Asad turned towards the stacked monitors.

"No!" Salem said.

"Hana?"

"You should know by memory. I trust you to navigate and operate this ship. Free your mind of all other clutter and focus."

"Yes, Hana."

"How far, in miles and time, moving at five knots, are we from the *Zafar's* path?"

Asad's eyes darted to the corner of their sockets as he accessed his cortex.

"Our shortest distance to their track is one hundred and sixty nautical miles. Thirty four hours at five knots, although closer to thirty seven with the current."

"Good," Salem said. "And where will the *Zafar* be in thirty seven hours? Don't look. Give me your estimate."

"I don't know, Hana."

"Will it be at least two days away?"

"Yes, Hana. I'm sure of it. Three days or more."

"Then we have time to rest and study the manuals for future tasks we might take, such as shooting weapons."

"I see, Hana."

"Take your rest. I'll remain here with Latakia. And when you awake, you will begin with a new focus on understanding this ship and the world around it."

Six hours later, exhaustion took a grip on Salem, and he welcomed Asad's image at the berthing door. His face was puffy with sleep.

"I'm rested enough, Hana. You and Latakia can get your sleep. Yousif will replace Bazzi in monitoring the propulsion and machinery."

Salem glanced at the speed display. Three knots.

He stood, walked by Asad, and mumbled a hasty word of appreciation as he passed through the door. He slid down a ladder to the lower deck and walked to the captain's stateroom. He desired a shower but had precluded all men from risking the noise and strain on resources. Wearing his smelly jumpsuit, he crawled into his bed.

Two days passed without event. Academic personnel transcribed manuals, prior naval personnel read them, and everyone made whatever possible sense of any system that looked important. Confident that he had made his mark on his team that ignorance failed as an excuse, Salem gave himself time for a long sleep.

He dreamt.

He was five years old running around a white stucco wall of his childhood home outside Damascus. Fear compelled him to run from something beyond his capacity to understand, and he tripped. The dry, hard earth smacked his jaw, and he wanted to cry, but a voice comforted him.

"Hana," a lady said.

The soothing tone erased his fear and pain. Warmth overcame him and he knew he was smiling as he rose effortlessly to his feet.

A woman with a paisley blue dress and white apron revealed perfect white teeth. Her wavy dark hair framed a heart-shaped face and tanned skin while curving to her shoulders. Soft brown eyes glistened in the early morning sunlight as she stooped toward him and extended her arms.

He bowed his head, pumped his arms, and ran to her, watching the pebbles and patches of grass flow below him in a blur.

"Hana," she said again, half laughing.

"Mama!"

Death's cold voice caught him.

"Hana," it said.

He fell again and felt the sting against his face. He pushed himself up, bearing a mighty new weight. The thirty-nine year old professor of economics tasted the blood flowing into the corner of his mouth from the puncture a rock had inflicted on his temple. His head pounded.

"Hana!"

He turned and saw Hamdan, his eyes hollow sockets, dressed in a wetsuit with Asad kneeling at his feet. A knife reflected the sun's rays, blinding Salem.

"You must end this now," Hamdan said.

"No," Salem said. "I have a destiny. We have a destiny."

His vision returned and he watched Hamdan stab the blade into Asad's throat, over and over, with fantastic speed, and then toss the flailing victim to the ground, blood spurting through clenched hands.

"We end this now. Drive to infidel cities and launch the cruise missiles."

Thunder struck and engines whined over the horizon. Salem looked over a hill of olive trees and saw cruise missiles streaking across the sky. They ripped through the atmosphere with impossible speed and created mushroom clouds.

"That was Damascus, you fool!" Hamdan said.

"No!"

"Yes. You've ended this in shame!"

Salem glanced to his mother, a silver-haired corpse in a coffin consistent with his final memory of a woman driven by hard life to an early grave. Her peaceful face split, and the Mediterranean Sea shot forth from the wound, enveloping Salem, carrying him toward a horrific abyss, and pinning him under its mass to force him to await death by drowning.

He awoke.

"Hana!"

"What," he said. "What is it?"

Asad's head appeared in the doorway.

"You wanted me to wake you when we reached the *Zafar's* track," Asad said. "We're there."

"Have we turned on course?"

"Yes, Hana. And the *Zafar* will overtake us in twenty-three hours at our present speed of four knots."

"When did we last confirm the *Zafar's* agenda?"

"It's been a while," Asad said. "You've slept ten hours. Nightfall will be soon."

Asad appeared confident, and Salem knew that challenging him two days earlier had been correct in stimulating his competence.

"Good. Well done."

CHAPTER 9

Being raped at knife-point and infected with HIV while cracking an Eastern European sex slave trafficking ring had put Olivia McDonald's field work on hold until Jake Slate. Then, her life spiraled out of control, carrying her into the murky and uncertain worlds of romance and submarine combat. She had considered it a wild ride, but she welcomed the chance to tuck the chaos into her past and return to her roots as a psychologist doing analyst work.

The sun shone through CIA headquarters windows and cast a heavy shadow across her desk. She raised her gaze to her old boss, Director Gerald Rickets, who towered over her.

"Why me?"

"Because you're the best with submarine profiles."

She glanced at the surrounding cubicles and saw inquisitive faces seeking glimpses of a bigwig in a dark suit, a direct report to the Director of the Central Intelligence Agency.

"And because you've been on a submarine," he said. "You know how they think."

"You're sure you're not just doing me a favor?"

Thick ebony fingers scrunched against her desk, stabilizing Ricket's leaning torso. His voice took on a tone too meek for a man of his stature that she recognized as the enduring shame he couldn't shake.

"I'm going to do you favors until you're running the agency or I'm pushing up daisies, whichever comes first, young lady. I still owe you for what I did to you in Paris. But this is a perfect match for you."

"How fast do you need answers?"

"As fast as you can. Two days. Three tops."

"Gerry!"

Rickets stood, and the inquisitive heads slid back into cubicles like scurrying gophers.

"I know it's fast, but you'll have at least a dozen people," he said. "Top analysts are being gathered now."

"What if I'm not up to it?"

"You are. Just split up the crew's dossiers evenly and get the best people on the senior crew members."

"What's the goal?"

"I don't know," he said. "We're playing a game of diplomacy with Tel Aviv while we have a submarine playing chicken with one of theirs. The goal is to find whatever you can as fast as you can and give me reports every six hours—sooner if you have a breakthrough."

She envisioned a coffee-fueled sleepless night.

"Yeah, Gerry. It sounds like something perfect for me. Can I have half an hour or so to cancel my life for the next three days?"

"Sure," he said. "What do you have going on?"

"Well, um, I kind of have a date."

His stare cold, he leaned on her desk again.

"What about you know who?"

"He sort of broke up with me in Charlotte."

"Sort of?"

"Yeah, and I sort of liked it. This transcontinental secret love thing was exciting at first, but then it just got old."

Rickets' tone turned to paternal suspicion.

"Who is he?"

"A cop," she said. "We met in a cop bar where my dad used to hang out."

"Good. I like him already. Wait. Is he…"

"No, he's not. I wanted to try dating a normal person instead of restricting myself to the HIV club."

"Have you told him?"

"No. I was going to tonight, but I guess that'll have to wait."

She stood, and her chair rolled out of her cubicle.

"I know the timing stinks," he said. "But this is a good opportunity for you to show the agency what you've got. You know it's a great assignment."

"You're right, Gerry. My flailing social life will still be there when I get back."

Lieutenant Commander Robert Stephenson jogged up the stairs to the upper decks of the *Bainbridge*. His palms slid across metal railings as the soles of his black shoes clapped and rang against serrated steps. Even inside the ship's superstructure, the evening's cool salt air smelled sweet as he caught his breath.

He entered the radio room and closed the door. A petty officer stood by a high-speed printer.

"Almost ready, XO," the sailor said.

"No hurry. I like coming up here myself to get incoming message printouts," Stephenson said.

"The exercise, sir?"

"Sure, but it also gives me time to think about what I read before presenting it to the captain. It's a good practice to bring solutions and insight when playing messenger."

"Hell, sir. You know the skipper's gonna piss and moan no matter what you do. He's just a…"

"That's enough!" a man said from the shadows.

"Senior Chief Wilson?" Stephenson asked.

"Yes, sir," Wilson said.

A lean man with a senior chief petty officer's anchor and star on his camouflage collar turned to the sailor and nodded toward radio equipment control panels.

"Go line us up for the twenty-one hundred satellite download," he said.

The sailor ducked away.

"I'll deal with him later," Wilson said.

"I know you will," Stephenson said. "There's a healthy amount of complaining, and then there's destructive attitudes. I'm seeing too much of the latter case."

Sadness clouded Wilson's face.

"You seem down, senior chief. I've noticed for a while now, actually. Something bothering you?"

"Can we talk? In private?"

Stephenson balanced himself against a bulkhead while looming over the senior chief petty officer. His head in his hands, Wilson sat at his desk in the corner of the radio room.

"I don't know if I should be telling you this, sir."

"Trust your instinct," Stephenson said.

Wilson lifted his head, exposing ruddy palm imprints encasing bloodshot eyes.

"I used to date the skipper's fiancée."

"Well, dang," Stephenson said. "That's a tough one."

"That's why I've been hiding in the radio room and doing everything possible to avoid him. A guy can tell when another guy's been with his woman."

"Was this before or after the skipper met her? Or in some gray area in between?"

Wilson waved his hands in defense.

"No, sir. It's not like that. Totally before. I'd never snake a man's lady. I've always played straight up, even if I have gone overboard since my divorce and become, well..."

"A playboy. Some of your recent exploits are becoming *Bainbridge* legend. It's just a phase a lot of people go through after divorce. When you're ready, you'll evolve out of it."

Wilson's head returned to his hands.

"I haven't so much as been on a date since Farah."

"How serious was it?"

"You want a chair, sir?" Wilson said as he arched his back and stretched.

"No, I'm good. Thanks."

"Well, sir, I'd say we were in pretty deep. It was fast but it was intense. She's a real intense lady. Smart, confident, and driven as all hell."

"Driven to what?"

"To finding a husband, best I can tell. Maybe her biological clock is ticking. You know. Woman passes her mid-thirties, looks back and realizes her career kept her from a family, and then it's scramble time. I have to admit, if I wasn't gun shy from my own divorce, I'd probably be calling her my fiancée instead of that jackass."

"Wilson!"

"Sorry, sir."

Stephenson gave Wilson a moment of silence to ponder his mistake.

"Nobody should be talking about their commanding officer that way, especially to their executive officer."

"I know, but she didn't even give me a chance, sir. As soon as I said I wasn't ready to get married, she went cold. Next thing I know, a month later she's crossing the brow to visit. I'm thinking she's going to give me a second chance, and she's here to surprise me. Then rumor spreads like wildfire about the skipper's new girl."

"I understand. That's tough."

"Excruciating, sir. If you haven't been through it, you have no idea."

"Fair enough. But I'm surprised that news about you having dated her first didn't spread just as fast."

"I didn't tell a soul," Wilson said. "The other girls I've dated, sure. I play basketball with kids half my age, and that buys me quality time with the younger ladies. But that's just fun with bragging rights. I could tell from the moment I met Farah that she was all business. Classy, intelligent, strong. I didn't take her to Navy hangouts."

"Why not?"

"Maybe I was afraid she was too hot, even hot enough to attract the younger guys. I mean really just attractive in every way."

"But if she was so intent on getting married, she wouldn't start flirting with other guys," Stephenson said. "And I've met her many times for lunch with the commanding officer and multiple guests, and she's never once taken her attention away from him."

"But she can turn it on and off like a switch. The night I met her, she sat at one barstool, made eyes at a bunch of guys, and each one came to her on command. She gets a free drink and then brushes them off. When she catches my eye, I'm thinking I'm no sucker, I'm gonna resist. Next thing I know, I'm saying hello and slapping a twenty on the counter. Then I'm thinking it's my lucky day because she's letting me stick around."

"What made you different from the others?"

Wilson scratched his head and smiled.

"Well, sir, I'm older and more mature than most of those kids, but I'm in better shape. Plus I ain't too bad looking, got a bachelor's degree and a full head of hair. Not to mention, I have a pretty good career. When I told her what I did, she perked up."

"Somebody must've known that you were dating her."

"Nope. Guys knew I was going out and that I had a girlfriend, but I never mentioned her name. It's so uncommon and she's sort of a public figure, being on faculty at Old Dominion. I wanted to protect her privacy."

"How did she like being kept a secret?"

Wilson's brow furrowed.

"Heck, I hadn't thought of that. She never made it an issue. In fact, she seemed to like it that way. Never pushed to meet my Navy friends."

"But you were considering marriage."

"She was. Looking back, she played me like a fiddle. I'm pushing forty, and she practically had me all gooey in puppy love. Now she's doing it to the skipper."

"That's your judgment, senior chief, and best not to be repeated. But I'm glad you shared. It'll help me understand his mindset and give him the support he needs. Commanding officer is a lonely job. I have to imagine it's an emotionally vulnerable one, too."

"Still stinks, seeing a woman I loved or at least think I loved with my skipper."

"I know that hurts, but it's no excuse to call your commanding officer a jackass."

Wilson curled forward and plopped his head back into his palms. He sounded defeated.

"Hell, you're right, sir. I'll put myself on report and…"

"No, I've got a better idea."

Eyes peered over fingertips, and Stephenson noticed a spark of hope cracking through knuckles.

"I'll take any advice you've got, sir."

"A new focus. Your mind is somewhere between a rock and a hard place thinking about your lost love and a commanding officer with whom you share—call it a personality clash—getting ready to marry her. That's tough if you brood over it, but maybe it's better to think that you're better off this way."

"I can't think how it could get any worse."

"Well, you were having a pretty good time with your playboy phase, right? Instead of thinking about your loss, focus on your freedom. Maybe you need to go back into that mode, have a little bit more fun, and see if the real Miss Right steps up."

Wilson stirred and sat up straight.

"Maybe you're on to something. Or maybe I can think that they deserve each other. I mean, she was pushy and manipulative, and he's..."

"Your commanding officer."

"Right, sir. Thanks."

"No problem. That's what I'm here for."

"I feel a little better."

"Great! You'll need the energy, because I think a just response for expressing disrespect towards the captain is to come up with the five most effective traits you admire about his leadership and steps you can take to promote that respect throughout the ship."

"Sir!"

"Would you prefer an official report?"

Wilson's head landed again in his hands. He mumbled.

"How long do I have to come up with my answers?"

"Before we take over anti-ballistic missile defense coverage."

"That's only three days."

"You're a sharp guy," Stephenson said. "You'll think of something."

Olivia McDonald gulped tepid coffee from a Styrofoam cup and gazed at her wristwatch. Fatigue blurred her vision, and she strained to focus on the hands that indicated three o'clock.

The windowless room lined with egg carton, sound-proofing foam gave no hint of the sun's absence overhead, and the stench in her armpits provided the best clue that it was early morning, almost forty hours after Rickets had offered her the project.

She led a team of analysts in studying the personal histories of the entire crew of the *Leviathan*. Half of her team held greater tenure within the CIA, and a few approached the ages of her parents.

The analysts worked with zeal—while awake—but only a handful of the fifteen joined her at a table. The remaining members sprawled across the floor in blankets and cots, catching a few hours of cortex-recharging sleep.

A portly man with a balding scalp and penetrating eyes seemed impervious to fatigue. Tapping his fingers, he jammed his thumb into the deeper pages of the dossier for the *Leviathan's* captain. He periodically reminded Olivia that he had dissected Khrushchev, Castro, and Khomeini before she was born.

"Shall we move on?" he said.

Olivia disliked his condescending tone but accepted it in exchange for his brilliance. She thought she could dissect dossiers fast, but he was lightening. She appreciated his backup in reading that of the captain.

"Sure," she said, stifling a yawn. "Let's wrap it up."

The other elder man at the table was in his late fifties and lean, and thick glasses made his head appear misshapen with an undersized jaw. He seemed detached from reality, living in the abstract of his mental machinations. He cleared his throat, nodded, and pointed his nose into a folder.

The other two at the table were young twenty-somethings of either sex who seemed too nervous around agency veterans to do anything but answer questions.

The portly CIA veteran opened the dossier for the captain of the *Leviathan*.

"I've been through this guy's file twice, and I don't see it," he said. "Israeli officers are loyal to a fault, the country is filled with patriots, and the military has a sense of duty that rivals ours. There's nothing to suggest that the captain was susceptible to treason."

The lean veteran cleared his throat and spoke with a monotone mumble that hypnotized Olivia to the edge of consciousness.

"Absolutely concur. Nothing on the executive officer either. I took a look at all the officers, in fact, and saw nothing. Not that our information is perfect or complete. It never is, and we may be unaware of an acute shock to a crewmember's life, but there certainly is no trend leading to treason for any of them."

"I know," Olivia said. "What about you two?"

"We didn't have as much data per person on the enlisted crew," the young female said. "But there was enough in most cases to determine little to zero risk of treason or mutiny."

"This is the conclusion from everyone," the young man said. "It's been a thorough effort."

Olivia inhaled slowly to grant her lagging mind time to process information. She recalled that if she had read Jake Slate's past dossier, she would have judged him incapable of stealing a Trident missile submarine. Then again, his dossier omitted a crucial shock, and one event could change a man.

"Each crewmember's information has been read at least twice by three people," she said, "and we've broken into groups to discuss and brainstorm extreme possibilities. But there's not a danged hint of evidence that any Israeli sailor aboard the *Leviathan* would have the slightest motivation to break from state control."

"The Israeli submarine fleet is a small, elite, well-trained, well-screened, and cohesive force," the portly man said. "It's like trying to find traitors among Navy SEALs. You don't find them being bred. And if one snaps, changes motivation and allegiance, the warning signs aren't always obvious, and the ones most likely to see the signs are his colleagues—not an analyst sitting across the ocean who's never met him."

The lean veteran droned.

"Sorry, Olivia. Sometimes the accurate answer is disappointing, but accurate for the available information nonetheless. You can wake the others for a final read through, but I don't see it going anywhere."

"No," she said. "Neither do I. I'll call Rickets and let him know we didn't find anything. Unless he protests, we'll wake up the others and tell them we're done."

Olivia earned time off for pulling one and a half all-nighters, but Rickets demanded that she come in by noon the same day. After a half night's sleep, she felt like a zombie.

She retraced her steps to the secure room in which she had just spent many hours and punched in her access code. The door seemed weighty as she nursed her tiredness.

Gerald Rickets sat alone in the room, which remained a mess with files and notebooks strewn about, while he flipped through the dossier of the *Leviathan's* captain.

"I wanted people to get rest," she said. "The room is still secure for the *Leviathan* project. I'll have them do a proper clean up tomorrow."

"You're sure there's nothing?"

"Nothing," she said.

"I know," he said. "You wouldn't have called me at three in the morning to call it quits unless you believed it. But I had to ask again. After at least a little sleep, do you still think this is a dead end?"

"Yes."

"But you would have said the same thing about Slate if you had a chance to analyze him before the 'Colorado Incident', right?"

"Yeah. Maybe. I don't know. His accident was documented but not the HIV part of it. It's unlikely that the accident alone would have motivated him to steal the *Colorado*, but I would have at least questioned it. There's no accident or analog thereof for anyone on the *Leviathan*, Gerry. No careers turned short, no bad medical news, no second cousins hanging out in the wrong circles, no fortunes given or taken, no travel to suspicious places, no nothing. I'm sorry. There's just nothing."

Rickets stood and buttoned his blazer.

"It's okay," he said. "You did good work. Maybe great work. Only time will tell. You've just ruled out the possibility of mutiny, or at least lowered our estimation of its probability. That's a big piece of the puzzle."

"I still feel like I failed."

"You didn't. This might be your first assignment that turns up nothing, and that's a good learning experience for you. Discovering nothing when nothing is the correct answer, is something."

He started for the door but she stopped him.

"Gerry?"

"Yes."

"You didn't bring me in for a pep talk, did you?"

"Oh yes, I had almost forgotten. I wanted to see if you were interested in a new case that's perfect for you. I thought you deserved a slow pitch after this two-day sprint with *Leviathan*."

"Sure. What is it?"

"Thirty-eight year old female. Iranian professor of psychology, on a teaching visa at Old Dominion, apparently making every effort possible to marry a sailor in Norfolk. She landed a big fish, the captain of the USS *Bainbridge*, an Aegis destroyer, who is now her fiancé."

"Slow pitch?" she said. "That sounds more like a yawn. She may be older than the average husband-hunter preying on sailors, but that's what it sounds like."

"Husband hunting?" Rickets asked. "It doesn't fit a self-made woman."

"She's probably seeking American citizenship. Or something else boring."

"The executive officer of the *Bainbridge* thought enough of it to call NCIS from his deployment."

"Sounds like a career limiting move by the XO."

"That took some guts, but NCIS will treat it like an anonymous tip, as will we," Rickets said. "And it was the right call. Apparently, this woman has quite an effect on men and is on a mission."

"Yeah, to get married and earn her citizenship."

"Maybe. But NCIS investigated some local bars, and she has a peculiar taste for destroyer sailors, regardless of rank. There might be a pattern suggesting something beyond snagging a husband."

"Why doesn't NCIS keep it?"

"No evidence of a crime. Assessing foreigners for the possibility of committing a future crime is something you do. You're one of the best."

She sighed.

"I'm still one of the best, even after coming up with zip on the *Leviathan*?"

"Yes," he said. "And let the *Leviathan* go. Some of our top minds were on that team, including yours. If you found nothing, the answer is nothing. Move on."

"Why me—for this?"

"You'll see similarities between yourself and the professor. You're both psychologists, and you both have unique perspectives on the opposite sex."

"You mean because I was beaten and raped."

He curled his lips.

"That experience gives you insight that few analysts have," he said. "We're looking at an educated female from a male dominated society. That experience may come in to play."

"Okay, I'll do it."

"Great," Rickets said.

"Any hurry?"

"No, not really."

"Good. I'm taking the next twenty-four hours off."

"Okay, you deserve it. I'll let your boss know."

"You know," Olivia said, "analyzing her might be a bigger challenge than you think. A woman is more complex than a man."

"How so?"

"I can't count on her to think with her penis."

CHAPTER 10

The twisting dirt path took Jake Slate by a young couple resting against a rock outcropping.

"Hello," he said.

"How are you?" the man asked in the sunny French of the country's southern provincial region.

"Good. You must have started at dawn," Jake said.

"When we reach the summit, I'll be proposing to this beautiful woman."

"Do you think she'll say yes?"

"Of course!" the man said as he turned to kiss his smiling future bride.

He bid the couple farewell and started toward the summit of Mount Saint Victoire, the peak glorified by Cézanne. An updraft from the valley blew the scent of lilac across his face.

Enjoying the risen sun's rays, he squatted against an olive tree and felt it bend. Hungry, he reached into a backpack for a baguette and wedge of Camembert. After mashing cheese against bread, he swallowed a mouthful and heard boots crunching dirt.

Looking up, he saw Renard, dressed in flannel hiking garb, laboring against the incline. His French friend winced and wheezed. Concerned, Jake moved toward him.

"You okay?" he asked.

Jake felt Renard's weight trembling on his arm as he struggled for breath.

"I'm fine. Perhaps I overdid it trying to outpace the others. We're not all athletic marvels like you."

Familiar men came into view on the trail below. The last time he had ascended the mountain, Jake met Renard's entourage of veteran French submariners under clandestine auspices. After uniting with them as a crack mercenary submarine crew, he considered them his closest friends.

"You'll be fine," he said and released Renard.

"Indeed."

"I'm running ahead again."

*   *   *

At a turn, a chapel came into Jake's view. He crossed the doorstep and smelled stale oak. Except for a statue of Christ and a few rows of pews, the chapel was bare with a floor worn by decades of random visitors.

In the grassy yard outside the chapel, a dried-up well attracted his attention. He walked to it and peered between the bricks. Dirt filled the hole.

He turned toward a structure that resembled a misplaced barn but which served as a gathering room for climbers resting within a stone's throw of the summit. Inhaling, he smelled dampness and age.

As his party's strongest climber, he carried the bulk of its goods. He plopped his backpack onto a wooden table, withdrew laminated presentations, and spread them in front of the benches. Next he slid out a thermos of coffee, a bag of baguettes, and wheels of Camembert.

He flipped through a presentation as he waited.

A man entered the structure. Having expected Renard, Jake was surprised to see Henri Lanier, retired expert submarine mechanic and Renard's closest French confidant. A stickler rivaling Renard with his penchant for upscale dress, Henri wore a flannel Abercrombie shirt and designer jeans.

"Hello, Jake," he said.

"Hello. Where's Pierre?"

"I passed him five minutes ago. The mountain seemed to get the better of him."

Henri lowered a knapsack to the table, and Jake helped him distribute coffee cups, knives, and napkins to those yet to arrive. Within minutes, the room filled with French-bred undersea mercenaries.

Lumbering into the room behind the others, Renard moved to Jake's side.

"Are you okay," Jake asked.

"Splendid," Renard said.

Jake ignored the incongruity between Renard's appearance and his words. He slapped his arm around Antoine Remy's back and tossed his leg over the bench. After watching Remy provide solid service on an advanced diesel *Agosta* submarine, Jake agreed with Renard that he was among the best sonar operators he had known.

"Pass me some coffee, buddy," he said. "I need it to stay awake while Pierre talks."

*   *   *

His stomach filled with breakfast, Jake turned his attention to Renard at the head of the table.

"Gentlemen, please," the Frenchman said. "Open your handouts. Skip the first page, which is a facade, but return to it at once if someone enters the room. Begin on page two."

Jake flipped to the second page and saw a cutaway diagram of the *Scorpène's* trim and ballast system.

"Dang, that thing is small," he said. "The whole thing would fit inside the missile compartment of the *Colorado*."

"Yes, we know," Remy said, rolling his eyes. "You believe that every submarine of French design fits inside a Trident missile boat. But I must remind you yet again that nothing fits inside the *Colorado*, specifically, because you blew it up."

"Technically, the USS *Miami* blew it up," Renard said. "We merely encouraged its demise. However, Jake's point, however crassly made, is valid. The *Scorpène* class submarine is comparable in size to the *Agosta* with which we are accustomed."

"I'm relieved to see a MESMA unit," Jake said.

"The MESMA air independent power generation system on the *Scorpène* benefits from lessons learned from earlier units on the *Agostas*. Slightly better efficiency, and supposedly easier to manage."

"So we'll be snorkeling a bit less than we did with our prior *Agosta*?" Claude LaFontaine said.

Jake welcomed the presence of LaFontaine, who was the engineer officer on the nuclear-powered *Rubis* when a younger Renard was its executive officer. He had also impressed Jake with his rapid grasp of diesel submarine operations while aboard the *Agosta*.

"Indeed," Renard said.

"It hardly matters," Henri said. "I can keep any submarine floating gracefully with its conning tower a mere meter below the waves, should you need to snorkel all day and all night."

"And you will know the trim and drain system better than anyone," Renard said. "All *Scorpène* systems are descendants or replicas of those upon which we have all become familiar."

"You have ship handling data?" Henri asked.

"At the shipyard and on the ship itself," Renard said.

"Then I will be your expert after digesting them."

The young couple that Jake had passed during his ascent strolled into the room. Jake smiled and raised his thumb in anticipation of the soon to be engaged couple.

"Flip back to the first page," Renard said in English.

Jake glanced at the page that held meaningless graphs of European stock indices. He looked up, saw Renard eyeing him, and remembered his queue.

"Your investment strategy looks strong against recessions, but I'm concerned about lagging behind in times of economic recovery."

Through the corner of his eye, Jake saw the young couple rehydrating from squeeze bottles. They seemed unable to understand English or uncaring if they did.

"It's fine," Jake said. "They have more important things on their mind. He's going to propose."

"Best of luck to him," Renard said.

Moments later, the couple departed.

Forty-five minutes passed as Renard's team covered a dozen systems. Familiarity with the precursor *Agosta* submarine design made for easy understanding of the pre-commission *Scorpène* class boat they would call the *Mercer*.

"Are we ready to review our prey?" Renard asked.

"Supposed prey," Jake said. "Nothing's sure yet."

"We'll be prepared to engage the *Leviathan* in battle whether or not we are granted permission to deliver the final blow. This is most certainly a hunt regardless."

"Seems complex," Jake said. "Too many things we don't know yet. Too many permissions pending."

"Assume that our mission will develop, and be ready for it," Renard said.

"Fine. Let's do it."

"Very well," Renard said. "Begin with the *Leviathan's* torpedo tubes and weapons. It carries only six spare weapons, but ten bow mounted tubes allow for great speed of fire and flexibility in engaging multiple targets. Reload from the spare racks is expected to be rapid. Under two minutes—highly automated reload."

Jake studied a listing of the *Leviathan's* characteristics.

"This ship looks tough," he said.

"Comparable to a *Scorpène*," Renard said. "Assuming comparable crews. We're safe to assume, however, that if the *Leviathan* has gone rogue, it has done so with degraded staffing. I can't see an entire Israeli crew mutinying."

"But there's only eight of us. That's a stretch to run a submarine designed for thirty."

"Optimized for thirty," Renard said. "It can run with fewer, and we have new recruits to our team coming from French Navy veterans. We'll have sixteen."

"So where are they?"

"On the ship, familiarizing themselves with the systems and making ready to sail. We will employ the use of a few shipyard experts to shakedown the ship, return the experts to shore, and then the ship will be ours."

The group studied and discussed the details of the *Leviathan* for an hour. There would be time to delve deeper underway, but Jake appreciated that his brain would process and sleep upon the first wave of knowledge it acquired through Renard's lecture.

"Very well, then," Renard said. "Are we ready to enjoy the view from the summit before we hike back down to the vans?"

"Sure," Jake said. "A few hours, the drive to Toulon, then what?"

"Stow gear on the ship before a late dinner," Renard said. "Then a night in the finest hotel Henri could find. It will be our last sleep on dry land for some time, and I thought we would enjoy the comfort."

As the team stowed gear and hoisted backpacks over their shoulders, Jake saw the young couple reenter the structure. The man smiled, and the lady raised the diamond ring on her finger. Renard's mercenaries erupted into applause.

While clapping, Jake whispered to Henri.

"That was a long proposal."

"No," Henri said. "You notice that their jeans are wrinkled and dirtied."

"You notice fashion details," Jake said. "I don't."

"Fashion or not, I believe there were extracurricular celebrations beyond the proposal itself."

Jake raced down the mountain ahead of the others. His thighs aching, he lifted his cell phone and sought a signal. Successful, he called his brother Nick and heard a groggy voice.

"Hello."

"Sorry, I forgot the time difference. Did I wake you?"

"Yeah, but I should have been up already. It's almost eight here. I've got a Reiki appointment at ten."

"Giving or getting?"

"Conducting a session for a friend. I've got a couple massages scheduled this afternoon, too. Business is picking up a bit."

"Good. If you ever need money, I can get some to you whenever."

"I appreciate the offer, but you don't have to keep asking. I'll be fine."

"I can't believe people pay you for what you do," Jake said. "I guess that's a good thing though."

"Many people see a lot of what I do as hocus pocus, but there's truth to it all. I help people feel better physically and spiritually."

Jake ran his hand through his hair.

"Yeah, that's kind of why I'm calling. I'm about to do something that could be dangerous."

"Who? You?"

"Be serious. I'm scared. For the first time I can remember, I'm scared like something's not right. I'm not sure if it's because you planted a seed in my head that gloom and doom was around the corner or what."

Jake waited in silence while he knew that Nick tapped into whatever third eye or energy field served as his wellspring of insight.

"Sorry," Nick said. "You know I stink at lying. I still sense danger. There is something wrong."

"Shit."

"I'm sorry, Jake. I'm concerned, too. Maybe you should back out of whatever you're planning."

"I don't back out of anything."

"I know. And I can't guarantee that backing out is the safer route. All I know is that your heart senses danger, and only your heart knows what your next move is."

"So what the hell good does that do me?"

"Connect with your heart and you'll know."

"Maybe in my next lifetime. I don't have time in this one. Not now anyway."

"If we had more time together, I could…"

"Never mind, Nick. Just let it go."

"Don't you want to know how Joey is?"

"No. He can take a flying leap… I mean, I'm glad you're okay. Look, I gotta go."

Jake hung up and wondered if his brother knew something that he was too dense to understand.

The next day, Pierre Renard examined the *Scorpène* submarine's operations room.

Six dual-stacked French-designed Subtics system tactical monitors spanned the compartment's left side. Seated before one panel was Antoine Remy, his longtime sonar expert. Short with a thick nose, Remy wore a sonar headset that made his head appear wide. He reminded Renard of a toad.

"This system is just like an *Agosta's*," Remy said. "It's easy."

"As it should be," Renard said. "Let me test the periscope."

Renard stuck his eye to the optics and saw the dreary Toulon waterfront. He toggled the magnification back and forth and stepped back.

"The periscope works," he said. "Submarine construction continues to amaze me with its efficacy and reliability. Sea trials seem almost anticlimactic."

"Who knew all those years of slaving away on old *Agostas* were preparing me for a life of riches earned by working for you on these new luxurious hulls?"

"I knew," Renard said. "I could feel it even back then, my friend. I was proud of our naval uniforms, but I sensed that someday we'd be setting sail on our own terms."

"Bullshit," Jake said.

The Frenchman spun around the periscope and pressed his palms against the railing surrounding the elevated conning platform. His American friend looked troubled.

"Bullshit?"

"We're doing this on your terms, not our terms," Jake said. "Just like our last venture and even on the *Colorado*, everyone is doing your damned bidding. You're a manipulator, and we're just pawns."

"At last count," Renard said, "my so-called pawns included eight millionaires. More than twice that many if you credit me with enriching my informants and moles."

"Hello, Jake," Remy said. "We all know he's a bastard. That's why we adore him. Didn't you sleep well last night? You seem more irritable than normal."

"Hi, Antoine. I slept like crap."

Renard saw Henri, his back straight with dignity in each step, enter the control center behind Jake.

"It's like I'm on an *Agosta*," he said. "I know I'm not, but I can feel and sense it. Things aren't located exactly where I want them to be, but the ship is familiar."

"Henri, my friend," Renard said. "I know you will adjust. It's our American colleague that concerns me."

"I'll be fine," Jake said.

A shipyard worker, a design expert in the Subtics system, slid by Henri and took a seat beside Remy. Renard watched him open a manual under Remy's nose and tap keys to run a pre-underway system diagnostic."

"You had better be fine," Renard said. "I need my executive officer at peak performance."

Two hours later, a second shipyard expert joined Henri by the ship's control station, and a veteran sailor, new to Renard's team after leaving the French Navy, sat with Remy and the first shipyard expert in front of the Subtics monitors.

Jake hovered over the group as an extra set of hands and as its human data aggregator. A sound-powered headset covered his ears, keeping him in communication with LaFontaine in the propulsion spaces.

Renard stuck his eyes to the periscope optics but pulled back and glanced at a monitor showing the outside world. He swiveled the periscope controls and panned the view in the monitor down to a tugboat escorting their submarine through the short egress channel. Taking a ship to sea quickened his pulse.

"Ha! How do you feel now, Jake?" he asked. "Once again, we are leading a ship to sea."

"Yeah," Jake said. "It's not so bad."

The tug had departed, and swells rocked the ship.

"Are we at the dive point yet?" Renard asked.

"Two minutes if you want to be perfect," Jake said. "We can submerge anytime you want though."

"Perhaps we should name our vessel prior to its first dive."

"I thought we agreed to call it the *Mercer*, at least for this one mission," Jake said. "Grant's paying for it."

"And so it shall be," Renard said. "Henri, submerge the *Mercer*. Make your depth thirty meters."

Renard watched turquoise envelope his optics and yellow rays dance in the subsurface waves. The *Mercer* slid below the swells as he lowered the periscope.

"We're steady at thirty meters," Henri said. "Speed five knots. So far, this ship behaves like a dream."

CHAPTER 11

Brad Flint watched Alex Baines flip a microphone toward his mouth.

"What's that? Okay, got it," he said.

"What's that you got, XO?" Flint asked.

"Possible target zig, INS *Leviathan*."

Sound frequency data shifted on across a monitor.

"You see it?" Flint asked.

"Yes, sir. Down-Doppler on their reduction gear frequencies and an increase in blade rate. It's too early for wave front data to give us information on their new range, but I'm sure they're accelerating."

"We'll let them open distance a thousand yards before reacting."

"Yes, sir."

"In the meantime, give me an update on merchants,"

Baines toggled a button, flipping through monitor views. He pointed at fuzzy traces.

"We've lost contact with three merchants in the last half hour and picked up only one. We're still close enough to a shipping lane to be concerned."

"This whole sea is a shipping lane, except where the trawlers are tossing nets over the side just to complicate our lives. Keep an eye out."

"I will sir," Baines said. "Sonar has a new speed for the *Leviathan* of eight knots, based on blade rate."

"After cutting holes in the ocean on their tip toes, they now all of a sudden need to get somewhere."

"Looks like it, sir."

"They might be in cruise missile launch range of coastal Egypt, right?"

"Depends on who you believe on the range of a Popeye missile," Baines said. "We might have just validated that it's in line with the longer range estimates, assuming they just simulated a launch."

"We didn't hear them opening outer doors, but they already proved they can simulate a launch sequence near Syria. They might just be making sure they can hang out and await launch orders without being caught. "

"Yes, sir."

"Okay, match their course and speed."

While Baines had the crew accelerate the *Annapolis*, Flint scratched his chin and stood. His disheveled hair brushed piping, and he curved his lanky frame forward. He gestured to Baines who slid his headset to a seat and met him at the polished railing of the conning platform.

"I'm going back and forth in my head, XO."

"You mean—are we trailing a ballsy and clumsy commanding officer or are we witnessing something else?"

"Bingo. And not an iota of insight on this from back home. You'd think someone would've lit a fire under the Israeli ambassador's ass for some answers."

"We have to let the bigwigs play the diplomacy game."

"Shit. If that's our only hope, we're in trouble."

Salem scowled.

"They're taking forever to slow," he said.

"As expected," Asad said. "A ship of that size is difficult to stop. Coasting to a standstill takes time."

"It's useless now to argue, but tell me why they aren't ordering their engines in reverse."

"Suspicion. A commercial tanker would never do so unless trying to avoid a collision, and any sonar system within a hundred kilometers would take notice."

"How soon until nightfall?"

"Two hours."

"This is trying my patience," Salem said.

"I sense the unrest among the men, too," Asad said. "The Russians warned us of psychological stress on a submarine, as did Bazzi. He remembers the old days."

"I'm starting to feel it myself. I pray that the *Zafar* will reinvigorate us."

"Me, too, Hana. And some of us will at least get fresh air tonight."

"We'll all get fresh air. If the *Zafar's* captain has a shred of decency, he'll send stores along with the tow lines. We'll use everyone to carry food down the hatch."

Ali Yousif twisted his rotund mass atop a seat before a stacked monitor.

"The *Zafar* is three miles away," he said, "and still probably moving. If we assume a three mile stopping distance, they have another two to drift."

"It could be as long as five miles," Asad said. "This isn't a parameter commonly tested on tankers. Braking distance, yes, but drifting to a stop is less known."

"But we need to know it now," Salem said. "Ali, what can you do for us in getting us near the *Zafar*?"

"Well, I believe I've figured out how this system works when we hear a ship. Our hull sonar picks it up and displays it here."

He pointed to a fuzzy green line running up the monitor. Salem moved behind his shoulder.

"Yes, I know," he said. "But are you making sense of it? Data we can apply?"

"Well, yes and no. I mean not really me. It seems automatic. If this line is the *Zafar*, it passed very close to us, as it should have. The direction to it changed rapidly as it passed, and this system volunteered parameters describing its motion and location in relation to ourselves."

"And?"

"And I was able to adjust a variable, an assumption on the *Zafar's* speed. Since we know it to be ten knots, I was able to insert that value into the system, and it accepted it. That's how I know where they were."

"Were?"

"Yes. You see, our sonar system seems to no longer hear the sound source I was monitoring."

"Which confirms that they secured their propellers," Asad said. "This is good news. Latakia thought he had heard them on the sonar system, but was unsure. This helps confirm that he heard and then stopped hearing their blades, meaning they are now drifting."

"So the system can tell us where they are and when they will finish their drift to a stop?" Salem asked. "I intend to take position behind them without keeping our periscope continuously exposed, but I would hate to drive into them."

"Perhaps," Yousif said. "But if so, I don't know how. However, I'll take their location when their propellers fell silent and extrapolate a simple exponential decay of speed. Assuming that three miles is their drift distance…"

"No, no," Asad said. "Why not instead ascend to snorkel depth, raise our radio mast, and ask them where they are? Since they are close, we can dial down transmit power to avoid snooping ears. If they cannot hear us, then we dial up power until they do."

"I like that much better than guessing," Salem said. "Take us shallow."

The *Leviathan* rocked as Salem peered above the waves. The sunlight seemed bright and foreign.

"I don't see them" he said.

"Me neither," Asad said. "The contrast on my monitor is excellent. They're just not in sight. Would you like Latakia to take us shallower to give you a greater height of eye?"

"Why?"

"You see farther when the periscope is higher."

"No. Just send them our greeting and a request of their position."

He heard one of his linguists speaking Farsi into a microphone. The ensuing silence weighed on him.

"This periscope has a radio antenna on it, right?"

"Yes, Hana," Asad said. "You used it last night to send rendezvous coordinates to the *Zafar*."

"Apparently they only partially listened," Salem said. "Either that or they grossly underestimated their stopping distance."

A voice crackled over a loudspeaker, and Salem's pulse raced. His linguist's voice became animated.

"They've acknowledged our message. They are at one and a half knots, still slowing. They are located at... please, someone write these numbers down... I believe they are coordinates."

"I'll write them," Yousif said.

Salem heard scribbling as the academics dictated and scribed numbers.

"They're estimating another mile before full stop," the linguist said.

"Tell them we'll be in position soon," Salem said. "I'm lowering the periscope. Asad, take us down to thirty meters."

An hour later, Salem had the *Leviathan* within half a mile of the drifting tanker.

"We should slow, Hana," Asad said.

"I agree. Two knots?"

"Yes, until nightfall."

"Will we see them?"

"Yes, I hope so. They are supposed to leave their stern light on. It's white with a narrow field of illumination, but we should see it from our position."

"And nobody else should see them?" Salem asked.

"Only those who would be directly behind them, and so what if they do? If interrupted, we'll wait until an intruding ship passes. Our visual signature at night is almost imperceptible. We won't be seen."

"Nightfall is when?"

"Thirty minutes," Asad said. "This is perfect timing."

*   *   *

The *Leviathan* had drifted to a stop behind the tanker *Zafar*. Salem peered through the periscope at a white spec.

"I see its light," he said. "But I can't see them."

"Let your eye adjust, Hana. It will take time, but you will make out their silhouette."

"It's time to contact them. We need to make sure that they are lowering the skiff."

"Perhaps we should surface now," Asad said. "If we do not, their skiff will be challenged to find us."

"I'll surface once I'm sure their skiff is approaching," Salem said. "No sooner."

With the *Leviathan's* high frequency radio set at a minimal power setting, the linguist contacted the bridge of the *Zafar*. As he reported that the tanker had lowered a skiff, Salem made out the white outline of the tanker's monstrous superstructure. He had failed to see it while darkness dilated his pupil and his mind refused to acknowledge the tanker's girth.

"Surface us," he said.

After running a blower to push air into ballast tanks and lift the ship, Salem ordered a battery charge. Two of the *Leviathan's* diesel engines ran, drawing air through the snorkel mast while Salem donned an Israeli officer's uniform and had his linguist do the same.

"Pressure is equalized," Asad said.

"What?"

"I equalized outside air pressure and hull pressure. This will keep you from flying out of the ship as you open the hatch."

"It's good you thought of it."

Salem opened and passed through the hatch. The night enveloped him in a half moon glow. The linguist joined him by his side, pointing a flashlight in the direction of the obelisk floating a football field away.

With the close proximity, the skiff from the *Zafar* found the submarine with ease. The twenty-five foot motorized vessel approached close enough for Salem to see its pilot's moonlit face.

His four Hamas soldiers brushed by as they moved to the *Leviathan's* bow. In pairs, they knelt with socket wrenches and flipped over a cleat on either side. He admired their efficiency and looked back to the skiff.

The small watercraft's pilot seemed nonplused by the lack of convenient mooring as he pulled aside the submarine and ran twin outboard engines in reverse. A thick towing line rose from the water, the skiff struggling against the line's neutral buoyancy.

Placing his fingers between his lips, the pilot unleashed a piercing whistle. A deckhand beside him tossed a baseball-sized rubber sphere at Salem, who dodged it and watched it bounce on the hull and splash into the sea. Unsure what to do, he welcomed Asad who rose through the hatch and examined the activity.

"Take the rope and pull," he said. "I'll get the soldiers to help. You'll need help and gloved hands."

Assisted by the linguist, Salem pulled the rope and looked to the skiff for guidance. He noticed a capstan on the watercraft's bow rotating and paying out towing line as it redirected it from the *Zafar* toward the *Leviathan*.

As he pulled, an oval, metal-clasped eyehook bumped up against the hull. The soldiers arrived, and he gestured for their help. They took the small rope from him and pulled it in unison to the deck.

The soldiers grabbed the hook and shuffled toward the bow when another piercing whistle shot from the skiff. Shaking his head, the pilot gestured for additional pulling. Nodding, Hamdan barked out commands and had the soldiers redouble their efforts.

As their reward for ten meters of yanking, the mooring line presented a split. Added tugging lifted the split half to the deck, revealing a second eye hook. As the soldiers dragged both eyehooks to the bow cleats, the pilot nodded approval.

Asad darted toward an eyehook and reached for a tumbling black box dangling from a wire. He cradled it while following the soldiers forward.

As the soldiers lay the hooks over the cleats, Salem watched Asad unfurl coiled cord that swirled around one of the hooks. A perplexed look on his face, Asad came up to Salem.

"It appears to be communications equipment."

Salem glanced at the pilot who cycled his gaze through the soldiers, his watercraft's slicing toward the front of the submarine, and a deckhand paying out tow line to the cleats with the capstan.

A voice rang from the box in Asad's hand. It spoke Arabic in a dialect Salem recognized as Iraqi but with an accent of a native Farsi speaker.

"Are the ropes over your cleats?"

"How do we answer?" he asked.

"I don't know," Asad said.

Asad depressed a switch, and a green light illuminated.

"I guess that's it. Yes, the ropes are on."

"Thank you. Stand by."

The pilot waved his hand, and two deckhands on the skiff pried the mooring line turn by turn over the top of the capstan until it fell into the water.

A lookout high on the *Zafar* caught Salem's eye. His lips moved in front of a bridge to bridge radio, and Salem heard the voice again from the box.

"We're taking up slack on the tow line."

To Salem's dislike, he noticed that the weight-bearing capstan that would tow the *Leviathan* had been installed ten meters above the waterline. Any observer could see it and speculate that the *Zafar* was towing something behind it.

He pressed the button for talking.

"Is there no other mooring point? That capstan is very high."

"It's all we could do with the ship's design."

"Who are you?"

"The captain. Who are you?"

"The captain," Salem said.

"You can take this communication box with you through your hatch. It is an ultrathin design and should work even while compressed through a watertight seal. It will let us speak."

"An excellent idea, if it works."

"You'll have wrapping wires coming in the first box from the skiff. Draw figure eights around the cleats with the wire and clamp them down over the hooks."

"It will be done."

"Hana, come on!" Asad said. "Fresh food."

He turned and saw the skiff, unmated but pressed alongside the submarine, with deckhands dangling boxes on the ends of pole arms.

"No, not food yet. Have the soldiers open the first boxes and take the wrapping wires to the cleats. Figure eights and securing the hooks."

"Yes, I know what they mean. I will see to it."

Salem sent his linguist below to call on other men to retrieve the next boxes, filled with food, and to enjoy the fresh air he promised.

The *Zafar*'s captain spoke, his voice ringing from the box with clarity.

"I'm going to restart my engines and begin towing you. You can secure the hooks while I do so. The wire is merely to assure the hooks don't slide off the cleats at deep angles. We control the tension here with the capstan, and it's an automated and reliable design."

"An excellent decision to move onward. I thank you for the job well done and the provisions."

"And I thank you for what you will soon accomplish."

*   *   *

North of Libya in the Mediterranean Sea, the Trigger stood on the bridge of the supertanker beside the Captain. With the report of a successful mating between the *Zafar* and the *Leviathan*, he felt relief, excitement, and the persistent stab of sadness that reminded him of his connection with mass death. It hit deeply, and he winced, but he fathomed no other existence. It felt comfortable.

"This is impressive," he said.

"Yes," the Captain said. "Now if that whore professor can produce equally impressive results, I sense the odds turning in our favor."

"I am told that Salem visited the professor and the captain of the Aegis ship," the Trigger said. "He believes she is devious enough and him foolish enough to accomplish our task."

The Trigger looked through the window to the ship's moonlit deck for inspiration.

"Three armed missiles with destinies that will be masked and protected by seventeen decoy missiles," he said. "And now the possibility of finding and removing our greatest obstacle, the Aegis destroyer. How far behind us is the *Leviathan*?"

"Less than a day."

"Thus far," the Trigger said, "the plan is unfolding per design."

"Outboard engines?" Flint asked, his eye pressed against the periscope's eyepiece.

"That's what they might be," Baines said. "There's probably just some high speed pleasure craft on the same bearing. Heck, the guys in the sonar room barely heard it. It could be miles away and have nothing to do with the *Leviathan*."

"This is screwed up. *Leviathan* disappears, then surfaces, and then disappears again. And now you say we might have heard outboard engines."

"Just the blades. High speed screws. Outboard engines are loud as heck, but the sound hardly penetrates the surface. I saw that in counter-narcotics ops as a junior officer."

The *Annapolis* rolled.

"Right. I stand corrected. You don't see anything on the monitor? No *Leviathan*? No cigar boats? No drug runners, *Titanic*, or *Flying Dutchman*?"

"No, sir. It's dark and lonely up there. I suggest that we lower the scope and begin a spiraling outward search for the *Leviathan* from its last known datum."

"After we get a note to squadron. Draft one telling them about high speed screws after the *Leviathan* surfaced and we lost contact with it."

"Aye, aye, sir."

"What about that merchant we regained on the bearing of *Leviathan*."

"I don't know sir. We had it solved at a range of twelve miles. Given that it turned up on the same bearing as the *Leviathan*, it's probably even farther than that, or moving a heck of lot slower than fifteen knots."

Flint sighed.

"We're going to need everyone from this watch section involved in reconstructing what we think we know."

"Even while we search for *Leviathan*?"

"Yes. The next watch section can manage the search. There are answers in front of us we aren't seeing that I want everyone rethinking."

"Aye, aye, sir. I'll take care of it."

Flint pinched the bridge of his nose.

"Shit, XO. This is getting tough. I'm not sure who's in charge of a highly capable submarine that we just lost track of less than four miles away. I don't know if I'm tracking, trailing, or hunting, and I'm waiting for some bureaucrat in Washington to at least give me permission to decide for myself."

"We'll be fine, sir. *Leviathan's* bound to make noise. We always picked them up again within a couple of hours. You'll feel better after we regain it."

"I hope you're right, but I got a feeling you ain't."

CHAPTER 12

Olivia McDonald yawned and stretched her arms behind her chair. She leaned forward and lifted a cappuccino off her desk. The foamy froth and strong taste woke her senses.

She flipped open the dossier of Farah Ghaffari. A doctoral thesis comprised the bulk of it, and her history before entering Tehran's university system spanned two paragraphs of conjecture. Beyond the two-page summary of the NCIS investigation into her unusual husband chasing behavior, Google could have provided the entirety of her history.

Ghaffari's headshot—taken from the Old Dominion faculty directory—showed a woman whose smile concealed a sinister secret and formed a semi-sneer. The eyes radiated with intelligence and anger. She was attractive with sharp features but intimidating and haunting, Olivia thought.

From Iran's Khuzestan province on the Iraqi border, she was raised bilingual in Persian and Arabic. She also had been a young girl witnessing the brunt of atrocity and destruction during the Iran-Iraq War. Either orphaned or sent away for her protection—the dossier falling short on the distinction—she moved in with her uncle in the safer Tehran province at the age of sixteen.

She scored in the top five percent of students on her admissions tests to the University of Tehran and finished equally high in her undergraduate class. In her post-graduate work, she achieved no special honors while earning her doctoral degree in psychology.

Olivia found Ghaffari's doctoral thesis to be vanilla, as if sanitized of its strongest insights and emotions. Its subject of youth rebellion and escape from home caught Olivia's eye, but a quick online search showed the thesis subject's prevalence among a small minority of Iranian doctoral students.

Based on the subject matter, she expected to read a tirade of protest. Instead, Ghaffari's work was a sterile numerical analysis predicting the future exodus of Iran's youth from homes to streets and violence. It bordered on macro-economics in its supplanting of passion with numbers, and she found the categorization of reasons driving the exodus—rebellion against conservatism, accepting the futility of economic disadvantage, and susceptibility to recruitment by organized radicals—to be stale.

The reasons that caught her attention by their omission were those that young women trampled by war often face—violence and sexual abuse. Having suffered both horrors herself, Olivia wondered if luck or foresight had spared Ghaffari during the Iran-Iraq War, or if she had repressed their damaging effect too deeply to reflect in her thesis.

Olivia read on, seeking evidence of Ghaffari's psyche in her lectures and in the reviews thereof. She found mundane subjects supported by centerline arguments delivered in mechanical doses. Ghaffari seemed to seek and achieve career mediocrity, but Olivia sensed that an ugly truth concealed a greater ability with energies directed elsewhere. She wanted to know where.

A two-minute search through the CIA employee database and a five-minute walk later, she leaned against the desk of a tall man in his early twenties with acne marking a face glistening in permanent perspiration.

She recognized Matt Williams from pleasant smiles in the hallway and from occasional cafeteria sightings. She had never said a complete sentence to him.

"You're an expert on Iran, right?" she asked.

Williams looked up, and his eyes opened with surprise.

"Yeah. What do you need?"

"Oh, my name's Olivia, by the way."

She extended her hand. His palm felt like sushi.

"Yes, I know your name. You're sort of a legend. Olivia McDonald. I'm Matt."

"What it's like growing up as a girl in the eighties? Khuzestan province."

"Geez," he said, rotating his chair to face her. His arms reached behind his neck and he made no attempt to hide his joy of serving as an authority.

"Normally I'd say, life in Iran depends on the particular village, but if you're talking in the eighties, Khuzestan province, during the Iran-Iraq War, or any of the other names it's been called…"

"Yes," she said. "During the war."

"Then life sucked."

"How bad could it suck?"

"As bad as it can get for a woman."

Olivia stared at him with eyes that had seen a slave trafficker hold a knife to her throat while raping her. Williams took the hint, leaned forward, and assumed an air of business.

"Statistics obviously aren't very good, but reasonable assumptions and reports of survivors indicate that it was hell. There were abuses of all sorts."

"Namely?" she asked.

"Violence. Beatings. Rapes. Mutilations. Your subject was lucky to walk out alive."

"My subject left the province at sixteen and eventually went to school at the University of Tehran. PhD in psychology. Her life turned out amazingly successful for what she might have gone through. I'm trying to figure out what that was and if it's driving her now."

"It's obviously a male-dominated society, and there generally wasn't much chance for women to rise in any social strata until the last decade or so, when they started becoming mainstream in the universities. Whatever she went through in the war might have forced her to turn away from family life in search of broader education."

"Turning on family? That could lead to an emptiness on top of any permanent psychological damage from the war..."

Olivia felt a lump in her throat. Analyzing a potential rape victim hit too close to home. Williams picked up on it and rescued her.

"I'm no psychologist, but you are, and a damn good one I hear. It looks like you're trying to figure out if this woman is damaged and taking it out on someone. My guess is that you're on to something based upon her background."

"Okay," she said, recovering. "That makes sense."

"Cool," he said, smiling. "Can you observe her?"

Olivia contemplated Ghaffari's proximity.

"Yeah," she said. "That's a good idea."

The next day, she drove to Norfolk and met a navy intelligence officer at the headquarters of the U.S. Atlantic Fleet. Commander Roger Sanders had been a helicopter pilot before joining the intelligence community. His lean, tall frame had hard, powerful lines, and he moved with precision as he walked in a starched white uniform to Olivia. A smile covered a face of soft features.

"Commander Sanders," he said, extending his hand.

"Olivia McDonald. Pleased to meet you."

She judged his mannerisms warm and casual for a naval officer. He had a deliberate ease and a sense that everything in his world was right.

"Director Rickets left orders with my boss to greet you personally and escort you to our Sensitive Compartmented Information Facility," he said.

"That's great."

"Do you need a moment? You've had a long drive."

"No, I'm good."

Alone with Sanders behind the egg carton walls and shelves filled with special compartmented information publications, she sat in a Naugahyde chair and noticed that he seemed out of place. His eyes were compassionate, unlike those of the cold and stern stares she had seen from military personnel. She wanted to know him, but she denied herself the indulgence.

"Did someone explain my business to you," she asked.

"Briefly. An Iranian professor of psychology engaged to the captain of a *Burke* class destroyer. Possible questionable motives. Sounds interesting and less stressful than what I've been dealing with otherwise."

"The *Leviathan*, you mean? I'm cleared for it, you know."

"I know," he said. "My boss told me you worked your tail off on that and that you're on your present assignment as a sort of break from the action."

"Yeah, that's what Gerry thought was best for me," she said. "I went with it."

"Gerry? Director Gerald Rickets? You're on a first name basis with him?"

"We go way back."

"You're more interesting than I'd hoped," he said.

She watched a smile spread over his face and blushed.

"Look, Commander Sanders…"

"Roger, please," he said. "Everyone calls me Roger. At least in private."

"Okay, Roger. Call me Olivia, at least in private."

"Deal."

"Roger, how did NCIS bring Doctor Farah Ghaffari to your attention?"

"Oh yes," he said, stiffening. "Very discreetly. She's engaged to the skipper of the *Bainbridge*, who I know by reputation as a well-connected tyrant. I'm glad the guys in the bars are paying attention and noticed that she was on a mission to get married, but there's no crime in husband hunting and latching onto the biggest fish."

"Husband hunting exclusively for destroyer sailors?"

"I wrote that off as coincidence," he said. "Well, sort of. I mean, guys from the destroyer community will hit the same bars. Same for the helo pilots, same for the fixed wing jocks, and et cetera for each community. She may have just been hunting by location. But to be honest, I didn't give her much thought because the *Leviathan* incident hit right after NCIS told me about her."

"I'm wondering if she was doing more than husband hunting," Olivia said.

Sanders leaned back in his chair, and Olivia felt his eyes probing her for wisdom.

"I'd like to hear why," he said. "I'm sure any time soon I'll be buried under a new review of the *Leviathan* data. So this will be my only distraction for a while."

"My analysis of Ghaffari is that she has a deep-rooted hatred of something, and that something is probably authority figures, especially male authority figures."

"Her fiancé fits the description."

"What about the others?" she asked.

Sanders flipped through pages of a folder.

"You know," he said, "you may be on to something. I didn't see it until you mentioned it because I was focusing on demographics like age and rank, which seemed random. But if you look at the photos of the guys she targeted, all of them look like authority figures. Even the young guy, Petty Officer Wendell, who's only twenty six, has gray hair and an air of distinction. Everyone else is over thirty."

"May I?" she asked as she reached for the folder.

"Sure."

"They all look distinguished with age," she said. "Most men pick up an air of bitterness or weakness with age, but not these guys. Proud. Actually, more proud looking than distinguished."

"She's had sex with all six men," Sanders said, "over a period of nine months. And that's just the guys that admitted it. I'm no PhD, but for a woman her age, that sounds like deep issues, husband-hunting or not."

Olivia folded the pages of the folder and stared at Ghaffari's victims of seduction. She felt something clicking in her mind.

"Commander Pastor is the only commanding officer," she said.

"Yes," Sanders said.

"She had extended relationships with two other men, Senior Chief Thomas Wilson of the *Bainbridge* and Lieutenant Commander Howard Reardon of the *Truxton*. Two months each."

"Yes," Sanders said.

"The fleeting relationships with the others were at most three weeks. She moved with purpose and skill through the men until she found one to…"

"Yes?"

"To take the bait."

"But what bait and why?" Sanders asked. "What makes this more complex than seeking a husband?"

"Destroyer sailors, all of them. Positions of authority or at least an air of presumed authority. Her body given freely, detached, used as a tool."

"Or a weapon."

"Wait," she said.

She flipped through pages and scanned the testimonies from each man.

"The three men with the fleeting relationships stated that she broke of the affair with no apparent ongoing interest in the man, right?"

"Sounds right," Sanders said. "I admit that I haven't yet given much time to look into this."

"But Wilson and Reardon state that she pushed them for marriage before she cut off the relationship."

"Still smells like textbook husband hunting."

"What's common among the three she wanted to marry—Wilson, Reardon, and Pastor—that's missing from the other three?"

"Are you asking me or quizzing me?"

"You're the navy guy. Is there something about their jobs?"

She slid the folder back to Sanders and watched him flip through pages.

"Reardon and Pastor are an executive officer and commanding officer respectively. So they have full access to almost anything on the ship. Wilson's a radio chief."

"What about the other three?"

"Engineering petty officer, deck chief, sonar chief."

"There's nothing in common between the last three, is there," she asked.

"Not really."

"What about pay?"

"The officers make the most money, of course, but Wilson is young for a chief. The deck chief and sonar chief that she ditched quickly have bigger paychecks. Money doesn't define her search."

"How about roles on their ships?" she asked.

"Communications," Sanders said. "The senior officers have access to anything on the ship, but Wilson narrows it easily to ship to shore communications. That's what they all have in common, and that's interesting."

"Maybe," Olivia said. "I need to learn more."

"How?"

"By meeting her. I need to figure out if she's chasing down a man to fill a life function or if she still thinks she's a young girl in a war zone seeking a way to fight back."

"How do you plan on that?"

"I'm going to find her on campus. Maybe start by going to one of her lectures."

Sanders nodded towards a desktop computer.

"Go ahead and log in as a guest. See if you can find her schedule."

Olivia logged in and browsed the Old Dominion site.

"Look," she said. "She's giving a public talk tomorrow night on self-esteem, poverty, and youth. Can you help me arrange for a room on base for tonight?"

"Sure. You don't waste any time, do you?"

"No, I don't. And as long as I'm here, I'd like you to keep me company. Can you take me to dinner?"

"Well, sure. Do you always get dates with guys just like that?"

"I just know how to read body language and knew you'd say yes."

"It was that obvious I was impressed with you?" he asked.

"From the moment you saw me."

He seemed flattered but then took on a somber tone.

"Look, Olivia, as long as we're sprinting down lover's lane, but I have to be open about something. I'm HIV positive. I earned it from a whore during a drunken port call, I lost my wife from it, and I make no excuses about it. This scares off ninety percent of the women I meet, and I make it a practice to lead with candor instead of wasting time."

"Gerry requested you personally?"

"Well, yeah, Director Rickets asked for me personally to work with you on this, but it makes sense since–"

"Damn him!"

Sanders stared at her blankly.

"Sorry," she said.

"Whoa. It's okay. What's going on?"

"I'm HIV positive, too," she said. "We've been set up."

"You mean Director Rickets."

"Yes, Gerry is trying to play Cupid."

"Oh," he said, blushing.

"I want to leave now," she said.

"Good idea."

Sanders stood and escorted her into the hallway. She heard his heels clapping the floor as he kept pace.

"You know, Olivia, you asked me out before you knew I was HIV positive."

"I know," she said. "I had no business."

"You had every right."

"But I don't need Gerry playing daddy and moving people around for me like pawns. I've thought about this every second of every day that I can't force myself to think of something else, and I want to do this on my own."

"Since when?"

"What?"

She stopped abruptly.

"Since when?" he asked. "You said you've thought about this every day. Since acquiring the virus or since some time later than that?"

She remembered Jake and wondered who she was outside of the relationship with him. She felt free but vulnerable.

"Since I became free," she said.

"Interesting."

"Yes, and I want to tell you more over dinner, assuming you'll have me. I want you to take me out."

"Of course," he said. "My pleasure."

A full bird captain approached, scowling. He brushed by Olivia with a curt greeting.

"Excuse me ma'am," he said.

He turned to Sanders.

"Please escort your guest to the quarterdeck, commander. I need you to round up the entire staff for a briefing. It's going to be a long night."

The captain turned and departed.

"Rain check?" Olivia asked.

"Sure," Sanders said, "but from the looks of it, it's going to be storming for a while."

The next evening, Olivia arrived ten minutes late to an evening lecture Farah Ghaffari was giving on self-esteem, poverty, and youth.

The subject material complemented her course curriculum, and students from her daytime sections filled the front of the auditorium. Olivia counted three dozen other attendees from faculty, staff, and other interests. A handful of young adults scribbling and sharing notes were clustered together, probably making an appearance from a local community college.

Olivia slid into a center seat ten rows from the podium and opened a notepad into which she feigned interest. She switched on her psychological radar, listening, seeing, feeling, and dissecting the speaker.

Ghaffari scrunched forward with white knuckles grasping a wooden podium and a makeshift dowager's hump pushing her head into a microphone. Olivia sensed an inner tension constricting a normally erect posture into a coil of discomfort.

Ghaffari's mouth was tight as she spoke, and her pupils were dark abysses surrounded by the intense radiance of brown irises. When she blinked, crow's feet formed by her eyes and her brow furrowed.

Olivia glanced around the room to see if any other listener reacted to the anger and pain she felt from the Iranian professor, but everyone else in the auditorium showed bland interest out of perceived duty or worked to understand the content of the lesson. She was alone in being in tune with Ghaffari's suffering.

The concepts she explored in discourse included reserved judgments on the reasons why leaders create poverty, why people accept it, and how people can compel themselves to rise above it. Other than noting the austerity of the content, Olivia found it dry.

She heard the professor rattle off concepts in words that were neutral. Her voice droned with the clarity and cadence of rehearsed repetition. Her face was plasticized, but Olivia caught the bulging veins of her neck throbbing. Ghaffari held back an emotional force, and Olivia waited for it to reveal itself through a crack.

Finally, it surfaced in a brief, involuntary snarl when Ghaffari mentioned the word "mankind". Her eyebrows furrowed, her head drooped, and her lips tightened. It happened so fast that Olivia second guessed herself in having seen it. She shifted her weight and intensified her attention on the facial expressions.

She saw it again on the word "manpower", and she recognized the anger. Then she saw subtler, quicker expressions each time Ghaffari mentioned the word "man", "men", or any male-centric term.

She folded her notepad and left the auditorium.

Back at her office the next day, she called Rickets.

"She's angry at men," she said. "And it goes deep. There's something powerful and unresolved inside her."

Olivia waited and could hear Rickets trying to detach his mind from whatever he had been pondering.

"The Iranian psychologist?" he asked.

"Yes. The one engaged to the commanding officer of the *Bainbridge*," she said.

"Right," he said. "Go ahead."

"I want surveillance on her communications."

"Why?"

"She's been husband hunting destroyer sailors with no rational motive. She's got a teaching visa that's good for years, enough prestige to earn invitations to teach in other wealthy countries, and all the money she needs. She doesn't have a maternal bone in her body, and I can't see her seeking or holding a serious relationship with another human being without tons of therapy. Her only motive, conscious or unconscious, is the expression of anger."

"At whom?"

"Men."

"All men?"

"Any men, or any man," she said.

"She may intend harm to her fiancé?"

"Possibly."

"You learned this from reading her dossier?"

Olivia reflected upon how quickly she had arrived at her conclusions. Intuition, training, and having been a rape victim facilitated her transfer into Ghaffari's mind.

"Her dossier and a visit to one of her lectures."

"You met her?"

"No, just saw her. It was all I needed."

"How sure are you?"

"About eighty percent."

"Good enough. You've got your surveillance, but this raises the sensitivity bar. I can keep this hidden, but we're approaching that fine line between the bounds of national security and harassing a senior naval officer's fiancée. You find anything, you bring it right to me."

"Thanks, Gerry."

"Sure."

"One more thing," she said. "Playing matchmaker with Commander Sanders. If you ever pull a stunt like that again, I'll kick you in the balls."

That evening, Olivia began pouring through emails and text messages between Ghaffari and her fiancé, Commander Richard Pastor. She discovered that the professor was taking a subservient role to a man with a tone so arrogant that a first year psychology student could see his childlike insecurities. That Ghaffari acquiesced to him riveted Olivia with the realization that she was playing a manipulative game.

Solving the nature of that game would have to wait. Olivia needed a mental break, and she drove home.

*   *   *

That night, alone in her bed, she guided her mind to thoughts distant from Ghaffari. She remembered sweet times with Jake—a ski trip to the Swiss Alps, a dinner atop the Eiffel Tower, and a motorcycle ride that had come a year later than promised but which had taken her to breathtaking remote sites in Europe.

The memories slipped into a mire of colors as her feelings for Jake drifted toward indifference. She felt a new sensation rising within her and an image forming in her mind. She shut her eyes tight against it to no avail.

She felt giddy as she pictured Commander Sanders smiling at her in his dress white uniform.

CHAPTER 13

Renard had hardly slept during his first night as captain of the *Mercer*.

The thrill of returning to sea on a high-performance vessel had energized him through a day and a half of testing the *Mercer* at high speed, deep depth, and under the strain of every angle and acceleration he could squeeze from its propulsion and controls surfaces. The ship obeyed his will like a steel-shelled symbiotic mate.

Surfaced and heading toward Toulon, he stood atop the *Mercer's* conning tower sail. A tug approached, took station beside the submarine, and threw lines to Henri and hired hands on the deck.

A brow flopped from the tug onto the submarine, and the shipyard workers walked across it with test data and reports stuffed in waterproof packs on their backs. A hand on the tug flipped the brow back, and the tug was gone.

Renard lifted a microphone to his lips and ordered the *Mercer* to turn around and head back to sea. As the ship heeled over, he heard Jake calling him from below.

"Pierre!"

"Yes!"

"We have news from Rickets."

"I'll secure the bridge and be right down."

At the bottom of a ladder, Jake greeted him with an earnest stare.

"The bridge is secure," Renard said.

"I'll make sure Henri knows and gets us ready to dive when he gets back," Jake said. "Can we decrypt this now?"

"Of course," Renard said.

Jake handed him a flash drive, and Renard took it to the privacy of his stateroom. He typed his password into his laptop and watched words form on his screen.

The message drained Renard's life force and left him shaking with anger.

"Merde!"

He launched a punch. The thud against the bulkhead echoed in his chamber, and avulsed skin burned his knuckles. He whipped open the door to his room and marched forward to the operations room.

Seated at the ship's control station, Henri looked up with concern, as did Antoine Remy from the forward-most Subtics sonar monitor. Jake turned from the periscope and approached.

"Well?" he asked.

Renard could muster no words but gestured for Jake to follow as he turned back to his stateroom.

Jake was pulling a chair to a foldout desk as Renard slammed the stateroom door shut. Jake cringed and seemed astonished and frightened.

"Don't ask," Renard said. "Just look."

He pointed to his screen. Jake leaned forward and read the message.

"You're fucking kidding me," he said.

Renard sensed himself trembling, losing control, and struggling for balance. He reached for his deck to stabilize himself, and he felt Jake clutch his shoulders.

"Are you okay, Pierre?"

"Dear god. I don't know why this upsets me so much."

"It's okay," Jake said. "It's actually good news, in a way," Jake said.

"For whom?"

"Let's talk about it when you're feeling better."

Catatonic, Renard let Jake think for him. Jake decided to submerge the *Mercer*, navigate the waters to the south of France, and gain familiarity with the ship's systems. There was little else to do.

Feeling the submarine submerge and commence the business of patrolling homeland waters dulled the bite of Renard's anger, revealing an underlying sadness. With the *Mercer* drifting into a tertiary supporting role of practical irrelevance, Renard sensed that the greatest days of his life were behind him.

He reflected upon the three topics of the note from Rickets. First, the Israeli's blinked during their last communiqué of diplomatic poker and admitted to the *Leviathan* behaving beyond its will. Second, the *Leviathan* had escaped its trailing American submarine and had spent the last two days at whereabouts unknown. Third, the last known track laid down by the *Leviathan* hinted that it was heading toward an American aircraft carrier task force steaming in the Mediterranean Sea.

Rickets had shared the information with an order for Renard to stand down the *Mercer's* hunt while American forces regrouped. A submarine had been detached from the task force to help find the *Leviathan*, and the *Mercer* had to stay out of the way.

Renard reclined in his rack, pondering that the loss of contact on the *Leviathan* signaled the end of the *Mercer* and his last chance to lead a submarine at sea.

He heard rapping at his door.

"Come in," he said.

Jake entered and pulled a chair beside Renard.

"I think I figured out why this is bothering you."

"Do tell," Renard said.

"Well, shit, Pierre, you're not getting any younger. I can see it in everyone else's faces, too. Even Henri looks bummed. This is the end of the gang."

"You seem rather relieved."

"Yeah," Jake said, running his hand through his hair. "I didn't have a good feeling about this."

"Indeed," Renard said. "That aura of charm protecting you since we first met had ebbed in recent weeks."

"My brother didn't help either. He filled my head with omens."

Renard rolled to his side and looked at Jake.

"That was a fine reunion."

"He didn't do it intentionally," Jake said. "He's a super-sensitive guy and into new age sort of stuff. When he talks about death, he means it."

"Then metaphorically he was correct. The *Leviathan* is indeed rogue, and if I were ten years younger I would find the means to place this ship within striking distance of a killing blow, regardless of Rickets' orders. But instead I feel defeated—dead if you must—and cannot muster the strength."

"I see what you mean. You look drained."

"And you," Renard said. "You were the spark I used to turn to, but you have decided that submarine warfare is in your past, have you not? I could not see it before, but now it's obvious. I've brought you here against your will, and you joined me out of loyalty alone."

Jake lowered his gaze.

"It's okay, my friend," Renard said. "You have many adventures and a long life ahead of you. But this is the winter of our adventures together."

"There's still a chance that the *Leviathan* pops up and we're needed for a kill shot."

Renard could sense that Jake preferred the more likely scenario where the *Mercer* remained useless.

"If everything is aligned as it appears," Renard said, "we will hear of the *Leviathan's* demise somewhere between its last known location and the steaming carrier task force. I fear that we will accomplish no more than the shakedown of this ship for its Malaysian customers. It's now time for me to think of... other things."

The next day, Olivia scrolled through six months of email confiscated from Farah Ghaffari's mail servers associated with the Iranian professor's accounts. She had little traffic beyond communications with students, staff, and faculty at Old Dominion and brief personal exchanges with her fiancé.

Mundane meanings filled most of Ghaffari's emails until her fiancé had headed to sea on the *Bainbridge* a week ago. Olivia read words of an emotional heart longing for a distant object of love, but she sensed that the professor was incapable of experiencing the feelings she claimed.

A recent and larger email file caught Olivia's attention. When she opened it, a picture of Commander Richard Pastor wearing his camouflage uniform appeared. She thought it odd that a man would send a photo of himself to his fiancée until she noticed that he was standing on the weather deck of a ship.

There were no identifying marks of the ship other than a doorframe through which the picture was taken, either by an assistant or a camera perched on a tripod with a timer. Based upon Pastor's supposed unapproachable personality and the meek puppy dog expression on his face, Olivia decided his portrait was a solitary effort.

The backdrop was purposefully romantic with the moon over his shoulder, a stuffed puppy dog with a big read heart on its chest under his arm, and a piece of construction paper with the phrase "195 days" written on it. Olivia surmised that the days represented a countdown to the wedding. After rummaging through an Internet search of wedding announcements, she verified her assumption.

She thought little of the photo until she came across a different email with a note from Pastor thanking Ghaffari for the little surprises she had planted in his sea bag. The email held a photo with him in the same pose, in the same place, but he held a giant Hershey kiss wrapped in red foil and a piece of construction paper reading "193 days".

Olivia leaned back in her chair and reflected. She leaned forward again and lifted a cappuccino off her desk. As the hot liquid energized her, she realized that she needed expert perspective on a question taking shape in her mind.

She called the few naval veterans she knew in the agency. Each verified that it was normal for a partner to leave cute and romantic gifts in a bag for her man while he was at sea, and that even the saltiest of sailors would cast aside his ruggedness and take pictures of himself to send back to a woman he loved, if asked.

Olivia finished scanning Ghaffari's emails and flagged Pastor's self-portraits as targets of future analysis.

She cleared her mind and let thoughts of a handsome naval intelligence officer creep into her head. After trying to thwart visions of Commander Sanders from growing in her mind and heart, she had given up. He had a hold on her.

She reached for her phone to call him but struggled to find a reason. Then she wondered if she could simply call him to say hello. She realized she could not and started down the passageway toward a break room in search of a snack to distract her from feelings she hadn't felt in years.

On her way to the break room, she decided to intensify the surveillance on Ghaffari. She would return to Norfolk and transform herself into a field asset to watch Ghaffari herself.

And it would remove the distance between herself and Commander Sanders.

Commander Brad Flint stooped over a navigation table in the control room of the *Annapolis*. He had spent three days spiraling, zigzagging, and repositioning his ship in search of the *Leviathan* but had found nothing.

With the Israeli submarine gone, he revisited the encounter where he had lost it. All the technology and brightest minds aboard his ship had reconstructed every known fact about the *Leviathan* when it disappeared. The verdict—the *Leviathan* had vanished without a trace.

The visual perspective Flint preferred for reviewing the *Leviathan's* disappearance was a simple hand-drawn graphing plot. Paper covered the navigation station's flat surface like a tablecloth. Ticked traces etched in colored pencils represented the Israeli submarine and all vessels occupying nearby water at the time.

He stared at the traces, struggling to make sense of what happened in the water almost four nights earlier.

Alex Baines appeared by his side.

"Still trying to make sense of it, sir?"

"Yup," Flint said.

"We'll find the *Leviathan* before it can threaten the carrier task force," Baines said. "Either we will or the assets from the task force will."

Flint grunted.

"Even if we don't finish this ourselves, we did our job, sir. Our work uncovered what was going on and allowed a task force to defend itself."

"If that's where the *Leviathan* is actually going," Flint said.

"There aren't many other interesting places for it. Maybe southern Europe to launch cruise missiles at what—Rome, Marseille, Barcelona? It's speculation, and given that the Israelis have admitted to losing control of the *Leviathan*, the carrier makes the best sense as a target."

Flint ignored Baines and tapped his finger on a thin, elongated oval that represented the uncertainty of the location of the high speed screws that had appeared in the direction of the *Leviathan* after its disappearance.

"We heard high speed screws on the general direction of the *Leviathan's* last known location, right?"

"Yes, sir. We've analyzed the heck out of them. They're the worst enigma in this mystery."

"High speed screws," Flint said. "You can make it from Cuba to Miami on a boat with high speed screws. So this could have been a sporting craft from Egypt."

"Could have come from Alexandria. Sure, sir. That's the verdict we agreed on. A small boat with high speed screws could theoretically make it from Alexandria to Beirut or Cyprus."

"But we would have heard it more consistently. It came and went, faded in and faded out too randomly. And then it was gone. We would have heard it pass by us with high bearing rate if it was making its way north or northeast."

"And it would have changed bearings if it was going any place else, sir. I know it. That's why it's not settling right for me."

"Nope. Not settling at all," Flint said.

Baines straightened his body.

"Well, sir," he said, "all we can do now is what we're doing. Head in the direction of the task force and see if we can catch the *Leviathan* before the task force does."

"Wait, XO."

"Yes, sir."

"We considered that one of the merchant vessels launched the high speed craft, right?"

"Of course, sir. It's possible, but unlikely."

"We've been dealing with the world of the unlikely since the *Leviathan* deployed."

"Agreed, sir. What's on your mind?"

"Some sort of interaction between a merchant ship, the high speed craft, and the *Leviathan*."

"We considered that, sir. We would have heard the high speed craft covering the distance between its mother ship and the *Leviathan* in that case."

"Not if the mother ship, as you say, was closer to the *Leviathan* than we thought."

"There were a couple ships that passed by the same bearing," Baines said. "But they were too far away to be factors."

"Humor me and let's see what happens if we change what we assumed about merchant speeds. Can we convince ourselves it's possible that one of these ships passed closer to *Leviathan?*"

Flint tapped a green trace and a purple trace representing the paths two ships had taken the night of the *Leviathan's* disappearance.

"What about these two?" he asked.

"We had blade rate for that one. So we know that its speed and tracking are accurate," Baines said. "We might have had blade rate for the other one, but since its screw noise faded, we just assumed it was far away. I can check on it with the sonar team."

"Yeah, XO. Go check."

The plot showed forty-two vessels in the water, and they served as extras in the movie in which the *Leviathan* starred. But Flint promoted the vessel of the purple trace into a supporting role by slowing its speed. He tightened the tick marks and pulled its track closer to the *Leviathan's* last known position. The tick marks correlated to ten knots.

Where the new purple trace passed in front of the *Leviathan*, Flint placed a straight edge on the plot and ran a mechanical pencil along it. The gray lead reached another merchant vessel that had passed to the west.

Baines returned.

"Dang, sir. We assessed the merchant from the system's stored data. It wasn't fifteen knots. Blade rate supports ten. I hadn't considered looking this deep at data for merchants because there was so much traffic, but it looks like I should have, given where you're going."

"Don't worry about it," Flint said. "I told you to focus on the *Leviathan* and the high speed craft—not the merchants. But look here. I've redrawn the merchant at ten knots."

"Closer, but still a couple miles ahead of *Leviathan.*"

"Now look at this other merchant here that we picked up about an hour after losing the *Leviathan.*"

"It's a ship moving in the same direction," Baines said, "but at fourteen knots, like most merchants."

"Right. Can it be the same ship?"

Flint watched Baines lean over the plot and work dividers along the merchant traces.

"At ten knots, this merchant passes in front of the *Leviathan*. Then we don't hear it for about an hour, but instead we hear high speed screws. Then a new merchant appears from nowhere, doing fourteen knots, but in reality, what we thought were two merchant ships is actually one."

Flint felt his heart pumping.

"Yes, that's what I mean," he said.

"There's a lot of conjecture between losing the first and regaining the second to make this work."

"The ship drifts to a stop, launches a craft with high speed screws, monkeys with the *Leviathan*, and then gets out of dodge at a cruising speed of fourteen knots."

"Plausible, sir."

"The fourteen knots was based on blade rate, right?"

"Most likely, sir. The bearing was constant because it had its stern to us driving away."

"We're trained to assume that blade rate correlates to a speed because merchants aren't stopping and starting in the open ocean. What if the blade rate meant that the screws were turning at the engine speed equivalent of fourteen knots but that the ship was instead accelerating from a drift or dead stop? "

"I see, sir. This is stuff I'd normally throw away as speculation, but with the *Leviathan*, we've seen that anything is possible."

"XO," he said. "Go back and have the sonar team assess these two merchants to see how likely they're the same ship."

Flint stood straight and watched Baines walk away. Minutes later, Baines returned from the sonar team's room and joined him by the plot.

"Can't prove anything either way, sir."

"I thought not. What's your gut tell you?"

"That we share what we know with squadron, and see what they can add to the picture."

"The picture, XO," Flint said, "is exactly what I'll ask them to add."

"Satellite support"

"Yup. To figure out if our two ships were one, who they are, where they're going, and, if I understand the capabilities of modern technology, what the skipper's eating for breakfast tomorrow. If something interesting comes of this, then I'll know we did our jobs right."

CHAPTER 14

Jake finished leading the *Mercer* back and forth along a submerged imaginary line a hundred miles from France's southern shore. The American assets searching for the rogue submarine had found nothing, and he began to wonder if a chapter in his life he considered closed began to creak open.

Renard greeted him and asked about the *Mercer's* status. Jake willed himself to utter data about systems in various states of advanced testing. Although Jake wanted to return to his apartment in Avignon and figure out how to begin the free decades of his life, Renard's face revealed that his immediate future would unfold on the *Mercer*.

"Each day the Americans fail to find the *Leviathan*," Renard said, "is an added day of hope that they will need us before this is done."

Jake nodded, swallowed, and walked away.

His stomach full of baked ham and green beans, Jake asked his lunch mates if they wanted desert. Henri Lanier and Claude LaFontaine nodded. They appeared weary but patient in their following of Renard.

"I'll get some ice cream," Jake said.

He entered the pantry and saw a tub of melting ice cream remaining from the watch section that had just eaten. As Jake reached into a cupboard for bowls, he heard a commotion. He peered into the wardroom and saw Antoine Remy's toad-like face jutting in from the passageway.

"Renard just received a message from Director Rickets," he said. "He's decrypting it now."

Henri snapped a comment to Jake about running the ship from the operations room in Renard's stead and shuffled away with LaFontaine on his heels. Expecting to hear of the *Leviathan's* demise, Jake scooped himself a celebratory bowl of ice cream and sat to enjoy it.

As he looked around the wardroom, he noted the barren walls. No leader and no country had yet claimed the ship, and nobody had imbued its officers' dining area with a personality. The entire ship had a skeletal persona and lacked an identity. It reminded him of himself.

Perhaps, he wondered, this is what his brother Nick meant by death and danger. He was on a dead ship that had yet to be born. He comforted himself with this thought as he awaited the desired news from Rickets about the *Leviathan* having been found and neutralized.

His ice cream half eaten, Jake sensed an energy throughout the ship that made him nervous. Renard burst through the door.

"My friend," he said, "I have news that will excite you to no end!"

"What?"

"The *Leviathan* is suspected to be towed by an Iranian tanker, a mere three days away from us."

"That's... how?"

"Likely an orchestrated hijacking."

Jakes heart skipped a beat.

"What's this mean for us?"

"We verify it."

"Verify what?"

Renard cracked an eager smile.

"Director Rickets has admitted that no American submarine is close enough to verify the presence of the *Leviathan* behind the tanker sooner than we can. He needs us to handle this delicate task. I intend to run it by you for your insight, of course, but I already have a plan in mind to achieve this."

"Oh really?" Jake asked. "Where are NATO submarines?"

"I don't care," Renard said. "Have you considered that we are on a state of the art vessel and that most submarines within arm's reach are not? Have you considered that Director Rickets is confining the information about a rogue Israeli submarine to as few people as possible? Dear god, this is the opportunity I had hoped for, and..."

"And damn it, Pierre, I don't give a shit."

Jake felt blood coursing through the veins of his neck during awkward moments of silence. He watched Renard reach into his breast pocket for a pack of Marlboros.

"I thought you quit smoking," Jake said.

Renard withdrew a gold-plated Zippo lighter and sparked flint into flame below the cigarette in his mouth.

"I must have started again."

"When?"

"Just now."

"Because of me?"

"No. I've been cheating. I may continue, especially if you no longer care about our fates being intertwined."

Jake glanced at the half eaten bowl of ice cream.

"That's part of the problem. I'm sick of being dependent upon other people for every step I take. The navy made me a submarine officer, you made me a traitor, and then you and Rickets made me a mercenary. I'm thirty years old now. When the hell do I get to say what I do and when?"

"A noble question, my friend, but this is hardly the time. You'll have plenty of time to ascertain your identity once this is behind us."

Jake looked away from Renard, and his finger began tapping the tabletop aside the bowl. Thoughts raced through his mind too fast to grasp. When his awareness returned to the room, Renard was seated in the Captain's chair beside him.

"Jake?"

"What?"

"Stop!"

Renard cupped his hand over the resonating finger. Jake ran his free hand through his hair and sat straight.

"I sense something in you I had seen before only in glimpses and snapshots, but now I see it as a constant, and it concerns me."

"Yeah?"

"Fear."

Jake shrugged. Renard reached for an ash tray and propped his cigarette on it. He looked at the lighting above, focusing his thoughts and words.

"It makes sense," Renard said. "I should have seen this. You've faced ungodly amounts of stress unwaveringly, but underneath your strength you are lost. Perhaps it was the omen from your brother or perhaps the fallout with Olivia, but something pushed you over this edge that I failed to see you approaching."

"Thanks, Freud."

"I believe the most disturbing part is that you no longer trust me to protect you. Even if I could guarantee your safety, you would reject it because you feel a need to branch out on your own."

"You're talking to me like I'm a teenager."

Renard stood and walked to the door.

"Where are you going?" Jake asked.

"To set a maximum speed on course for Gibraltar and to schedule a refueling stop."

"Then what?"

"Then I'm not sure you need to know what follows."

"Why not?"

"Because," Renard said, "when we reach Gibraltar, I'm setting you free."

"The battery is at one hundred percent charge," Henri said.

"Secure snorkeling," Renard said. "Lower the induction mast and prepare to dive."

Renard watched Henri flip switches in front of his seat at the ship's control station and heard the gentle rumbling of the *Mercer's* diesel engines subside.

"Ready to dive," Henri said.

"Make your depth thirty meters," Renard said.

The deck angled under Renard and settled again.

"Thirty meters," Henri said.

"That battery charge took us three hours and ten minutes, and we made twelve knots," Renard said. "We made twenty-two knots during our prior high speed run, and the battery lasted fifty minutes."

"Calculating now," Henri said. "Just over fourteen knots average speed, alternating high speed runs and snorkeling at those speeds. That's as fast as this ship goes following that pattern."

"And the tanker with the *Leviathan* is averaging what?"

"Fourteen and a quarter knots, based upon the last position," Henri said.

"I dislike a speed disadvantage."

"We could risk going faster while snorkeling," Henri said. "The snorkel mast may avoid damage up to twelve and a half knots."

Renard watched Henri jot down figures on a scratch pad and press keys on a pocket calculator.

"That would give us just under fourteen and a half knots average," Henri said.

"No," Renard said. "I suspect the battery discharge curves yield a better answer. We can likely make eighteen to twenty knots submerged with much more efficiency than a sprint at twenty-two knots. Perhaps enough efficiency to matter. Check the curves please, and see if we can make fifteen knots average speed with twelve knots snorkeling."

"The figures become more promising as we consider lower submerged speeds. More so than traditional battery discharge curves due to the MESMA system becoming a bigger factor. With our MESMA module providing that extra underwater power source, we can maintain eighteen knots for three and a half hours."

"If we believe the manufacturer's specifications."

"They were accurate for the twenty-two knot sprint."

"Very well," Renard said. "We'll test it. Note the time, and make turns for eighteen knots."

Renard felt the ship vibrating during its rapid acceleration. The trembling subsided as it passed fifteen knots and crept to its final speed. He passed through the after battery compartment and the after auxiliary machinery room and entered the hull section that contained the air-independent ethanol and liquid oxygen MESMA plant. The hiss of steam filled the section, and Renard felt heat waft over his body as he passed through.

His jumpsuit unzipped and flopped over his waist, Claude LaFontaine exposed a sweaty tee-shirt. He was examining gauges on a control station as a young and well-paid mercenary veteran of the French Navy, also in a tee-shirt, scurried between valves and gauges on the lower deck.

"How is our speed performance?" LaFontaine asked.

"Per the expected specifications thus far," Renard said. "We're testing battery endurance at eighteen knots now."

Renard glanced upward at an ominous high pressure oxygen tank—a bomb of compressed explosive gas.

"The MESMA system is improved since our last ship?"

"Yes," LaFontaine said. "This design is less temperamental. It is easier to control, but it will take a lot of my attention to keep it operating if you intend to make repeated high speed runs."

"And how will you fare without Jake?"

"Badly, I fear. The hour or two per day I hoped to receive his support will be missed. I will be lucky to sleep two hours a night."

"Yes," Renard said. "We will all suffer from his absence. But I must set him free."

Jake had spent most of the prior two days in his stateroom reading electronic books on his computer. He felt numb and detached from the burgeoning buzz of energy building on the *Mercer*. Though he was close to all but the newest members of the mercenary crew, they had become distant caricatures to him—even Renard.

The *Mercer* rocked on the surface as the ship neared Gibraltar.

Renard knocked on his door and opened it.

"We're approaching the channel, my friend," Renard said. "If you have not yet seen the Rock of Gibraltar, I recommend that you head topside. It is a magnificent view."

Jake closed his laptop.

"Thanks," he said, waiting for Renard to leave.

*   *   *

After avoiding his shipmates' faces on his climb topside, Jake felt the warm Mediterranean wind against his cheeks. He wore black slacks and a blue dress shirt that had acquired wrinkles while folded under his rack.

Out of earshot, Henri lifted a life vest and pointed. Jake shook his head, deciding that fate's sense of humor lacked the finesse to drown him en route to his final port call after letting him survive fire, ice, and torpedoes.

He reached into his pocket, withdrew his phone, and placed it against his ear. He heard his older brother's groggy voice.

"Hello."

"Sorry, I forgot the time difference again."

"It's good to hear your voice. Let me just get out of bed."

"Another Reiki appointment today?"

"No, business has slowed a bit."

"Do you need money?"

Jake cringed, realizing he was trying too hard to help someone who didn't ask for it.

"I appreciate the offer, but it will pick up. Can you tell me where you are?"

"I'm in Southern Europe," Jake said as he watched the towering rock that reminded him of the Prudential logo.

"Cool," Nick said. "What's on your mind?"

"I'm not sure."

"Big brother's counsel?"

"Yeah, sure. What the hell. I can't think of anything better to call it."

"Sounds windy," Nick said. "Where are you again?"

Jake slid behind the sail and the wind subsided.

"Gibraltar."

"Cool. What are you doing there?"

"I have no idea."

"That doesn't sound like you're still involved in whatever you were planning. Did your plans change?"

"Yeah. Kind of. Turns out I wasn't needed as badly as I thought."

"That's odd. It doesn't feel right."

"No, it doesn't. But nothing has for a while. I'm not sure what to do next."

"Are you asking me?"

"I think so."

"I don't see anything clearly. The danger I sensed isn't as prevalent, but it hasn't gone away. It's perhaps lurking in the shadows."

"That doesn't help."

"You're lonelier than our last talk."

"What? How could you possibly..."

"It didn't take a soothsayer," Nick said. "An idiot could pick it up by your tone."

"Okay. Fine."

"What are your options now?"

"The world," Jake said. "I can go wherever I want."

"That's not what I asked."

"What did you ask?"

"What are your options—for you? What do you see now? It's human nature to need to do something, to go somewhere, or to see someone. Pick your top three options for the next hour, day or week of your life."

Jake ran his hand through his hair. He found it peculiar that his transcendental-meditating brother found it necessary to coddle him like a lost child through the basic tactics of living.

"Shit, Nick. I don't know. Maybe see an old friend in South America. Maybe chill at my home in France."

"Did you want to visit me?"

"Maybe."

"Chilling at home is lame, and I can tell that you're not ready to visit me again. So you could visit your other friend, but that sounds like running away, and you're too driven to be lacking a stronger choice. What else is there for you?"

"I don't know."

"Guess."

Jake tapped the edge of his dress shoe against the damp metal of the *Mercer's* sail.

"Maybe the people who I thought didn't need me, need me," he said.

"People need to go where they're needed. If you avoid that, your spirit dies."

"What about the danger?"

"Life is dangerous, and I can't tell if the danger I sense lies on the path to your friend in South America, on the road to your home in France, or with the people who need you most, but I know it's still close to you."

"So I'm back to square one?"

"Yes. I'm sorry. I wish I could be more helpful."

"No, Nick. I think you helped."

After hanging up, Jake headed below and found Renard in the operations room.

"Have you enjoyed the view, my friend?" Renard asked.

"I'm staying."

"What?"

"With you and my friends here. I'm staying. I'll help you identify the *Leviathan* and send it to the bottom if needed. Whatever you need from me."

"Are you sure?" Renard asked. "I cannot ask this of you out of guilt or obligation. That is destructive. You must want this."

"I want this."

Renard extended his hand, and Jake accepted.

"Welcome back, Jake."

CHAPTER 15

Hana al-Salem dreamt.

He sat at the head of the table in the Captain's chair of the *Leviathan's* wardroom. The people of his personal selecting—all those aboard except the Hamas detachment—filled the other seats.

Lively banter filled the room until a bowl of unidentified flesh in a stew of crimson materialized on the table. He dipped his hand into the goo and rammed his fingers in his mouth. He tasted soft organ tissue and piquant blood, and in his dream he knew the flesh to be human. The mouthful repulsed him.

He looked to see if his companions enjoyed the macabre meal, but they had fallen silent. Each had his throat slit open and his head pulled back to expose bloodless vertebrae, with lifeless eyes gazing straight up. Standing, Salem reached for a holster by his waist to defend himself against an unknown assailant.

Movement at the room's door caught his eye, and he withdrew a pistol. As he pointed it, it transmuted itself into a black serpent that writhed free, thumped against the deck plates, and slithered into the passageway over the sneakers of the man blocking Salem's escape.

Adad Hamdan, the Hamas team leader, smiled.

"Look," he said, and nodded to the table.

The men with opened throats were now Israeli submarine sailors from the *Leviathan*.

"I don't understand," Salem said.

"You killed them all," Hamdan said. "Everyone. Regardless who lifts the blade or pulls the trigger, it is you who delivers death."

"My actions are just."

"As are mine."

With imperceptible movement, Hamdan appeared before Salem, who felt cold steel slicing into stomach.

*   *   *

121

Salem awoke to the sound of Ali Yousif's voice. The rotund engineering professor seemed concerned.

"Hana?"

Salem turned over in the sheets of the captain's bunk. He rubbed his eyes.

"Yes?"

"You wanted me to wake you for breakfast."

Salem realized that he had attained normal circadian rhythm sleep, and his dreaming mind was allowing itself to process his subconscious fears.

"Thank you, my friend."

"You were stirring in your sleep," Yousif said. "I had to repeat your name five times before you awoke."

"Thank you, Ali," Salem said.

Salem stepped into the jumpsuit he had procured from the *Leviathan's* prior captain and followed Yousif to the wardroom. One of the linguists had made a sizable quantity of powdered eggs, cheese, powdered milk, and toast. Salem and Yousif joined the linguist as did Hamdan and a younger Hamas soldier.

There was little energy in the conversation at the table, reminding Salem of the lethargic energy he noted throughout the ship.

Under tow of the tanker, the submarine required little effort to maintain. One man sat on watch in the operations room to adjust depth and to monitor whatever consoles happened to demand his attention, and another man sat in the engineering spaces watching the battery trickle electrons into its economized load.

Success in mating with the Iranian tanker had provided Salem's crew with a revitalizing spark that had shined but then flamed out. As the ship approached Gibraltar, Salem sensed that boredom was his men's greatest enemy. His mind raced for a topic of interest and found one.

"We have prepared too much food for this meal," he said. "We will store the excess for lunch. There is no need to waste."

"Hana," Yousif said, his eyes sullen, "we have more than enough stores."

"For what purpose?" Hana asked.

"We have at least thirty-five, perhaps forty days, worth of stores."

Hands and utensils stopped moving, and the room became silent. With his peripheral vision, Salem watched Hamdan's reaction as he spoke with Yousif.

"I didn't ask about timing. I asked about purpose. You said we have enough stores. For what purpose?"

"For achieving our mission, of course," Yousif said.

"Perhaps," Salem said. "But we must be ready for contingencies. Our escort tanker could fail for any number of reasons, and then we'd need more time to reach our destination."

"Even so," Yousif said, "we would run out of fuel before running out of food."

"No, damn it!" Salem said. "You're thinking with a closed mind. Use your creative mind. What if we find ourselves in a situation where we can cripple a merchant vessel and procure diesel fuel from it?"

"Then we could take their food, too, Hana!"

Salem caught himself forming a smile and let it happen. It was the first time in days.

"That's the type thinking I want to see more of," he said.

Hamdan and the younger soldier exchanged a silent and uneasy stare.

"For what situation, Hana?" Hamdan asked.

"Excuse me?"

"For what situation might we need to procure diesel fuel? We have plenty to reach our objective, do we not?"

"Of course we do," Salem said. "At least per plan. But not all plans survive contact with the enemy."

After breakfast, Salem stood below the *Leviathan's* forward hatch. Droplets trickled along the cord connecting the communications box with the tanker *Zafar*.

Salem depressed a switch on the box and saw a green light illuminate.

"Good morning?" he asked.

"Good morning."

He recognized the voice of the *Zafar's* first mate, one of several people aboard the towing ship that spoke Arabic.

"Has anything changed with our status?" Salem asked.

"No, but we are in sight of Gibraltar. It's a tight passage, and we may see new wind and seas on the other side once in the Atlantic Ocean. We will adjust cable length if needed."

"I understand. All is the same here. Nothing has changed. Thank you."

Salem passed through the operations room where Asad stared at a monitor.

"Good morning, Hana."

"How are you?"

"Well. The ship is well. It's holding its angle and depth automatically. There's little for it to adjust to."

"We figured out how these automatic systems work?"

"We're starting to. The manuals are easy."

"Even when you can't read them?"

Salem nodded at a screen of diagrams and Hebrew characters that appeared to be an electronic manual of the trim and drain system.

"My interpreter will be joining me after his breakfast. I memorize the drawings on my own."

"I'm glad that you are making use of otherwise idle time. Do you believe the others are doing the same?"

"The naval veterans are. So are the people from your university. It's the Hamas soldiers that seem reluctant. They have learned what buttons and valves to push for the purposes we demand, but they have no curiosity to explore further."

"I've noticed the same. This concerns me."

"I haven't thought about it much."

Salem sat at the console beside Asad. He examined the room to assure they were alone, and he lowered his voice.

"Have you considered our fate in the event that we succeed in destroying the *Bainbridge* and then survive?"

"I try to avoid such thoughts. They are distracting. My purpose is the *Bainbridge*. All else is speculation."

"Do you trust me to keep you safe?"

"I trust you, Hana, but I am aware of the dangers. I intend to return home someday, God willing, but I am prepared to meet whatever fate I deserve."

"I believe that most men aboard share your outlook."

"That's correct, Hana. We accepted our fates in this long ago in exchange for the opportunity to be part of something this important."

"But now that we have relaxed from the intensity of taking this ship," Salem said, "we have many days of transit ahead of us. Men's idle minds will wander."

"Perhaps," Asad said. "What is your concern?"

"I dislike the look in the eyes of the Hamas men. When I see them, I see conflict, and I see it especially in their leader."

"Hamdan strikes me as insightful and thoughtful for a trained soldier. He may simply be over-thinking his fate."

"That's the problem," Salem said. "The soldiers have nothing to do but to press buttons and twist valves, yet they all seem to have something weighing on their minds."

Asad frowned and leaned forward.

"This is a curious observation."

"I considered long ago, when I realized that we needed warriors, that such talent may not come with blind obedience to me or to the vision I follow."

"Go on."

"Consider," Salem said, "that the Hamas soldiers have been ordered to take matters into their own hands in the event that we, a team of veteran sailors and academics, should lack courage at key moments."

Asad leaned back and waived a dismissing hand.

"They need us. They couldn't possibly launch weapons from this ship. That's a feat that will require everything we collectively know, such as knowledge of manuals they have ignored. They have no ability in this area."

"Perhaps not," Salem said. "But perhaps they think they could ram the *Bainbridge*. A submarine's steel is thicker than the skin of a destroyer. Or perhaps they believe that after they help launch one weapon they can launch another—mimicking our actions without our assistance."

Yousif's thick frame entered the operations room.

"Am I interrupting?" he asked.

"No, please join us," Salem said. "And listen. Intently. I need your thoughts."

Yousif crouched between the chairs.

"I have been assessing a threat in my mind, and I believe it's real enough to share with both of you, but no others. I want your assistance in monitoring the Hamas soldiers."

"This is serious," Yousif said. "What do you fear?"

"I believe that the Hamas soldiers have conditional orders to scuttle this submarine, killing all of us by hand first if they must, in the event that we succeed in our mission. They may even have other orders to kill us if we take inappropriate actions with this ship at certain milestones."

"Hana," Yousif said. "Why?"

"Because," Salem said. "I believe their leaders who gave them their parting orders knew too little about operating a submarine and may have considered us expendable at some point."

Yousif's brow furrowed and his face became flushed.

"I am prepared to die for a cause, Hana," he said. "But don't ask me to throw my life away. You said that we would make use of this ship after the *Bainbridge*. That we would expend its resources in a new cause against targets of opportunity until our weapons were gone. That we would use the Gulf Stream to assist our journey home. I volunteered to face danger for you. I did not volunteer for suicide."

"I consider your mind an asset too valuable to waste, Ali," Salem said. "But if all unfolds as I foresee, there may be no need to flee. I cannot share the details, but I ask you to continue trusting me."

Yousif exhaled and appeared to relax.

"I respected your wish to keep the operations outside our submarine a secret," he said. "Knowledge is power but it is also danger. It will be difficult for my analytical mind to exercise the patience, but I have known you for years, and I will trust you."

"When we are victorious *Leviathan*," Salem said. "Rest assured that all will become clear."

Renard swallowed a bite of lobster tail, enjoying the sweet meat and buttery taste. He reached for a glass and swirled its purplish ruby colored Châteauneuf-du-Pape Charvin wine. As he lowered the glass to sniff the aroma of its contents, he glanced at a depth gage in the *Mercer's* wardroom. The ship was descending from its snorkel depth.

"The last meal before a special operation," he said, "is nearly as special as the operation itself."

"You always know how to add the right special touches, Pierre," Remy said from the seat beside Renard. "It's too bad Jake and Henri can't join us."

"They enjoyed an early dinner," LaFontaine said from his seat opposite Remy. "Someone has to drive the ship. Such is submarine life."

"From the looks of it," Renard said. "Jake has downloaded the satellite information we need and has just taken us deep. I expect that we'll hear from Henri soon."

Seconds later, heads at the table turned in response to a knock. Henri's silvery hair slipped through the door, and he had a stern look on his face.

"We have the *Zafar's* coordinates and track," he said. "They are in the shipping lane to New York, following the plan of the ship's manifest. They are making no attempt to deviate from their planned route."

"The tow cable?"

"Still taut, per the aerial reconnaissance of ten minutes ago."

"How far from us?" Renard asked.

"Twenty miles, and moving at fourteen knots. We have just over an hour."

"Deploy the towed array sonar and bring up all systems," Renard said. "Have Jake take us to two hundred meters depth and keep us one mile to the south of the *Zafar's* track. If you have to err, get us closer to the Zafar as opposed to too far. Our depth will provide us separation so that we avoid collision with their towed cargo."

Henri nodded and departed. Renard turned to the table and raised his glass.

"To solving two mysteries—that of the object being towed by the *Zafar*, and that of the missing *Leviathan*. Let their resolutions be as I expect—one in the same."

An hour later, Renard buzzed with the energy of tactical gaming.

Technical advances in data processing allowed a team of only four to gather and interpret sonar data. Jake drifted over the shoulders of Renard's mercenary team, assimilating, filtering, and presenting information gleaned from a world of sonic directions, propagation strengths, and frequencies, while Remy, with his impeccable wisdom, teamed up with two younger men who had joined the crew for a sizable payout after proving themselves competent to contacts Renard retained in the French Navy.

Jake stood over a vacant Subtics station, studying its monitor.

"How far?" Renard asked.

"Two miles," Jake said. "We hear the *Zafar* on at least five mechanical frequencies, blade rate, and broadband noise. No sounds of a submarine in tow."

"Is our depth still optimized for listening?"

"Unless you want to change assumptions about cable length and angle, but there's no reason to change."

"Indeed," Renard said. "I know this. I'm just realizing that listening for a submarine becomes a challenge when it's not responsible for generating its own propulsion. Keep listening."

"We need to speed up, or they'll pass us by."

"All the more challenging that we haven't heard anything from the submarine yet."

Renard braced his palms against the silvery railing surrounding the conning platform.

"Henri," he said. "All ahead two-thirds, make turns for thirteen knots."

"Thirteen knots, aye, sir."

Renard felt a mild shudder as the *Scorpène* class submarine accelerated. He checked with Jake that the *Zafar* remained one mile behind them, and one mile to the side, as the *Mercer* attained thirteen knots.

"This is ideal," Renard said. "They will overtake us to the north with a closest point of approach of one nautical mile. It will take them two hours to draw equal to us and then move ahead of us a mile down track. This gives us every opportunity to listen to what they're towing."

"Except that our systems are starting to become degraded at thirteen knots," Jake said, "due to our own flow noise. We may miss some of the quieter sounds."

"Indeed," Renard said. "But I assume there is a submarine with men aboard it being towed by that tanker. They are going to make a mistake that puts noise in the water—something as simple as dropping a fork or securing a door to a latch. And when they do, we will hear it."

An hour later, the *Mercer's* operations room held a musky scent of body odor and tobacco. Renard inhaled from a Marlboro to soothe the tension building inside him. The postures of the men before him sagged.

"Anything?" he asked.

Jake shook his head.

Another hour later, Renard sat in a foldout chair behind the periscopes on the elevated conning platform. He lit a fresh Marlboro.

"They're a mile ahead of us now," Jake said. "Whatever they're towing is passing us by now, too. They're pulling away, Pierre, and we haven't heard shit."

"I know," Renard said as he stood.

"Two and a half hours remaining on the battery at this speed," Henri said.

"How long until nightfall?"

"Four hours," Henri said.

Jake appeared in front of him.

"This is going to be tedious," he said. "We're going to have to snorkel soon, and we can't risk being seen."

"I know," Renard said. "It is unfortunate that we have yet to hear evidence of a submarine in tow, but it is not unexpected. We will let the *Zafar* open range to five miles and then snorkel under cover of night."

"And if they see us? It is possible. What if they are armed with anti-submarine weapons? What if the *Leviathan* is there, hears us, and the *Zafar* somehow signals it to send a torpedo at us?"

"Then they will have failed in whatever mission they hope to accomplish," Renard said. "Because they know we will respond with a salvo of our own. Because they also know that if a submarine is spying on them, there are likely other assets assisting us, as are presently two P-3 Orion aircraft patrolling within range."

"You know damn well that the Iranians may not care. A one for one exchange with a western submarine may be a bigger prize than whatever they're after."

"Unlikely, given that the *Leviathan* has four Popeye land attack cruise missiles aboard and is likely heading to New York under tow."

Jake ran his hand through his hair.

"We know the *Leviathan's* weapons load out?"

"Yes," Renard said. "The Israeli ambassador was recently authorized to share all information we requested about the *Leviathan*, its crew, and its ill-fated patrol."

"Nuclear tipped?"

Renard blew smoke into the overhead piping.

"No," he said. "The ambassador assured this. The Popeyes have conventional warheads, and that is comforting."

"Not comforting for the people of New York," Jake said. "Why isn't one of those P-3 Orions pinging the heck out of that tanker with active sonobuoys and pounding whatever it's towing with air-dropped torpedoes? For that matter, why the heck isn't somebody just crippling that tanker or at least boarding it?"

"That would happen," Renard said, "well before that tanker reaches Popeye missile range of the American coast, in the event that we fail. However, a decision has been made to retrieve the *Leviathan* in one piece."

"Shit, Pierre. Are you serious?"

"Of course."

"Why?"

"Several factors. The Israelis lost a submarine named the *Dakar* decades ago, and they had trouble finding it. It became a sentimental subject. And I don't need to remind you of the importance of proper disposal of the Israeli crew's bodies. If there are corpses still aboard, there are family members who want access to them."

"Emotional factors," Jake said.

"Not exclusively. Also consider the fallout to the German-subsidized submarine program that supplies Israel with its undersea fleet. Public knowledge of a hijacking and loss of a submarine will put the program in jeopardy."

"So people are actually going to try to keep this a secret," Jake said. "Return the *Leviathan* to home port in one piece and make a cover story for the crew?"

"Indeed. And pressure families of the crew to bite their tongues."

Jake shook his head and laughed through his nose.

"What's wrong," Renard asked. "Is this scenario sounding all too familiar, except that you're not on the rogue side of it?"

"Maybe," Jake said. "But what I don't get are two things. One—is there a submarine being towed behind that tanker. And two—a way to make it turn around and head back home if it's there."

"I'm as frustrated as you are about not having heard the *Leviathan*, but I have faith that it is there and that we will find it before it would have to be destroyed. We have several days yet."

"Sure, Pierre, I know we'll find it if it's there. But then what? I was expecting to have permission to blow it up and move on with our lives."

Renard smiled as he pressed an expended Marlboro into an ashtray.

"No, my friend," he said. "I expect that our fate and that of the *Leviathan* will be quite more intriguing than a simple torpedo detonation. Director Rickets informed me in our last communication of a plan under development to retake the submarine and lead it safely home."

"I'd love to know the details."

"We will shortly. What I know now, though, is that it will involve us, an *Ohio* class SSGN submarine, and a team of Navy SEALs. And we will no longer be taking orders from Director Rickets but from the Commander of the Atlantic Fleet. I trust you find this interesting."

"Yeah, of course."

"Then you will also find it interesting that there will be a new commanding officer of the *Leviathan* for its journey home."

"Oh yeah, who are they sending?"

"The operation is too dangerous to risk sending one of Israel's few seasoned, command-qualified officers," Renard said. "Instead, it appears that the *Mercer* will be my second to last command. You are looking at the future commanding officer of the Israeli Naval Ship, *Leviathan*."

CHAPTER 16

In the combat information center of the USS *Bainbridge*, Lieutenant Commander Robert Stephenson looked over the shoulder of a seated sailor. A monitor showed the *Bainbridge* in the center of a circle one hundred and fifty nautical miles southeast of Nantucket.

The ship's radar systems created dots on the circle representing fishing vessels and traffic in shipping lanes from New York and Boston. Information from distant radar systems added to the picture as far as Philadelphia and Halifax.

Whirring air conditioners kept the internal, windowless room cool. Stephenson pulled his sweater sleeves to his wrists and turned.

Behind him in a Naugahyde throne, the section's watch officer orchestrated the efforts of a dozen men who staffed the center. Stephenson had trained the watch officer and several like him to manage the overwhelming amount of data that the Aegis combat system could supply, and he trusted him to react when the ship was threatened. But when a situation required extended tactical action—the known likelihood of exchanging weapons—the throne belonged to Stephenson.

"Good evening, XO," the watch officer said.

"Good evening. What's our emissions status?" Stephenson asked. Stephenson knew that nothing had changed in days, but in the nerve center of a naval vessel, where one word launched missiles, specifics and confirmations mattered.

"The SPY-1D radar system is optimized for high-altitude targets, sir," the officer said. "All surface radar systems are off. The ship is dark and in modified emissions control."

"Very well," Stephenson said, translating the answer in his mind to mean that the *Bainbridge* was painting the sky with electromechanical radiation, searching from the horizon to the heavens for missiles and aircraft. In contrast, the ship's radar system was putting little energy into sea-level searches to minimize the chance of surface vessels electronically eavesdropping and finding the *Bainbridge*. The ship also had all outwardly visible lights turned off so that it could not be seen.

Stephenson wished the officer a quiet night and left the center. He climbed stairs to his stateroom where he sat at a desk and typed a letter to his wife and two daughters. After reading and rereading the note to verify it held no tactical information about the *Bainbridge* and its operations, he dumped the note into an email queue. At the next satellite communications uplink, his note would give his family a welcome and a smile.

Olivia found spying on Farah Ghaffari to be routine. The Iranian professor was completing her third day of following a mind-numbing pattern. She drove to Old Dominion University, parked near the Perry Library, and walked to the Mills Godwin Life Science Building where she spent her day.

Posing as a post-doctoral researcher, Olivia worked her way into the library and found a table near a window overlooking the life science building and Ghaffari's car. She read books of whatever topic came to mind while glancing out the window. On the third day of watching the professor, Olivia found the conservativeness of her day to be conspicuous.

In the late afternoon, an hour after her last class of the day, Ghaffari appeared in front of the life science building. Her head down, she marched to her car. As she drove away, Olivia raced out of the library.

Driving a rented gray Ford Fusion, Olivia sped down Hampton Boulevard behind Ghaffari's Mustang. Later, as she turned into a grocery store, Olivia parked, trailed her into the store, and followed her from two aisles back.

Through her peripheral vision, Olivia saw her glance in her direction. She held her breath, studying a jar of tomatoes until she looked away. Unsure if her spying skills had rusted, Olivia continued to shop for her dinner and checked out at a register far from the line in which Ghaffari stood.

She lost time waiting to check out and fell five minutes behind Ghaffari. When Olivia pulled into her newly rented apartment that had a view of the professor's home, she saw Ghaffari in her kitchen making dinner. Olivia strolled to her door and dropped her groceries on a rented coffee table.

Instead of settling in to a third night of watching the professor hide in the solitude of her apartment, Olivia placed her phone to her ear, called Commander Sanders on his cell phone, and heard his voice.

"Hello."

"Hi, it's Olivia McDonald. I met you at your office last week."

"I remember you. Of course. What can I do for you?"

"Take me to dinner on that rain check. I'm in town."

"Sure. But it has to be on base at the officer's club. I'm working late, but I could use a break. I can get out of here soon. Is seven o'clock okay?"

"Yes. I'll see you then."

At dinner, he wore his uniform and looked less energetic than their first meeting. He glanced around the room.

"I haven't been here in a while," he said. "It looks kind of plain. I think I had better memories of it than what it looks like now."

"I was thinking it's like an austere country club, which is probably the look you're going for in an officer's club. Just enough ambiance to know that you're dining but not too much to forget that you're in the military."

"Maybe. I'm just tired."

"You look it."

A waiter took their meal order, and Olivia tipped back a glass of water with a lemon wedge straddling its rim.

"I thought you were upset about us being set up by Director Rickets," he said.

"I was," she said. "But screw him. I'm a big girl."

He smiled.

"Sure. So what have you been up to?"

"Not much really. Just working an assignment."

He stared at her, waiting for details. In that moment, she realized the Achilles Heel of two people from the intelligence community trying to enjoy conversation. They could share nothing about the topics they cared about most.

"What about you?" she asked.

"Working hard. A lot of hours."

She nibbled on a buttered breadstick.

"So you flew helicopters before you joined the intel group, right?" she asked.

"Yep," he said. "SH-60 LAMPS helicopters off the back of destroyers. Anti-submarine warfare. And I was pretty darn good, too."

"I bet you were."

"Yep."

He looked at his breadstick, and she realized he was lamenting that a jaunt with a whore had cost him his love of flying helicopters.

"Hey, I'm pretty good on a motorcycle," she said. "Pocket rockets. I look pretty hot on them too."

"Sweet," he said. "I bet you do."

"Do you ride?"

"No," he said. "A close friend died on one and I swore... well, I just don't ride."

"No, it's okay," she said. "I get it."

She bit off another piece of her breadstick, mashed it with her teeth, and swallowed.

"You want to go somewhere... I don't know... secure?" she asked. "You know. So we can really talk."

"That's the best idea I heard all day," he said. "I'll get our dinners to go."

In the secure room where she had first gotten to know him, she felt more relaxed. She watched heat rise from Styrofoam carryout boxes he had removed from a microwave oven. She plunged a plastic fork into her salmon steak.

"I have some questions about Ghaffari," she said.

"Shoot," he said.

"For a woman who was a party animal while husband hunting, she's turned into a homebody. I've watched her for three days, and all she does is go to work and come home. Maybe stops to buy stuff like groceries and gas, but that's it."

"Sorry," he said. "You'll have to catch me up."

"Oh, yeah. Gerry let me put her under passive surveillance. Emails, cell calls, Internet. She's been streaming a lot of movies recently, sitting at home. And she's been getting emails from her fiancé where he photographs himself with a sign counting down the days until their wedding."

"Cute," he said.

"Yeah, and I asked a few guys from the agency if that was cause for alarm. They didn't think so."

She washed down buttered green beans with diet cola from a plastic cup.

"Don't you think it's odd that she's not out shopping for dresses, shoes, or stuff for her new life?" she asked. "Shouldn't a woman getting ready for a wedding in six months be making some fuss?"

"Depends on the woman, I guess."

"I know her motives are destructive, but I would still expect her to have some sort of celebratory activity. Buying trophies of having bagged her husband, gloating, or something. Sequestering herself at home seems wrong. It's like she's hiding, waiting for a bomb to go off."

"I'm no analyst," he said, "but it makes sense."

"Yeah, I just wanted to talk it out."

"No, I get it. You seem awfully lonely."

She raised an eyebrow.

"I mean on this assignment. You're all alone as its only resource."

"Yeah, Gerry didn't expect me to find much, but I've been kind of on a mission to find something since I came up blank on the *Leviathan*."

"Where'd you leave off on *Leviathan*?" he asked.

"Three days ago when I drove down here," she said. "I heard they lost it but found it again. There's a French submarine involved now, right?"

"Kind of. Technically French built, although it's a joint construction effort with a Spanish company. It's a pre-commission unit that's going to be the *Razak* when it gets to Malaysian hands, and that's what we're calling it. But it's a French submarine on a NATO-type of exercise operationally as far as we're concerned."

"Which means what?"

"Which means it's following the orders of our commanders," he said. "The Commander of the Atlantic Fleet has control, although I understand your friend Director Rickets is considered an integral advisor."

"Not surprising," she said. "He is a sharp guy and a mover and shaker."

"We have reason to believe that the *Razak* is trailing the *Leviathan* now," he said.

"Which is being towed by the *Zafar* towards New York," she said. "So why do we still just have reason to believe? We were that far three days ago."

"The *Razak* picked up a few transient noises from the *Zafar* that could have been from a submarine in tow, but it's unconfirmed."

She admired the way he ripped through a Porterhouse steak with a plastic knife as she took another bite of her salmon.

"Isn't this the sort of thing you confirm with a deep sea camera after you've crippled the *Zafar* and sent its towed cargo to the bottom?" she asked.

"When the Israelis came clean on everything," he said, "such as admitting that they have no idea who's running their submarine and telling us about its weapons load, they pleaded for us to bring the submarine back in one piece."

"I see. It prevents wasting a submarine, causing Israel to look weak, and upsetting the Germans who subsidize the program. I guess it makes sense."

"Not to mention the possibility of returning corpses home," he said. "At least one thing looks clear. Your analysis that this wasn't an inside job may stand up."

"It would be nice to know that I was right," she said.

"Yep. Hey, when this *Leviathan* thing is over, I should have more time. Do you like to hike?"

"Yes, actually. It looks like we've found something besides national intelligence that we both do."

"Sweet. Let's say ten days from now we hit a walking trail in a nature preserve about an hour from here."

"Sounds great, Roger" she said. "But why ten days?"

"Because I'll need some time to write up a report on the *Leviathan*. I want to leave some slop."

"Slop on what? I didn't know the end point was decided yet."

"Oh, yeah. I forgot. You don't know yet. There's a plan to take the *Leviathan* back. Would you like to hear about it?"

She sipped from her plastic cup.

"I'm all ears."

Jake watched Renard give the briefing in the *Mercer's* operations room. His old friend revealed his age by preferring colored pencils to tactical monitors. The Frenchman's silvery hair bounced as he moved in front of nautical charts and trace paper taped over the aft Subtics monitor.

Henri, Antoine Remy, and three younger mercenaries crouched and stood around the display with Jake.

"The USS *Georgia* is waiting in Norfolk, here," Renard said, pointing at a chart showing the Atlantic Ocean from Halifax to Bermuda to the coastal regions of the United States. "It's awaiting the delivery of special cargo and is the limiting factor on the timing of the operation."

"I think that the confirmation of an Israeli submarine behind that tanker is the limiting factor," Jake said.

"We've heard transients that had enough bearing separation from the tanker to suggest that they came from a vessel being towed. Phantoms don't make clanking sounds of doors being latched."

The omen from his brother weighed on his mind.

"Fine. Sorry. Keep going," he said.

"What is the *Georgia* waiting for?" Henri asked.

"The cutting instrument and the Israeli system experts."

"By system experts, do you mean special forces killing experts?" Jake asked.

"No," Renard said. "I mean system experts. Four men who know various parts of the *Leviathan* will be present aboard the *Georgia*. One will join the Navy SEALs in the insertion into the *Leviathan*. The SEALs will take care of the killing."

Renard blew smoke into the overhead piping and returned the Marlboro to his mouth.

"At least I pray they take care of it, since I shall be with them."

"When does the *Georgia* set sail?" Jake asked.

"No later than three days. They need the time to configure the cutting instrument in the SEAL minisub."

Renard tapped a red dot on the chart four hundred miles north of Bermuda.

"Okay," Jake said. "That pushes our fuel limit."

"Pushes, but does not quite exhaust, does it?"

"No, but damn close."

"You miss nuclear power, do you not, Jake?"

"Yes. No. Not really. What I really miss is dry land. I'm looking forward to nailing this and moving on with my life."

"Indeed," Renard said. "Nailing this, as you say, will simply take the patience and skillful submarine operations I've come to trust you with. The United States Navy will handle the delicate portions for us."

"Then why do they still need us?" Jake asked.

"As always," Renard said, "we are the hedge against a one for one exchange. Should we see sign of hostile intent before our operation is complete, we will send our adversaries to the bottom. Should our adversaries, in that event, retaliate successfully, then it is only an inexpensive submarine with mercenaries that is lost."

"And you want to be involved," Jake said. "You've been pushing Rickets to make sure of it."

"Almost as intently as you still appear to wish not being involved. I thought you had rejoined our team in both person and spirit."

Renard jabbed his Marlboro into an ash tray and reached toward his breast pocket for a fresh cigarette. Jake looked away but lifted his gaze.

"No, I'm with you."

"Good."

"But I still am concerned that we're missing concrete evidence of the *Leviathan*."

"In good time, my friend," Renard said. "We will continue to accumulate evidence. And no matter, in the final outcome, the SEAL minisub will mount them, per this scenario."

Renard tore off the Bermuda chart and revealed colored drawings of five ships. Concentric circles framed the *Leviathan* at the center with the *Zafar* ahead of it. The *Georgia* lay ten miles away, in apparent safety, while a minisub rested on the back of the *Leviathan*. The *Mercer* was even with the *Leviathan* and a mile to its far side.

"What's that line between the *Georgia* and minisub?" Jake asked. "Is it like a torpedo wire?"

"Precisely," Renard said. "For communications and with an electrical power supply as well."

"They're going to send power across a torpedo communications wire?"

"It's a design that's had some apparent success with the SEAL delivery from converted *Ohio* class submarines."

"So that's it?" Jake asked. "Looks simple enough except that it's happening at fourteen knots."

"I've been assured that the SEAL minisub can make sufficient speed with the electrical power from the *Georgia*. They will succeed even if the *Zafar* cannot be enticed to slow."

"Enticed to slow?" Jake asked. "How?"

"A ship will set sail from New York on a reciprocal path of the *Zafar*. The ship will send out a distress call when the *Zafar* is close enough and bound by maritime custom to assist. The ship will not call for the *Zafar*—its call for help will be universal, but the *Zafar* should volunteer assistance."

Renard replaced the original chart that showed Bermuda to Halifax. He traced his finger over a series of small arcs that faced major eastern population centers.

"We have until these boundary lines to conclude our business. Should the *Zafar* cross that line before we do, we will withdraw and let antisubmarine aircraft deliver the killing blow."

"What's that arc radius?" Jake asked. "Two hundred nautical miles?"

"Two hundred and fifty," Renard said. "The Israelis have shared with us the ranges of the Popeye missiles aboard *Leviathan*. Two hundred and ten nautical miles. I've drawn the two hundred and fifty mile boundary as a warning barrier. As you can see, our operation will be concluded before approaching even this warning area."

Two monitors forward, a young mercenary cupped his hands over a sonar headset. He then lowered his hands and twisted knobs at his Subtics station. Antoine Remy crept to his shoulder and listened as the man pointed at his monitor.

"The *Zafar* is slowing," Remy said. "Making turns for ten knots."

"Excellent," Renard said. "We shall slow as well to conserve battery. To your tracking stations."

Half an hour later, Jake leaned over a display of the darkness that Renard saw on the *Mercer's* periscope.

"Ten knots," he said. "Tankers never slow unless they have a reason. What the hell?"

"Patience, Jake," Renard said, his Marlboro dangling from his lips below the periscope optics.

"Remy?" Jake asked, looking over his shoulder.

"Nothing yet," Remy said.

Jake stared at the monitor again, trying to see the tow line but unable to spy it against the dark sky and the sea's blackness. Stars and the *Zafar's* red, port-side running light filled the screen.

"Fans!" Remy said.

Jake stood and glared at Remy.

"Fans!" Remy said again. "They're running fans. They're very quiet, but I hear them, and the system has them on a bearing that places them a quarter mile behind the *Zafar.*"

"Like a submarine ventilating?" Jake asked.

"Exactly," Remy said.

"Shit," Jake said. "They don't need to snorkel to charge their battery, but they need fresh air. Fans."

"Right," Remy said.

"See if you can hear something else, some other piece of machinery they'll keep running when submerged, now that we know they're there."

"Will do, Jake."

Jake looked up at Renard.

"Well, my friend," the Frenchman said. "You were correct that we needed to confirm our suspicions. And now they are confirmed. We have the *Leviathan.*"

CHAPTER 17

Renard had found the two days since confirming the *Leviathan's* presence behind the *Zafar* anticlimactic. He felt like a passenger on a ride and that his will had little imprint left to impart on the outcome.

He was reading the philosophy of Voltaire when Henri ripped open his stateroom door.

"Come quick! *Leviathan* opened its outer doors!"

Renard trotted behind Henri to the operations room where Jake stooped over Remy's shoulder at a Subtics monitor.

"You're certain?" Renard asked.

"Yes," Remy said.

"How have you responded?"

"I assigned a weapon to the *Leviathan* as a counter attack," Jake said. "Other than that, I did nothing. Opening our own outer torpedo doors could alert them or provoke them."

"Good response," Renard said.

Renard felt his heart rate slowing as he watched his protégé retain his sharp mind under stress.

"No sound of flooding a tube, yet, but that would be harder to hear," Jake said.

"Correct. Assign a weapon to the *Zafar* as well, just in case this turns against us."

Jake slid into a seat and tapped keys at the Subtics station with speed and competency that impressed Renard.

"Done."

Henri stood by his preferred seat at the ship's control station.

"You're happy with course and speed?" he asked. "Do we not want to distance ourselves?"

"No," Jake said. "If they know we're here and intend to shoot us, we're too close to flee. Any change in course or speed could produce noise that alerts or provokes them."

"Wait," Renard said. "That's a sound analysis except for one factor."

"Oh yeah," Jake said. "What's that?"

Renard saw the flush color in Jake's face and neck.

"The possibility that the present crew of the *Leviathan* are such incompetent submarine operators that they are attempting to launch a weapon but are proving themselves incapable."

"If that's the case, then it doesn't matter what we do," Jake said.

"Unless, of course," Renard said, "they are fast learners, learning from their mistakes as they go. If they are indeed trying to launch a weapon at us but failing in their attempt, I see the prudent course of action being to slow down and let the *Zafar* take them away from us."

"Cut our engines and drift?"

"Exactly."

Salem stood in the torpedo room with Asad, Hamdan, and a translator between the six spare reload weapons.

"You're certain this is necessary?" he asked.

"We are certain of it, Hana," Asad said. "There is no other way. Or if there is another way, we are unable to identify it in the manuals, but the torpedo hydraulic system seems incapable of supporting any other option."

"And it is safe?"

"No," Asad said. "No such operation is perfectly safe. But we have mitigated risks. It is you who must decide."

"And decide carefully," Hamdan said.

Salem noted that a perpetual cloud of doubt blanketed the Hamas soldier and that he was destined to dislike any choice he would make.

"I have told you my choice," Salem said. "The Harpoon missiles are to be the primary weapons."

"You understand the consequences?" Asad asked.

"Yes, and I'm willing to make the sacrifice, if it's indeed a sacrifice at all. If we can learn to manage the reloading of weapons, we may end up having more weapons available when we need them. It could be a net gain in armament during the critical time of battle."

"Okay, Hana," Asad said. "I understand."

"What are the risks?" Salem asked.

"That the weapon comes to life and considers us a target or otherwise accidentally detonates,"

"And how likely is this?"

"Highly unlikely. Torpedo designers have been mitigating this risk for decades."

"Any other risks?" Salem asked.

"There will be sea water pressure in the torpedo tube," Asad said, "which means that we will be testing the watertight integrity of the breach door for the first time. We have no choice but to trust the design and be thankful that we are testing the breach at a shallow depth if the design should fail."

"It will hold," Salem said. "The Germans make excellent submarines."

"Another concern is that we will have to cut the guidance wire. If we fail, then the wire will prevent us from closing the muzzle and outer doors, but this is a simple mechanism."

"So jettisoning a weapon is nontrivial, and it is an important learning experience for launching a weapon."

"That's correct, Hana."

"Then let's prove to ourselves we know how."

"Are you ready?"

Asad glanced at a speed gage showing the *Leviathan's* speed at nine point seven knots.

"The *Zafar* has slowed us to less than ten knots," he said. "We are ready."

Minutes later, Hamdan was reaching for and twisting valves with the linguist on his tiptoes verifying each valve's label behind him. Asad sat with Salem comparing the valves against a drawing in the manual of the torpedo tube system. They were beginning to recognize numbering systems in their ship's foreign language.

Asad stood and studied the room's monitor and control station that included sensors for torpedo tube status.

"The tube is flooded," he said.

Asad twisted hydraulic valves that opened the muzzle door, indicated with a circular amber light, and then he slipped a sound powered phone set over his ears. The unit's cord caught Salem in the throat, and he lifted it over his head.

"Yousif is in the operations room and ready to jettison the weapon," Asad said.

"We could do it from here if we so choose, right?"

"Yes, Hana. Is that what you wish?"

"No," Salem said. "Let's prove we can do it from our tactical center over the phone. Have him do it now."

Salem heard a loud whine as high pressure air pushed a slug of water from the impulse tank into the tube, thrusting the torpedo into the Atlantic Ocean.

"That's it?" Salem asked.

"If Yousif programmed the weapon correctly, that's all it takes, other than cutting the wire."

"Should we do that now, or should we wait?"

"We should wait."

"For what?"

"I'm not entirely sure, but I know that I would feel much better knowing that time has passed and we have gone a long distance from this spot. If we hear no high speed screws on our sonar system for twenty minutes, perhaps then I will relax. Until then, I would like the cord connected in case we need to ask the torpedo to shut down."

Salem walked to the operations room.

"Is it safe?" he asked.

"Yes, Hana," Yousif said. "It was safe the moment it left the tube. The torpedo accepted the command that it was to remain dormant, flood its ballast compartments, and sink to the bottom."

"We just can't prove this other than trusting the torpedo itself from the information it gave you?"

"That's correct. But it's also a good sign that we don't hear its screws. Without its screws, it cannot propel itself, and we are being pulled away from it."

"The wire cannot drag it?"

"I imagine that's possible but unlikely. Perhaps we should cut the wire to be sure."

"Asad says to retain the wire to be sure. You say cut it to be sure. Such is my dilemma."

On his return to the torpedo room, Salem stopped at the forward hatch and reached for his communication link to the *Zafar*.

"Hello, *Zafar*," he said.

"*Zafar* here."

Salem recognized the voice as that of the captain.

"We're done. Please return to normal speed."

"The weapon is gone then?"

"Yes."

"I am accelerating to fourteen knots."

Salem stepped forward and descended a ladder into the torpedo room.

"It's been long enough," he said. "Cut the wire."

"Yes, Hana," Asad said.

Asad pressed a button near the muzzle door.

"That's it?" Salem asked.

"Yes, the wire is cut."

Asad twisted small hydraulic valves, and a green light illuminated, indicating that the muzzle door had shut. He then repeated a similar sequence of twisting to open valves that drained the tube of its seawater.

"I'm ready to open the breach door," he said.

"Do it," Salem said.

The door opened, Salem snatched a flashlight from a bulkhead storage cradle and pointed it into the empty tube. Streams of moisture glistened within the metal cylinder, and the flat, round muzzle at the far end held the ocean at bay. He shut off the light and stepped back.

"It seems such a waste," Asad said.

"But we agreed that it was necessary to sacrifice one weapon to rearrange the armaments."

"Yes, Hana. There are six spare weapons and six weapons racks, and every tube was full. I saw no other safe way to create an empty rack to allow weapon movement."

"Then it was not a waste but a necessity," Salem said, "because I am seeing our objective more clearly as it approaches. The Harpoon missiles are the tip of our sword, and we must bring all of them to bear."

Salem pointed at the nearest Harpoon in its encapsulated, waterproofed sheathe.

"This one looks like the most logical missile to place into the empty tube."

"Yes, Hana, it is."

"Well then, let's prove to ourselves that we know how to reload a weapon. Load this Harpoon into the tube."

Salem watched his team move with deliberate patience while adjusting hydraulic valves to move the weapons rack to the open breach door. Hamdan positioned a hydraulic ram behind the Harpoon and used it to slide the weapon into the tube. The missile loaded, Asad mated an electronic ribbon from the tail of the weapon to a connector inside the breach door, and he verified with Yousif in the operations room that the ship's tactical systems recognized the Harpoon.

"The weapon is loaded and in communication with the system," he said.

"So we can launch this weapon?" Salem asked.

"Yes."

"That took us eleven minutes."

"That's not bad for our first time, Hana. We were moving slowly through the procedure on purpose while learning."

"Quite acceptable for a first time," Salem said. "But the manual says that a reload can be achieved in less than two minutes. You'll have several chances to practice while withdrawing the torpedoes from the tubes and inserting the Harpoon missiles into them. Call me when you're ready to insert the final Harpoon, and I will time you. Two minutes will be your goal."

Renard was still calming his nerves after a hostile submarine launched a torpedo from a mile away. Remy's assurance that the torpedo lacked high speed screw noise had felt like a stay of execution.

Since his scare, he had been struggling to understand the *Leviathan's* actions. He thought he understood but wanted Jake's insight before volunteering a theory.

"Bizarre, don't you think?" he asked.

"Heck, yeah," Jake said. "Could have been a hot run, a dud, or a command shutdown at launch. Could have been something entirely different."

"It was likely not a hot run," Renard said. "If the torpedo had started its engines within the tube, we likely would have heard the screws."

"True. Just brainstorming ideas before ruling them out," Jake said.

"Yes, of course. I understand. I also doubt it was a dud weapon. If they had a target in mind, they could have launched a backup weapon by now."

"Agreed."

"I do, however, find your command shutdown idea intriguing. Why would they launch a weapon and then shut it down before the engine starts?"

"Changed their minds?"

"Unlikely."

"A warning?"

Renard inhaled the taste of tobacco and exhaled.

"To whom?" he asked. "To us? They are in no position to warn anyone of anything."

"Then they jettisoned the weapon."

"Indeed," Renard said. "And by all appearances, it was a functional weapon."

"Training?" Jake asked. "Just to be sure they can get a weapon out of a tube?"

"Perhaps that and more. Perhaps they wanted to be certain that they could reload a tube. The net gain is then five weapons. The one is sacrificed, but they earn the assurance that they can reload the six in the reload racks. That would be a very mature move."

Renard saw a spark in Jake's eye he hadn't seen for years. Afraid or not, his protégé immersed his powerful and experienced mind into the moment.

"But take it one step further. There's meaning in which weapons are in the tubes and which are in the reload racks. We have no way of knowing which tube was opened, which weapon was jettisoned."

"No," Renard said. "We do not."

"But we could hear them empty and load each tube, right?

"Indeed. Remy is certain that he identified this as he counted breach doors opening and shutting. I trust his ears and mind."

"Me, too. So they took three weapons out, put four weapons in, and did a whole lot of moving weapons about the room. We know their starting load out, and we can now estimate their present load out."

"I see," Renard said. "That could be useful. I see your thought process. They cannot touch the Popeye missiles in the larger tubes, leaving the four torpedoes and two Harpoon missiles that were loaded."

"With a jettison, they removed four weapons and then promoted four to the tubes as their primary salvo. If we assume they moved each weapon only once, then they shifted from a torpedo-dominant load out to a Harpoon-dominant load out."

Renard flicked ashes into a tray, returned the Marlboro to his mouth, and pressed his hands against the machined metal surrounding the elevated conning platform.

"Consider that it would be folly to unload two Harpoon missiles just to load different ones into different tubes," he said. "If so, then we have our conclusion."

"They have all six Harpoons loaded."

"If our assumptions hold," Renard said. "This is interesting and worthy of sharing. We'll transmit this information to the fleet."

"What's it mean?" Jake asked. "If I'm a submarine commander, I always go with torpedoes. They are impossible to stop, and there's something more damaging about the torpedo hitting under the keel and its shockwave moving through water."

"But you're thinking like a man trained on a nuclear powered vessel that can approach the speed of a destroyer. Think in terms of a battery powered vessel, and you see the advantage in the distance and speed of a Harpoon. The *Leviathan* doesn't have the speed to chase a ship, but its Harpoon missiles can extend its attack radius and reduce its time to target from launching."

"What about land attack?"

"A good question," Renard said. "The Harpoon in general is capable of it with modifications such as a booster for added range, but the six about the *Leviathan* are generic anti-ship weapons."

"But anything that can hit a ship can hit a building," Jake said. "Even a sea-skimming missile like Harpoon could take out something on the coast of New York City, if the *Leviathan* got close enough to launch."

"Possible, but they won't get close enough to launch the Popeyes, much less the Harpoons."

"They don't know that."

Renard glanced at a Subtics monitor and saw icons representing the *Mercer*, the *Zafar/Leviathan* tandem, and the awaiting *Georgia*.

"True," he said. "But their window of blissful ignorance is closing. They will know about their failure in two days."

CHAPTER 18

Salem awoke to find Hamdan, the leader of the soldiers, standing over him.

"I am displeased," Hamdan said.

"How so?"

"You're taking us into missile range of major American cities, but you insist on striking a solitary warship."

"You have known since the beginning that nobody but I can know the full scale of our operation."

"This decision was made by men far away in the comfort of their homes and mosques. I believe that by serving by your side in combat, I have earned the right to know."

"Knowledge is as dangerous as it is powerful."

"And you have been graced with plenty of it," Hamdan said. "You have no right to keep it to yourself. Not anymore. Not this close to America."

Salem felt cornered.

"You are correct, my brother. I have no right. But I have a responsibility, and I will share with you why. Despite what you may have heard, the Americans—at least their best people, the ones who would interrogate us if captured—are cunning in their methods. They ascertain when a man is lying and break him. In the event that we are captured, I am sparing you from torture."

Ire rose in Hamdan's eyes.

"Capture? Why dare think of it? If you placed your purpose above your life, it would be far from your mind."

"War always has unpredictable outcomes," Salem said. "We must prepare for random contingencies."

"Are we carrying nuclear weapons?"

"No."

"There were radiation monitoring devices."

"The devices mean that the ship is capable of nuclear weapons. This load out is conventional."

"How can you be certain?"

"The tactical system indicates that the Popeye missiles have a range of only two hundred and ten nautical miles. This short range indicates a conventional warhead, which is heavier than a nuclear warhead. When using a nuclear yield, you would see a longer range."

"But we can still attack land targets. We have ten missiles loaded. You must tell me why we're wasting this arsenal and this ship on a single destroyer!"

Salem grew irate, forgetting his fear of the soldier.

"Wasting? No, you fool. I asked you to trust me, but I see you have discounted the courage and skill I have displayed. Well then, let me enlighten you, and let you bear the burden of the knowledge."

"There is nothing you can share that I am unwilling to bear."

"Very well. There is another tanker sailing to Halifax which is carrying Shahab III ballistic nuclear missiles on launch rails in one of its emptied oil tanks. We are attacking the *Bainbridge* to prevent it from defeating the Shahab missiles in flight. The missiles have a destiny with the people of America."

"Hana, I had no idea… This is…"

"Magnificent. Glorious. Brilliant. You need no more details to grasp the significance. America has become a void of purpose and integrity, and nature abhors a vacuum. A shock is required for America to regain equilibrium with its surroundings, and we are enforcing nature's laws. Are you now content that our destiny is proper?"

"Yes, Hana," Hamdan said. "And I will share this with nobody. The younger ones will take renewed faith in my renewed faith."

"See to it."

Renard checked the time, slowed the *Mercer* to ten knots, and ascended to snorkel depth. As the *Zafar-Leviathan* tandem steamed five miles ahead, Renard had Henri raise the induction mast and charge the batteries with the *Mercer's* diesel engines.

"You're not worried about the *Zafar* seeing our induction mast?" Jake asked.

"They have given no sign that they are looking behind themselves for such a danger, and we appear miniscule from their perspective. Why would you question it now when we've done this many times?"

"Because we're close to finishing this."

"Now is time for confidence—not paranoia. What happened to your aura of being charmed?"

"Hell if I know, Pierre. Doesn't matter anymore, though. It's time for me to hide. I'm going to the engineering spaces with Claude."

"You could probably get away with staying here and greeting the SEALs as long as you didn't speak. Your French is impeccable, but I'm afraid your lack of French accent when speaking English would be a dead giveaway."

"Probably."

"And your musculature might create suspicion as well."

"And knowing my luck, one of my naval academy classmates would be with them and recognize me. I'm heading aft."

Renard reached for Jake's arm.

"Not so fast," he said.

"What?"

"You're commanding this ship in my absence."

"I know. I've done it before."

"The men trust you. I trust you. I want you to know this."

"Why the drama?"

"Remain alert. Keep your wits about you. That's all I ask."

"Pierre, this is easy. Running from the U.S. Navy across the world in a Trident is hard. Chasing down a rogue Pakistani *Agosta* submarine across the Pacific Ocean is hard. This time it's a team effort, and the good guys have our backs."

"Regardless. When I've departed and you return to this room, you are commanding a warship. Prepare yourself mentally while you have the time to do so."

Renard watched his protégé walk away. As he turned to the operations room, he saw Henri standing before him.

"He's a good man, Pierre. A rare find. I remember when you first recruited him. You had no doubt. Why do you doubt him now?"

"Something about the reunion with his brothers. One of them planted a seed of doubt in his mind."

"He's stronger than that," Henri said.

"Perhaps it is more."

"How so?"

"The reunion may have been a catalyst for a rupture in his mind. I fear that his return to the states hurt him. It dashed his dreams of going back to the life he once had. His attempt to go home proved that he was homeless. I blame myself for allowing it."

"You had to help him try."

A young mercenary entered the room and gestured to Renard to follow him.

"Manage operations for me here," Renard said.

"Of course," Henri said.

*   *   *

Renard followed the mercenary to the aft hatch and climbed a step ladder. He turned an ear upward to listen. A gentle, high pitched note vibrated from above.

"You are correct, lad," Renard said. "Our guests have arrived. I would never attempt this unless I knew that experts were piloting a minisub above me. And if I'm wrong, I'll thank the next submarine designer I see for making hatches open outward. If there's sea pressure on it, it will prevent me from doing something stupid."

Renard twisted a ring of metal that unlocked the hatch. When it clicked, he rotated the metal ring further, held his breath, and pushed. He was surprised and relieved when he felt the hatch rise by its own will.

Backlit by fluorescent lighting and the familiar concavity of a submarine's interior, a stern face appeared above. After scanning the inner environs of the *Mercer*, the face locked eyes with Renard and transmuted itself into a smile.

"Good morning," it said.

"Good morning."

"Lieutenant Commander Tony Gomez," Gomez said. "United States Navy. SEAL Team Four."

"Pierre Renard, commanding officer of the *Mercer*."

"The what?"

"Excuse me. That's a nickname we've given the ship. This is the pre-commission unit *Razak*. You're welcome to come aboard."

Gomez' face receded from view, and a knotted rope fell into the ship. Moments later, a figure raced down the rope, swung itself aside the stepladder, and landed on its toes. It held a rifle pointed upwards but scanned the room for targets.

Renard blinked, and a second figure, bulkier than the first, slid behind the first, facing the other way. He noticed thickness at their chests suggesting body armor, and he was surprised to note that their camouflage employed colors of gray, sand, and beige. He had expected black wet suits, but the colors registered in his mind as being appropriate for the inside of the *Leviathan*.

"I would have offered you the step ladder," he said.

"Training," Gomez said. "The next time we do this it's for real."

"Understood."

Gomez' features had gone hard again but softened as he turned to Renard. Gomez was of average build and height, but even under his camouflage, Renard saw contours of lean muscle. The SEAL extended a hand that Renard accepted.

"Gomez."

"Renard."

"This is Chief Petty Officer Smith."

Smith spanned twenty percent more mass than Gomez in all directions. He turned and smiled.

"Pleased to meet you," he said.

"Likewise," Renard said.

Renard thought that the SEALs shifted states of mind from robotic to jovial too rapidly for him to comprehend, as if they shared a secret reality that would elude his understanding no matter how he might try to grasp it.

The knotted rope receded above Renard, and the hatch slid shut.

"Just in case," Gomez said. "Our minisub will hold, but no sense in leaving an open hole."

"Right," Renard said.

"Let's brief your tactical team and get out of here."

In the operations room, Renard watched Gomez drawing figures on trace paper. Henri, Remy, and two younger mercenaries observed the lesson.

Gomez looked up and seemed to be holding back a grin. Some hidden energy churned within him.

"You guys are the best dressed crew I've ever seen. Fitted shirts, designer slacks, and Nikes. Nice."

"We are a different breed than you are likely accustomed to," Renard said. "But we are professionals."

"No doubt," Gomez said as he looked down.

"The *Georgia* is here and will stay ten miles ahead of the *Zafar* and *Leviathan*," Gomez said. "The minisub is connected via command wire to the *Georgia*. We're taking power from them and we have communications with them."

"Taking power?" Henri asked.

"Yes. It helps us with propulsion and with our cutting laser. It allows us to sustain fifteen knots. We can sprint faster if we need, but it eats the battery. The wire to the *Georgia* can only be so thick, and that limits the power we can borrow from them."

"Will we be in communications with you?" Henri asked.

"No. But you shouldn't need to hear from us. After we've taken the *Leviathan*, we'll inform the *Georgia*, and they'll have other assets force the *Zafar* to stop. That should be the end game. If the *Zafar* disobeys, we'll have Mister Renard attempt to snap the tow line by shaking the *Leviathan* free. Worst case, we surface the *Leviathan* and disconnect its tow lines, under protective fire if needed."

"Whose protective fire?" Renard asked.

"Ours. Two sharpshooters in the sail. I'll take two of my guys rocking in the sail against whatever the *Zafar* can dish up trying to stop us."

"Where do you want us?" Henri asked.

"You're on the right course now," Gomez said. "But you'll have to speed up once we're gone. We want you on the other side than the *Georgia* so that any weapon the *Leviathan* fires doesn't threaten the *Georgia*."

"What if you fail to get aboard?" Henri asked.

The stern image cascaded over Gomez' face.

"In that unlikely event, you'll destroy the *Leviathan* with a torpedo."

"How would we know to do so?"

"If you hear us banging on the hull of our minisub. Repeatedly. You'll also likely hear us driving away fast, but if you don't, don't hesitate. We're expendable."

Remembering he'd be in the minisub, Renard swallowed.

"And if we fail or don't hear you?"

"The *Georgia* will attempt to contact you via underwater communications. If you still don't fire a weapon at the *Leviathan* after that, they will."

"And if they fail?" Henri asked. "They are deliberately far away for their own self-preservation. Their shot landing on the *Leviathan* would be no guarantee."

"Then we all drive the hell out of here and hope we don't get caught in the weapon storm that's going to fall from the sky. I plan on being onboard that submarine within the next three hours. But if I'm not, this patch of water is going to be a mess of every sensor and weapon in the U.S. arsenal, and you're going to want to be sprinting in the other direction."

Salem's subconscious mind freed his dreams of demonic soldiers, and he had dreamt of a world of peace. But the peace was overwhelming like a cold winter void of life. As he awoke in the morning, he sensed that he was fearless but numb, as if awaiting sedated annihilation.

He ate breakfast in silence with Hamdan and Hamas soldiers who seemed to carry a newfound aura of respect. When he had finished half of his powered eggs, he excused himself and went to the operations room where Yousif sat at a tactical monitor.

"How was your night, Ali?" he asked.

"Quiet. I believe I have read all I can about the systems that matter. I'm reading material for the third and fourth time."

"I know Ali. You are prepared. We all are. Get some breakfast and get some rest. I'll take your place here."

An hour later, Salem sat at a monitor beside a linguist who joined him after cleaning the galley. He was working through a system manual on launching and targeting Harpoon missiles when the communication unit with the *Zafar* chirped. Concerned, he walked to the hatch and grabbed the box.

"Leviathan here."

"Captain?"

"Yes," Salem said.

"This is the captain of the *Zafar*. We have encountered a problem."

"What's wrong?"

"A ship ahead of us in the transit lane has caught fire and is preparing to abandon ship."

"Why is this a problem for us?"

"We are one of the closest ships capable of rendering assistance."

"Let someone else help them."

"I see only one ship on radar that is closer to the vessel than us, and they have already passed it by. I would not blame them to feign not having heard and to continue."

"But we cannot feign not hearing because we are approaching the vessel and will see it?"

"The smoke will be visible if the ship is not."

"So what happens?"

"The United States Coast Guard will echo the call for all vessels in the vicinity to assist. If another vessel is found that can manage, we may be released of our obligation to help."

"What obligation is that?"

"Centuries of custom and several agreements and maritime laws."

"Curse customs and laws. Ignore the vessel and deal with the legal issues when you arrive in New York."

"I would, but the Coast Guard will also send aircraft to investigate, and this aircraft will have radar discerning the location of all vessels within reach of assisting. They will see us, and they will identify us by matching our location with our manifest. Then they will contact us and remind us of our obligation."

"Curse their reminder. Tell them you have a tight schedule. Use any excuse you know to continue."

"I could do that, but we will be passing by an area that will involve the watching eye of at least one Coast Guard aircraft. They will likely see us and our tow cable. That will arouse suspicion we cannot afford to arouse."

Salem's heart sank.

"I see."

"We have but one choice. We have to release you."

"This will delay us," Salem said.

"The delay is only slight. We will inform the Trigger, and he will adjust his timing to compensate."

"I understand."

"What speed can you sustain toward the Gulf of Maine?"

"I believe the ship can go faster, but I'm comfortable with ten, at most twelve knots."

"It's best that you go slowly while evading the attention that will be surrounding us. Ten is fine."

"What about the tow cable?" Salem asked. "Can you cut us loose now?"

"Yes. That is no problem."

"We'll risk having it catch in our screw."

"We'll reel you in first before cutting, to shorten the length so it can't reach your screw."

"We'll have to come shallow and slow."

"Yes, this is just as planned, only sooner than hoped. Ten knots. I'm slowing now."

"Excuse me for a moment," Salem said.

He darted to the operations room and asked the linguist to fetch Asad and Bazzi. Then he returned to the communications unit.

"I'm back," Salem said.

"The Coast Guard already has an aircraft en route."

"You've foreseen events well," Salem said.

"You have little time. I need to speed up again to render assistance. Make haste in coming shallow."

Asad appeared beside Salem.

"Bring us to snorkel depth," Salem said. "The *Zafar* is slowing to ten knots. I'll have Bazzi bring up propulsion. Use Latakia where you see fit."

"You look concerned, Hana. Is everything alright?"

"There is a change in plans," Salem said. "But we will be okay. Bring the ship shallow."

Asad marched away. Salem grabbed the communications unit.

"We're coming shallow," he said.

"While we cut the line, we will have to hold it taut around the capstan. You may feel your ship being jerked about. That cannot be helped. Make sure your pots and pans are stowed."

"What's wrong?" Bazzi asked as he approached.

"We must part with the *Zafar*," Salem said. "Prepare the propulsion system for operations. Wake everyone you need. Make haste. I don't want to linger in this area."

"Yes, Hana."

"Also, have a soldier walk about the ship and make sure everything is stowed. We may get jerked about while detaching from the *Zafar*."

Minutes later, Salem prepared to release the *Zafar* from its towing obligation.

"We're at snorkel depth, ready to be released."

"Very well. I'll secure the towing capstan. You may feel jerking soon."

"This is our last communication then?"

"Yes. Possibly a few jerks while we cut, and then we will be separated."

"I thank you for a job well done."

"And I thank you for a task to soon be accomplished."

Salem returned to the operations room and felt ripples in the *Leviathan's* speed. He found his balance by shifting his weight between the balls of his feet and heels, and then he felt nothing.

He walked to the communications unit and hailed the *Zafar* to no response. Then he stepped back to the operations room.

"We are alone again," he said. "Is Bazzi ready?"

"Not yet, Hana," Asad said.

"No matter. We will change course now regardless, since we are now responsible for our own journey. We will drift to our new course."

Salem bent over a keyboard and called up a chart. He sought the course to point the *Leviathan* at the southwestern tip of the Gulf of Maine.

"Come to course three-two-zero," he said.

Asad jostled a joystick, and Salem felt the deck heel under him and settle even again. A digital gage showed the *Leviathan's* speed at eight and a half knots and slowing.

"Bazzi is ready," Asad said.

"Have him bring us to ten knots."

CHAPTER 19

Olivia's phone woke her, and she peeked at it through her half open eye. It was an automated message from a CIA central watch post. She flipped open the phone and checked the message telling her to log in to her secure web folder.

Tapping the keyboard of a laptop computer, she saw its monitor illuminate. A few clicks and passwords later, she was reading a message stating that a man using a disposable cell phone had called Ghaffari and left a voice mail. The Farsi words translated to 'Publish Your Work'.

Electronic surveillance had tracked the call's source to Iran. The voice was being frequency-analyzed to recordings of people of interest, but Olivia knew that finding a match was speculative.

Olivia compressed her morning routine and emerged showered and clothed in time to see the professor passing by a window. Moments later, Ghaffari was marching to her Mustang, a duffel bag slung over her shoulder.

She waited until the Mustang pulled away and then darted to her Fusion. The sun had risen, but the roads remained fast before rush hour. Keeping the Mustang in sight, Olivia sped through the commute to the university, pondering a suspicious voice mail, a duffel bag, and Ghaffari's early morning egress.

On campus, Olivia slowed as she watched the Mustang glide into a parking slot. Ghaffari sprang from the car without the duffel bag and hastened toward the library.

Olivia parked, slung a backpack over her shoulder, and walked to the library. She climbed stairs and swept upward, scanning each floor for the professor. She found her on the third floor at a computer, and she sat at a distance where she could see Ghaffari's face.

She slid her backpack to a table and withdrew a psychology text. Olivia peered over the book's edge and studied Ghaffari's expressions as the professor jabbed her jump drive into the library computer, clicked the mouse, and tapped the keyboard.

Her habitual brooding ire became contempt as Ghaffari seemed displeased with the computer's speed. She wiggled fingers beside a mouse in a subconscious attempt to hasten the machine. In juxtaposition to her subject's inquietude, Olivia became patient in observing the professor's intense fixation on the monitor.

An expression cracked the grimace congealing on Ghaffari's face, and Olivia tagged it as happiness, the first indication of joy the professor had revealed as she yanked her drive from the computer, logged off, and sauntered away.

The professor out of site, Olivia trotted to the computer and logged in. She dialed her phone and held it to her ear. After a sterile greeting, she rattled off her badge number and awaited technical support. A man with a young geeky voice greeted her.

"How can I help you McDonald?"

"I need Ghaffari's Old Dominion web account data."

"One moment while I access her info. Okay... got it. Are you ready to memorize or write?"

"Yes. Go."

Olivia asked the man to remain on the line while she typed. Ghaffari's computer session revealed its nature when Olivia opened a browser. She discovered a new webmail account and relayed its information to the man on the phone.

"That's a Google account," he said.

"Can you get in?"

"We have access to all major accounts—golden keys to email servers. Give me a second... I've got the emails sent from that account, three minutes ago. It looks like five emails were sent. Big ones. About fifteen pictures in high resolution. I'm forwarding them to your account now."

"Can you describe them to me?"

"Sure, let me open the first. It looks like a sailor with a teddy bear. He's holding a sign..."

"I've seen it," she said. "Can you trace the addresses of the recipients?"

"Just one recipient. The trace is being run and... it's going to be a dead end for now. This thing went to a blacklisted domain in Iran."

"I need to run," she said. "You'll keep tracing the email to a better defined recipient?"

"Someone in our office will. We get more emails to blacklisted domains than you might think. Do you want me to bump this up to an urgent priority?"

"Yes. Urgent. Can you forward these to a naval officer I want to review them?"

"If you give me permission, I can."

"You have my permission. Get ready to write down his email address. His name is Commander Roger Sanders."

Olivia held her phone to her ear while driving.

"Gerry?" she asked.

"Now's not a good time," Rickets said.

"I'll be quick. Ghaffari just received a message from a disposable cell phone in Iran telling her to 'Publish Your Work' and then sent a bunch of pictures of her fiancé on the *Bainbridge* to a blacklisted domain in Iran. She also raced away from the university to god knows where while she's supposed to be teaching this morning."

"What do you need?"

"A few things."

"Go ahead."

"I need someone to make sure we follow those emails to their destination."

"I'll take care of it," Rickets said. "No guarantees that anything comes up, but I'll see that the appropriate avenues are followed. What else?"

"Someone to arrest Ghaffari."

"I'll have a cop bring her in. You found enough for us to hold her."

"I also need someone to figure out what's so interesting about those pictures. I'm going to join Commander Sanders for his opinion, but I want eyeballs from our experts on them. Tech support forwarded them to my account. You can get to them, I'm sure."

"Done. Anything else?"

"That's it."

"Good job. When you see Commander Sanders, ask him about your last project. You'll like what you hear."

Olivia sat with Sanders in a soundproofed room at the headquarters of the U.S. Atlantic Fleet.

"Check these out," she said, "and tell me what's interesting or dangerous about them."

She rotated a computer monitor showing fifteen pictures that Commander Pastor had taken of himself over two weeks and had sent to Ghaffari. He glanced at them.

"I don't like these," he said. "You mentioned these earlier, didn't you?"

"Yes."

"Let me print them out."

He fingered through the images as a high definition printer spat them out.

"They didn't set off alarms when you told me about them, but looking at them and knowing where they're going, I know something is wrong. I need to look at these for a while to pinpoint it."

"Do you think the *Bainbridge* is in danger?"

"Hard to say," he said. "But it's obvious that someone is plotting against it or its captain. He's done himself no favors by being manipulated by his heart strings. He'll probably get administrative punishment for showing poor judgment. I'm going to make sure the destroyer squadron commodore knows about these."

"You'll be ending his career, right?"

"Maybe, but I've got to do the right thing."

He grabbed the printed photographs and slapped them onto the table. He pulled a monocle magnifying glass from his pocket, slipped it into his eye socket, and stooped over the first picture.

"These look like really simple pictures," he said. "A guy in love. The trick is figuring out what's hiding behind the obvious."

"That's what you do, isn't it?"

"Yeah, but the eye and the mind make for a tricky connection. You have to know what to look for. It takes training, and it's best done as a team sport. You have CIA people looking over this, don't you?"

"Yes."

"Good. The more the better. I'm gonna get some local help, too. I'm good at this, but there are some guys in our building who are whizzes. They're just sitting around waiting to see if the ops guys need them for *Leviathan* anymore."

"What's going on with the *Leviathan*?" she asked. "Gerry told me to ask you."

"The end game."

"Why are you here then?"

"Operations," he said, dropping his monocle to his hand and looking up. "My job ended when I helped the operations guys figure out who to take down and why."

"Sounds like a letdown."

"I can always watch it happen. You can watch it too, if you want."

"How?"

"In the fleet operations room," he said. "You're cleared for it. You get a bird's eye view from windows above. We're the lowest priority viewers, but there's usually room. I can escort you in."

"You sure do know how to please a woman."

"Maybe we can talk about that hiking date now."

"Well," she said. "Maybe not. Let's figure out where this Ghaffari thing goes, first."

"Good idea," he said.

He returned the monocle to his eye and slid each picture below it in sequence.

"Shit!" he said.

"What?" she asked.

"The moon," he said. "The stars."

"Romantic, huh? She played him."

"Romantic, but also essential to celestial navigation. These photos are clear, and I bet there's enough star and moon data to get a pretty tight fix on the *Bainbridge* in every picture. This is a common tactic in the intelligence community. I just didn't think of it at first while looking at a friendly ship. We usually do this for neutrals and bad guys."

"Navigation by the stars?" she asked. "How bad can it be for a ship that fast?"

"Bad enough if it's following a predictable pattern. Someone could theoretically use these to take good guesses of where it will be in the next few hours or so."

"They need to be warned," she said.

"I'll take care of it."

"Warning them is going to be difficult," she said.

"True. We don't know what we're warning them about. But at least they can shift their mode of operation to heightened alert."

"That's not what I meant," she said.

"Oh?"

"I meant that by warning the *Bainbridge*, you're telling the captain that he was betrayed by a fiancée and that his career is at risk due to his own stupid moves."

"Nobody said being a naval officer was easy. He'll have to suck it up and keep commanding his ship—assuming his squadron commander keeps him in command, which I think he will. Commander Pastor is one of the best tacticians we have. It's how he made rank despite being an arrogant prick."

"You better tell the destroyer squadron commander."

"Wait here," he said. "That's where I'm going now."

The Trigger watched the Captain point to the sky in a photograph of the *Bainbridge's* commanding officer, questioning a fix drawn by one of his mates.

"The angle of declination for the moon is too high here. Bring it down five degrees and compute again."

The Captain left the mate and his companions to continue their celestial analysis of the *Bainbridge*.

"You are making sense of this?" the Trigger asked.

"Yes. I'm taking extra care with the more recent photographs, but I want accuracy with the older ones as well. This helps us identify a patrol pattern."

"What do you see?"

"Come. I'll show you."

The Trigger walked to the chart and observed the Captain's pencil pointing to dots.

"I don't see anything but dots and numbers," he said.

"Let me be so bold as to connect these in order."

The Captain drew lines that zigzagged inside the lines of an invisible slanted rectangle.

"I see," the Trigger said. "The *Bainbridge* steamed to the northern end of its patrol boundary near the entrance to the Gulf of Maine, and then it has been cutting east to west on its way to the southern boundary."

"Correct. We don't know where that southern boundary is, but we have all the information we need, assuming the double-checking of these fixes proves them accurate."

"Meaning, we will drive to the vacated northern edge of their patrol boundary to launch our missiles?"

"Precisely. We know that's a weak point in the American missile shield by the presence of the *Bainbridge* filling that weakness, and we know the *Bainbridge* is now steaming away from that point. It's our perfect launch point."

"And what of the *Leviathan*?" the Trigger asked.

"They are in a strong position to help us. We'll send them an estimate of the *Bainbridge's* course and speed, and let them do what they will. The *Bainbridge* is within their reach."

"Then the board is set," the Trigger said, "and the pieces are moving."

"I've deviated from our track to Halifax and have set course for the *Bainbridge's* northern patrol boundary. We'll need the helicopter's radar if we are to find the *Bainbridge*. Shall I launch it now?"

"Yes, but keep it at low altitude until we've made contact with the *Leviathan*," the Trigger said. "When that's done, have your pilot fly high with his radar at maximum energy directed at our best estimate of the *Bainbridge*."

"We are arousing suspicion," the Captain said. "There is no turning back. The missiles must fly."

The Trigger felt a stab of sadness and swallowed.

"I'm sure my missiles will fly as planned," he said. "They always have, and I guarantee them."

Renard found the SEAL minisub to be spacious and his shipmates elite company.

Four SEALs joined Gomez and Smith in the vessel, and two sailors from the *Georgia* operated the craft. Also present was a naval officer, fluent in Farsi and Arabic, who would serve as a translator, and an Israeli man of average build who Renard understood to be the premier expert on the *Leviathan's* systems.

Introductions were curt as the SEALs demanded silence while seeking the *Leviathan*. Renard strapped himself to a seat against the hull and watched Gomez and Smith slide a bulky mass along weight-bearing railings in the overhead.

Smith's muscles bulged as he slowed the device above the vessel's lower hatch. The two SEALs lowered the mass as it extended from a hydraulic arm. They flipped switches to activate it in a brief diagnostic check and then they lifted it again. Its size and movement reminded Renard of an X-ray machine.

"I can hardly wait to see what it does," he said.

"You'll want to look away so that you don't" Gomez said. "You'll see the effect soon enough."

"How long will it take?"

"We've programmed it for a two-foot diameter cut," Gomez said. "Forty seconds."

"And then?"

"And then we pull the cut piece away and rain down hell on whatever's waiting on the other side."

The vessel's pilot called out to Gomez, who crouched and walked forward. Gomez returned to Renard.

"We just got word from the *Georgia*," he said. "The *Zafar* cut the *Leviathan* loose. The *Leviathan* turned to the northwest and is now making ten knots. I don't see this changing our plans at all, and neither does the skipper of the *Georgia*. Does this mean anything to you?"

"It means that the *Leviathan* is now capable of its top speed, which is probably twenty-two knots."

"Twenty-three," the Israeli expert said.

"Who are you?" Renard asked. "I'm afraid in our haste that we were improperly introduced."

"Doctor Gabi Marom," Marom said. "I was responsible for delivering the *Dolphin* class submarine to our fleet."

"A man after my own heart," Renard said. "I did the same for Pakistan and the *Agosta* class."

"Gentlemen," Gomez said, "the *Leviathan* is free under its own power."

"Of course," Renard said, "it can sustain its sprint speed for only about forty minutes."

He glanced at Marom.

"Forty-two minutes," Marom said, "by design. They pushed it to forty-five minutes in sea trials but damaged a quarter of the battery cells."

"You are quite a useful man," Renard said.

"I can advise about the ship, but I am no operational commander. This is why you will be commanding the *Leviathan* to bring it home where it belongs."

"But it's not going to sprint and snorkel, is it?" Gomez asked.

"No," Renard said. "If its intent is to launch Popeye missiles against New York City at the maximum weapons range, then its optimum navigation to drive into range submerged for the entire trip would be twelve knots for approximately twenty hours."

"That's correct," Marom said.

"And it would have to travel almost due west," Renard said. "Its present course of northwest seems odd, unless Boston is its target."

"I'll let the *Georgia* know your opinions," Gomez said, "but this change in direction and decrease in speed means two things for us."

"Yes?" Renard asked.

"Our closing speed to catch the *Leviathan* is twice as fast as planned, but now we have a tougher job in finding them. It throws a monkey wrench into our timing, and you need to get ready in case we find them sooner rather than later."

"How do I get ready?"

"Put this on."

Gomez handed him a camouflage vest with a Kevlar chest protector while Smith handed a similar garment to Marom. Renard wiggled into the protective top and let Gomez assist him with harnessing it around his torso. He considered Marom and himself to be ragdolls as the SEALs dressed them.

"Take this, too," Gomez said.

He handed Renard a standard nine millimeter pistol.

"What do I do with this?"

"Stick it in your pocket here."

Gomez slid the barrel into a vest pocket and sealed the handle into a snug fit with a Velcro tie.

"There's a pocket on the other side for your clips," Gomez said. "But you don't get those until we're inside the *Leviathan*. There's a greater chance of you shooting one of our own team than shooting a bad guy if you run around with loaded weapons. So you only lock and load in an emergency. Got it?"

"Got it," Marom said.

"Well, no," Renard said. "I loathe firearms. What constitutes an emergency?"

The content smile appeared on Gomez' face that hinted at a hidden energy.

"If one of my guys tells you to shoot something, that's an emergency," he said. "And you also have permission to start shooting in the unlikely event that you happen to see me or one of my guys dead."

CHAPTER 20

Lieutenant Commander Robert Stephenson handed Pastor a copy of the latest patrol orders while summarizing them, but his commanding officer stood motionless.

"Sir?" he asked. "This is a significant change."

The sun was rising through the bridge windows of the *Bainbridge*. Stephenson squinted as Commander Richard Pastor's backlit face took on an expression he had never seen. He thought that Pastor was pouting.

"Yeah, XO," Pastor said. "I know."

"Do you want me to take care of it? Come up with a new patrol pattern?"

"No, XO, I'll take care of it. You've been up all night. Get some sleep."

Pastor turned his back and waved his hand. Stephenson took the hint and left the bridge. He climbed to the radio room and found Senior Chief Wilson chatting with a sailor wearing a blue and gray camouflage uniform.

"Senior Chief?" he asked.

"Yes, sir," Wilson said. "What can I do for you?"

"Did the captain just get a personal message?"

"Yes, sir. From squadron, about fifteen minutes ago. Whatever it was, he took it hard."

"How so?"

"He was upset when he read it. His eyes got big, he turned red, and he was shaking mad. Worse than I've ever seen him."

"I noticed he was shaken on the bridge."

"I hate to say it, sir, but his fiancée is a dangerous heartbreaker. If I know her like I think I do, she did something to him, and that's what's under his skin."

"Good to know, Senior Chief," Stephenson said. "I'll keep an eye on him."

As he walked to his stateroom, Stephenson let his responsibilities to the crew and the captain slip from his shoulders. He felt the fatigue of sleeplessness and of having tended to the *Bainbridge* throughout the night while Pastor slept.

He slid under crisp sheets and questioned the significance of the last patrol order to avoid a new allied submarine operation at the southern edge of the *Bainbridge's* patrol boundary. Accepting that Pastor would update the *Bainbridge's* direction away from the operation, Stephenson fell into a deep sleep.

Renard wondered if his fellow passengers felt his level of anxiety, but he read nothing in the faces of the SEALs. He watched Gomez moving between the silent seated statues of the minisub's other occupants and tap the shoulder of the vessel's pilots. The SEAL exchanged inaudible words with the sailors and then crouched, walked, and knelt before him.

"The *Georgia* has good track on the *Leviathan*," Gomez said. "But it's not gnat's ass tight. We're supposedly five hundred yards behind them, if you trust that there's no slop in the tracking."

"There's always slop in the tracking," Renard said, "unless you use active sonar. And even then you find that there is still slop."

"We have an active sonar system designed for fine tuning our approach to targets. It's not designed for listening. We can only use it as a range finder, and it's only good at short range."

"I imagine."

"We essentially rely upon cameras and active sonar to guide us in to targets."

"You have external lights and cameras?"

"Yes, with limited range," Gomez said. "Usually good for the last ten yards. My concern is getting from here to camera range with our active sonar. It's high frequency, low range, but I want to be sure they don't hear us."

"When transmitting active, you run the risk of being heard," he said. "That cannot be helped. You mitigate this by using minimal power settings and quick transmission bursts. It is also advantageous that it's a high frequency system."

"We have some leeway in selecting frequencies."

Renard wiggled in his seat, attempting to find comfort in his vest. He looked at the Israeli systems expert seated beside him.

"Do you know the *Leviathan's* fathometer frequency?"

"Yes," Marom said. "Thirty-five kilohertz is the center frequency."

"Can you transmit at that frequency?" Renard asked.

"Yes," Gomez said.

"Then," Renard said, "I suggest we transmit like the *Leviathan's* fathometer in its default mode. If they should happen to hear us and be paying attention, then they'll have no reason to believe we're anything beyond a scattered echo of their own hardware."

Thirty minutes later, Gomez was scowling at Renard.

"The *Georgia* just updated their solution to the *Leviathan*," he said. "It's tighter, and we're repositioning now. Hopefully this unplanned goose chase will end now."

"I understand that the *Georgia* is constrained in maneuvering by the need to retain our command wire, but that solution should be accurate now," Renard said.

From the corner of his eye, he saw one of the two sailors seated in front press his finger against a monitor and turn his head. Gomez sprang across the cramped compartment and bent over the sailor's shoulder.

For seconds that passed with lethargy, Renard held his breath, twisted himself in his seat, and watched. As his lungs began to burn, he saw Gomez' profile and noticed that a smile had melted his scowl. The *Leviathan* lurked directly below.

During the descent to the Israeli submarine, Renard craned his neck to peek around Gomez and the minisub's operators at the monitor showing its illuminated deck.

He felt the Israeli expert stir beside him.

"I don't suppose you can see anything?" Marom asked.

"Hardly anything. But I think we're close."

Renard dug his palms into his seat as the minisub lurched and heeled.

"It's okay," Gomez said. "The *Leviathan* is coming shallow. We're just getting out of the way."

"Is this a concern?" Renard asked.

"This will actually make our life easier."

"How so?" Renard asked.

"If they're going to snorkel depth, they'll probably stay there for a bit," Gomez. "No drastic changes in depth. We'll mount them and infiltrate while they're up."

The minisub's motions were imperceptible as its pilots maneuvered it over the back of the shallow *Leviathan*. At ten knots, Renard expected a drastic thump, but he heard and felt nothing as the vessel settled on a slight incline on the Israeli submarine's back.

"We're on," Gomez said. "Draining the mating skirt."

A pilot flipped a switch, and a motor by Gomez' knee whirred. Gomez reached and illuminated halogen lamps aimed at the minisub's hatch, and he motioned to one of his SEALs. Renard cringed as Gomez' man flipped the circle of metal back over its hinges and exposed the aqua green paint of the *Leviathan's* back.

Gomez and Smith grabbed handles and guided the laser cutter downward on its hydraulic arm. When its axial tip passed through the hatch and stopped against the submarine beneath it, the SEALs unfolded tripod arms and braced the instrument against the minisub's deck.

"Cutting!" Gomez said.

He depressed a button on the device, and Renard saw a laser cutting an arc around the tip. He looked away from the brightness, heard air swooshing through the growing metallic incision, and felt his ears pop as the minisub and *Leviathan* equalized air pressure.

"Energize magnets!" Gomez said.

Renard heard thumps echo from both ends of the minisub as it bolstered its connection to the *Leviathan*. As the SEALs crouched behind Gomez in preparation to greet the inner world of the *Leviathan*, Renard felt thankful for being seated at a distance from the hole.

Stephenson was dreaming of his wife when a knock at his door woke him. Senior Chief Wilson entered his stateroom and handed him sheets of paper.

"I had news that couldn't wait, sir."

Stephenson rubbed his eyes.

"What is it?"

"Warnings from squadron about violating our patrol area. The captain said to ignore them since it was just a squabble between some destroyer admiral and submarine admiral. He said the submarine guys can go to hell."

"Where are we?"

"Southern end of our patrol area."

"Damn it," Stephenson said as he slipped his camouflage shirt over his white crew neck.

"There's more, sir."

"What else?"

"From the Atlantic Fleet Intelligence to your personal inbox. I wanted to deliver it myself. I couldn't help but see as I printed them for you. They're weird pictures of... Well, you'll see."

Wilson dropped the pictures of the *Bainbridge's* captain on a desk. Stephenson paged through them.

"These are embarrassing and show poor judgment."

"Read the note, sir."

"It's from a Commander Sanders," Stephenson said. "It states that these were sent by the captain's fiancée to a blacklisted domain in Iran. We're the subject of an unknown operation."

"Dang, sir."

"Are we still in modified emissions control?"

"Yes, sir."

Stephenson darted for the combat information center.

Salem's linguist held the high frequency radio handset, translating Farsi into Arabic, as he conversed with a man whose voice he recognized from an important meeting long ago.

"Yes," he said. "I have just inserted the coordinates of the *Bainbridge* into my system. I am ready to launch."

The linguist translated the Trigger's response. The supertanker serving as the launch platform had just fired two dozen Chinese-designed C-802 anti-ship missiles at the *Bainbridge*.

Salem knew that the C-802 missiles would not reach the *Bainbridge* or explode if they did, since they had no warheads or terminal guidance systems. They were pre-production skeletons that the Trigger had selected to overwhelm the destroyer in a calculated decision-making overload. As part of the coordinated attack, Salem had to launch the *Leviathan's* Harpoon missiles now.

He wished the Trigger good fortune and turned to Asad.

"All Harpoons are programmed for the coordinates of the *Bainbridge* and released for launch," he said. "Launch all Harpoons immediately."

"Yes, Hana."

Asad turned and stopped at the sound of deep thuds from above that sounded like metal hitting metal.

Salem looked at the petrified Asad and then gazed into the overhead. His pulse quickened as he saw smoke billowing through the hull's insulated lagging.

Focusing beyond the smoke, he noted a black line tracing a tight circle through the lagging. He tapped Asad on the shoulder, startling the young naval veteran.

"This room is dangerous. Go to the torpedo room and launch the weapons," Salem said. "I will deal with this."

As Asad marched away, Salem told the linguist to fetch the Hamas soldiers with their weapons.

"Get out of here, Ali," Salem said.

"Hana, I don't understand," Yousif said.

"Our destiny lies with launching weapons. There is only danger in this room. Join Asad in the torpedo room."

Yousif departed as Hamdan returned with his three younger combatants. The hole in the operations room had been half cut, and the instrument making the cut nicked a hydraulic line, shooting a stream of glistening fluid.

"Hana?" Hamdan asked.

"I don't know who or how. I just know that we must defend ourselves."

Hamdan positioned himself and his soldiers at four quadrants of the growing circle with rifles pointed up.

Salem envisioned an instant massacre of the Hamas team.

"No," he said. "Follow me. Now! Make for the torpedo room. Slow their advance so that we can launch all of the ship's weapons!"

The soldiers backed toward Salem as he passed under the forward hatch. He slid down a ladder to the torpedo room and saw the soldiers stop above the ladder and assume firing positions.

Hamdan appeared above the ladder and extended two pistols to Salem.

"You may need these," he said. "We'll use rifles."

"I need three minutes more than I need bullets," Salem said, cradling the weapons under his arm. "Three minutes to launch the Harpoons and to reload. The *Bainbridge* is in torpedo range."

Hamdan's face softened.

"It is my destiny," he said, "to protect you for those three minutes. It is your destiny to ensure that those three minutes matter."

Salem locked eyes with the soldier and clenched his hand. If Hamdan concealed secret orders to kill him, Salem forgave his companion.

A rapid change in air pressure and a hiss from the torpedo room diverted his attention, and Hamdan disappeared above the ladder.

Behind him, Asad's voice verified Salem's hopes.

"First Harpoon is launched," he said.

"Are you sure?" Jake asked.

"Yes!" Remy said, his hand pressing his sonar headset to his ear. "The *Leviathan* just launched a weapon. And now another!"

"Open the outer door to tube one," Jake said.

Remy nodded to a young mercenary beside him who handled the task.

"The outer door to tube one is open," Remy said. "Three... wait, now four weapons were fired thus far."

"Any coming at us?"

"Wait. Six weapons total!"

"Tell me if any are coming at us, damn it!"

"I think they're all missiles. I heard weapons broach the surface, but I hear no high speed screws and no seekers."

"Encapsulated missiles," Jake said. "Either Popeye or Harpoon, but out of range of any targets."

"Who are they shooting at, Jake?" Remy asked.

Jake wondered where Pierre was and what he would do if their positions were reversed.

"Doesn't matter. Targets over the horizon we don't know about. Prepare to launch tube one at *Leviathan*."

Faces in the *Mercer's* operations room turned cold. Henri turned from his ship's control panel.

"You're sentencing Pierre to death," he said.

"We don't know that."

"In that minisub, the shockwave to his broadsides would be his demise."

"He's my friend, too Henri. But the *Leviathan* is probably reloading right now."

Henri looked to the deck, showing his straight silvery hair, and the returned his attention to his panels

"Do what you must, Jake. I will support you."

A final hiss, whine, and rumble reverberated throughout the minisub's hull.

"What was all that?" Gomez said.

"The launching of weapons," Renard said.

"I know, but what type?"

"Missiles, most likely. I counted at least four weapons but probably more. A torpedo salvo is unlikely, but given our hijacker's lack of sophistication, I cannot rule it out."

"Shit!"

"Indeed," Renard said. "We must hurry."

Whiffs of smoke swirled from the circular incision as Renard watched Gomez and Smith elevate the laser cutter up its hydraulic ram. A third SEAL pressed a suction handle onto the *Leviathan's* green metal and squatted to jerk it upward. Smith and Gomez knelt, bracing themselves on one hand each and holding a grenade in the other.

The SEAL with the lifting handle yanked the severed metal as Gomez and Smith rolled their grenades into the gap. The SEAL dropped the metal back into place and pressed down on it. Moments later, Renard heard the cracks from within the *Leviathan*.

"Again," Gomez said, clutching a new grenade. "Open!"

He and Smith pushed the grenades deeper into the gap, the third SEAL closed the gap, and again grenades cracked under the metal.

A SEAL presented Gomez a handheld electronic periscope, and Gomez had the circle of metal removed a third time. He slid the periscope's neck down, watched its battery-powered monitor, and swiveled the device.

"The room's empty," he said. "The way is blown clear."

He signaled for two SEALs to enter the *Leviathan*. In a flash, a rope unfurled from the minisub's overhead, and two men followed it through the hole. As he lined up his next two men, a pilot called to him. Renard missed the verbal exchange, but Gomez crept to him and explained.

"The *Georgia* just ordered us to abort," he said.

"Dear god, man! Why?"

"Your submarine just shot a torpedo at us."

"Jake," Renard said, his voice tapering.

"Whoever you left in charge makes up his mind fast," Gomez said, "The *Leviathan* blows up in two minutes."

Stephenson entered the combat information center and picked up a phone.

"Captain speaking."

"Sir, this is the XO," Stephenson said. "I need to inform you that you're violating orders from squadron and patrolling restricted waters."

"Noted. It's already in the deck log. What do I care about a submarine exercise? We can annotate in the log that you protest, if you want to protect your career."

"I'm more concerned about a note with photographs I received from fleet intel. I won't insult you with the details, but it's possible our patrol locations have been compromised. I recommend abandoning emissions control and lighting up in full defense."

"You know how to protect this ship from any supposed threat, right?" Pastor asked with anger and insecurity in his voice. "That's your job, isn't it?"

"Yes, sir."

"Then do it. Any damn way you see fit."

The captain hung up. Stephenson walked toward the combat information center's watch officer to order him to beef up the *Bainbridge's* defense status when a tense voice from a console operator stopped him.

"Low flying aircraft—inbound! Low on the horizon."

Stephenson continued to the watch officer and stood before his throne.

"Secure modify emissions control," he said. "Raise the ship's defenses to full alert."

The officer barked out commands to set Stephenson's will in motion. When he was done, he relinquished the throne to Stephenson, who had a sick feeling that the fully awakened Aegis system would recognize the contact on the horizon as something more sinister than a low flying aircraft.

CHAPTER 21

"Can you lock the hijackers out of the weapons systems from the operations room?" Renard asked.

"Yes," Marom said.

"And then what?" Gomez asked. "The *Leviathan* isn't going to be here in two minutes."

"Perhaps not," Renard said. "But if Jake still has the command wire to his torpedo, I can inform him via underwater voice to shut down the weapon."

"The underwater voice should reach him at this distance," Marom said. "This is possible."

The glare remained hard on Gomez' face. The lack of his secretive smile concerned Renard.

"Let's do it," Gomez said. "You two go in after me and Smith. Marom first. Straight to the control panel. My last two guys after you. Watch for bent metal and wires in the overhead on your way in."

Gomez and Smith disappeared into the hole, and Marom shimmied his way after them. Renard began his descent, hand over hand, curling his legs around the rope. He saw hydraulic fluid dripping from a depressurized line and an electrical bundle shredded with its metal brackets twisted by a grenade.

As his feet touched the deck, he saw Smith and Gomez guarding the forward door and the first two SEALS guarding the aft entrance. Marom leaned into a system monitor while tapping keys.

Renard saw a microphone clipped against a control box to the underwater communications. He marched to it and examined its dials. The writing was foreign, but he understood its function.

"This is the underwater communications?" he asked.

Marom looked up and nodded.

"Don't call off the torpedo until he's locked the hijackers out of the weapons," Gomez said.

"Bad news," Marom said. "They've taken local control of two tubes, which they are reloading. They will be able to launch these reload weapons, and there's nothing we can do about it."

The last two SEALs landed in the operations room.

"Yes there is," Gomez said. "We can let the incoming torpedo sink the ship."

"Not in time," Marom said.

"Give me some good news," Gomez said.

"I've locked out the other eight tubes."

"Okay," Gomez said. "What did they fire?"

"Six Harpoons. They reloaded two torpedoes. I recommend that the incoming torpedo be shut down and we take the torpedo room by force. They will likely fire the next two weapons, but we might be able to shut them down."

Gomez nodded.

"We'll take the torpedo room," he said.

He barked out orders, and four of his SEALs disappeared through the room's forward door. Smith moved to guard the rear door.

"Marom," Gomez said, "help Renard get that incoming torpedo shut down. Go!"

Marom sprang to the unit, adjusted the controls, and handed the microphone to Renard.

"Speak, and quickly please," Marom said.

Renard spoke with deliberate clearness in his native tongue so that the echoing and reverberating energy of his voice would reach the *Mercer's* sonar with clarity.

"Jake, Pierre, I have the *Leviathan*. Shut down your weapon. Jake, Pierre, I have the *Leviathan*. Shut down your weapon."

On his third iteration of his mantra, Renard cringed as a torpedo alarm whined.

"Seeker of inbound torpedo is active," Marom said as he walked across the room to silence the alarm.

"One minute estimated until impact," Gomez said. "We still have time to get out and take our chances driving away in the minisub."

Renard shook his head while repeating his prayer into the communications unit, trusting that Jake would answer.

"The inbound aircraft is now identified as twenty-four inbound hostile missiles," Stephenson said. "The bogey is reclassified as twenty-four subsonic vampires. Engage all vampires with birds."

The watch officer he had just relieved moved below him, orchestrating the efforts of people seated at consoles and concerned faces entering the room in response to the *Bainbridge's* call to general quarters battle stations.

"Two birds per vampire?" the officer asked.

"Yes," Stephenson said, confirming the advantage he allowed the *Bainbridge* in using two Standard SM-2 Block IV missiles against each incoming weapon. He wanted the doubled probability of knocking down the incoming attack, and he judged it worth expending half of his defense arsenal.

"To the bridge," Stephenson said, "All ahead flank, come left smartly to course zero-nine-zero."

He clenched the arms of his chair as the deck tilted and thunder rumbled from the *Bainbridge's* forward vertical launch cells. A coffee cup hit the deck and shattered as the *Bainbridge* inclined through its turn, and alarmed voices clamored.

Weapon exchange scenarios and probabilities became images flipping through his mind, and, for the moment, he trusted his defenses. A sailor announced that ballistic missiles appeared on the same northeast bearing as the inbound vampires. The discovery sent Stephenson into a new mental calculation of a scenario that bordered on the surreal.

Another man's voice penetrated the din, emphasizing that new inbound missiles approached from the south.

"Silence!" Stephenson said.

The room quieted, and Stephenson pointed at his watch officer.

"Report!"

"Six sea skimming vampires," he said. "Range two miles. Impact in sixteen seconds. I launched twelve birds at them from the rear launcher."

"Popping chaff?"

"Yes, sir!"

The ship heeled to the left.

"We're turning again?"

"To bring the cannon and close-in weapon system to bear on the six vampires. The twenty-four to the north splashed on their own."

Stephenson looked beyond the shoulder of his officer at an overhead display of icons showing that twenty-four inbound missiles stopped dead in the water.

He gripped his chair's arms to steady himself in the turn. His heart pounded as he grasped that synchronized attackers tricked him into wasting forty-eight missiles on decoys, diverted his attention to the north, and exposed him to an attack from the south.

Playing new probabilistic scenarios unfolded his mind's eye, he disliked the results.

As Stephenson heard the five inch cannon's rhythmic popping and the close-in weapon system belching a chainsaw chorus of depleted uranium sabots, he realized the six new incoming missiles were near.

He clenched his jaw as he accepted that some of them would slip through the *Bainbridge's* defenses.

"Jake, Pierre, I have the *Leviathan*. Shut down your weapon," Renard said.

He released the speaking button and hoped to hear Jake's voice. As he repeated the sequence a fifth time, he heard grenades cracking forward of Gomez' position.

"Forty seconds," Gomez said. "Screw this. I'm pulling my guys..."

Jake's voice, amplified and garbled by its journey through water, came through the box above Renard's head.

"Command shutdown completed," Jake said.

Renard exhaled and relaxed his shoulders. He looked to Marom, who nodded with verification that the *Mercer's* torpedo had ceased its search.

"Thank you, my friend," Renard said to the ocean.

His gratitude waned with the familiar whine and pressure change that accompanied the action of a torpedo tube's impulse tank.

"They just launched a torpedo," Marom said. "From the information in the system, it's launched at a ship eight miles away. The same ship they shot the Harpoons at. For the moment, the command wire is still connected."

Renard walked to the console, stooped beside the Israeli systems expert, and looked at the screen.

"It is a well-placed shot in wake-homing mode."

"Shit," Gomez said.

"I fear this torpedo will be a challenge. But if your men hurry," Renard said, "you may be able to spare the target from having to dodge the next one."

The crack of gunfire and the report of rifles rang in Renard's ears. Gomez glanced forward and leaned back.

"They're doing fine," he said. "Two enemy casualties. Two to go. Give them thirty more seconds."

"That may not be fast enough," Marom said.

Renard walked to a panel that he recognized as controlling the *Leviathan's* trim and drain system, its rudder and planes, and its high-pressure air. He scanned for the switches that lingered in the back of mind of every submarine sailor.

Two silver knobs protruded from the top of the panel.

"Marom, do these control the emergency blow valves?"

"Yes."

"May I?"

"Yes. Feel free."

"Wait!" Gomez said. "What's this going to do to my guys? They're in a fight."

"The deck may shift, but not much, since we are already at snorkel depth."

"Why bother?"

"So that the targeted vessel might see us and know that we are the launch point of the torpedo they need to evade. Plus, I'm going to hail them. It will instill trust in our communications if they can see us."

Gomez nodded in cadence with the clamor of small arms fire. Renard pulled the switches and walked to the elevated conning platform as high-pressure air groaned and hissed throughout the *Leviathan*. He pointed.

"High frequency voice transceiver?" he asked.

"Yes," Marom said.

Renard snapped the transceiver's microphone from its clip and curled his fingers over it as he pressed his palms into the periscope control levers. He stuck his eye to the optics and swiveled the periscope toward the targeted ship.

A deep but muffled boom reverberated throughout the room.

"That sounds bad," Gomez said.

"I believe that a Harpoon has found its target," Renard said.

As the *Leviathan's* rise expanded Renard's horizon, smoke came into view.

"Damn," he said. "I see mast heads and smoke. It appears to be a warship. *Burke* class, if I'm correct."

"One of the Harpoons hit, then?" Marom asked.

"No, I see two plumes. One must have hit too high above the waterline for us hear."

"That can be crippling, can it not?" Marom asked.

"Possibly, but those ships have respectable armor and skilled damage control teams. However, if our torpedo finds its mark, they are all doomed."

Renard felt the air moving around him and withdrew his eye from the optics. Gomez stood before him, his face frozen in a glare.

"What can a *Burke* destroyer do against our torpedo?"

"They have but one option, I'm afraid."

"What is it?" Gomez said.

"Run."

*   *   *

Salem's ears throbbed from the grenades and small arms as he leaned into Asad's ear.

"Did you cut the wire?"

"Yes."

"Excellent."

He watched Yousif tapping keys at a weapon control panel. The rotund academic proved adept at applying his knowledge of the operations room consoles to the local console in the torpedo room.

At the room's far end, Hamdan appeared at the bottom of the ladder. One of his younger soldiers propped his feet on the ladder and reclined against the lip of the gap to the upper deck, his torso exposed while he returned fire at the team that was retaking the *Leviathan*.

Salem picked up a sound powered phone and dialed the engineering spaces. Bazzi's voice revealed terror.

"What's going on?" the elder naval veteran asked.

"The ship has been breached and is being retaken by a commando team."

"We're dead then?"

The body of the young soldier on the ladder went limp and thumped the puddle of crimson fluid forming at Hamdan's feet. Hamdan squatted, aimed a rifle upward, and fired.

"I give you permission to surrender," Salem said. "That goes for all of you who retreated into the engineering spaces."

"Hana?"

"I've protected you with ignorance. None of you has information of value to captors. I will not ask you to sacrifice yourself in an act of misplaced faith or valor."

"What they do to prisoners…"

"Is better treatment than many see in the free world," Salem said. "You will be a living inspiration instead of a dead and forgotten myth."

"Inspiration? Did we succeed?"

"Did you not hear the explosion? One of our Harpoons hit near enough the waterline for us to hear with naked ears. The *Bainbridge* is damaged and slowed, and our torpedoes will finish the job."

Bazzi's voice carried relief.

"Thank you, Hana."

Salem hung up while Yousif raised a plump finger.

"Stand back. I'm firing the weapon!" he said.

Salem covered his ears while a torpedo tube whined and spat out its payload.

Asad stood by the breach door awaiting a command to cut the guidance wire. Salem moved toward Yousif to verify that the torpedo had ignited its engine and headed toward the *Bainbridge.*

As he walked, time stopped.

Meters away, Hamdan convulsed and collapsed.

Before his lifeless head smacked the deck, a man dressed in desert-like camouflage leapt down the hole.

In midair, he twisted his torso, scanned the room with his rifle, and sent two rounds into the linguist whose fatal optimism drove him to raise a pistol in anger.

Salem raised his palms as his attacker straddled Hamdan's corpse.

The assailant walked his rifle barrel across the room and squeezed out three rounds. Each round landed in lower torsos. Asad fell to the ground first, followed by Yousif, who fell back against two tubes.

A second assailant landed behind the first and both men approached with smoking but quiet weapons. He feared they would kill him if he lowered his hands, but instinct compelled him to clasp his belly.

He felt sticky goo and a sharp jab of pain consume him. Numbness supplanted pain, and the cold, hard deck of the torpedo room slapped his face.

"Silence!" Stephenson said.

Chatter in the *Bainbridge's* combat information center fell to a murmur.

"We have no more inbound weapons," he said. "We've taken one hit to the starboard side of the engine room and one in the bridge. We've lost friends and shipmates. Honor them now by doing your job. We have fifteen ballistic missiles to deal with. Carry on."

His watch officer appeared before him.

"The engineer officer reports that we're still capable of twenty-two knots, sir."

"Very well."

"Sir? The captain is gone. Nobody on the bridge survived. You're in command."

"Yes. I know," Stephenson said. "But call me the executive officer. Calling me the commanding officer would remind the crew that we've lost our captain."

"Yes, sir."

"Where are the ballistic missiles going?"

"We're seeing the trajectories now. They're all heading over America, and we're identifying them as hostile."

Again scenarios flashed in Stephenson's mind. None please him.

"We only have twelve anti-ballistic missiles," he said. "Can we reach any of these hostiles with our conventional missiles?"

"Negative, sir. Out of range."

"How long until we need to launch?"

"Two minutes, but the sooner the better."

"Very well. Overlay the Patriot missile coverage of the entire United States over the trajectory of the fifteen hostiles. Figure out which three of the fifteen come closest to Patriots—whether they're within range of the Patriots or not. Target the other twelve."

The officer walked away and exchanged words with a sailor at a console whose fingers flew into a rhythmic tap dance over a touch screen. He came back to Stephenson.

"Twelve missiles targeted, sir."

"Take twelve hostiles with anti-ballistic birds."

Stephenson heard the rippling drone and hiss of the *Bainbridge's* vertical launch tubes.

"This isn't adding up," he said. "Only major states have this many ballistic warheads in their arsenal."

"Sir?"

"Some of these are decoys. They used decoys in their attack against us, and they're using decoys now."

"They can't all be decoys. That would be pointless."

"That's what's bothering me."

An agitated sailor at a console beckoned for the watch officer. Stephenson dismissed him and awaited his return.

"Sir, one more ballistic missile," the officer said.

"Going where?"

"Almost straight up and down. It'll land in the water."

"Say again."

"Straight up and down, sir."

"Is it in range of our conventional weapons?"

"No, sir."

"Well then," Stephenson said, "Let's make sure our twelve anti-ballistic birds do their job. And make sure fleet command is alerting every Patriot battery that has a prayer of helping us protect the country."

"The second weapon from the *Leviathan* has just shut down," Antoine Remy said.

"What about the first?" Jake asked.

Remy shook his toad-shaped head.

"It's a trailing shot headed for their wake. The damaged ship might outrun it if they make full speed."

"You've identified the ship?"

"Yes. *Burke* class destroyer."

"They took two *Harpoons*. Their speed may be limited. How fast are they going now?"

"Ten knots."

"They're probably slowing to prevent fanning flames. They don't know there's a torpedo coming at them."

Jake heard his brother's warning in his head about death, accepted it, and released a sardonic smile.

"All ahead flank," he said.

The *Mercer* trembled with power.

"I think I know what you're doing, Jake," Henri said. "And I don't like it."

"We're going to broach and warn them, ask them to turn to us, and then sprint at them."

"How can this work?" Henri asked. "You're pushing our luck. When we did this in Hawaii, I had no intent of a repeat performance."

"Not a repeat performance," Jake said. "We'll drive straight at them, get in their wake, and absorb the torpedo. Simple."

"Jake," Henri said. "This is suicide."

Stephenson received confirmation from fleet command that Patriot missile batteries would assist in the defense. A crew in Maine would attempt to engage two of the other three, pushing the limit of their system's range, and a crew in Virginia would do the same for the fifteenth inbound ballistic missile.

Probabilities plagued his mind, telling him to expect four missiles to hit their targets on American soil.

The phone beside him chirped.

"XO," he said.

"Sir, it's Wilson."

"Are you okay up there?"

"Barely, but yeah. Listen, sir, there's a guy on HF voice. Says he's on a submarine to the south."

"Patch him through."

As Stephenson stood and reached for a transceiver in the overhead, his watch officer moved to him.

"Sir, surfaced submarine on radar and visual, bearing one-nine-five. Eight miles. There's a minisub on the back of it."

"They shot at us?"

"Probably. There's nothing else out there."

"Target him with two Harpoon missiles, one torpedo, and the cannon. Get our helicopter in the air and move it over him."

The watch officer indicated his understanding and turned away. Ire rose in Stephenson as he spoke into the microphone.

"Surfaced submarine, this is the naval unit to your north. Identify yourself."

"Naval unit, this is the Israeli Naval Ship, *Leviathan*. This ship was hijacked and used against you, but the ship has been retaken by friendly forces."

"How do you expect me to react to that?"

"I don't. I must warn you that two torpedoes were launched at you before my team retook the ship. I have shut one down, but one is beyond our control and headed for your wake. I recommend that you make your best speed and steer course zero-five-five."

Stephenson released his speaking button and called to his watch officer.

"Inbound wake homing torpedo. Conduct a torpedo evasion. Have the engine room give us top speed."

"Aye, aye, sir."

Stephenson pressed the button and continued his radio conversation.

"If it's a wake homing weapon, what difference does my course make? I need freedom for evasive maneuvers."

"This may take a while to explain, but I have a plan. Or I at least see one unfolding. I beg for your sake that you trust me."

Stephenson released the button to put his radio conversation on hold. He called again to his officer.

"Is our helo up yet?"

"Just launched, sir."

"What about the ballistic hostiles?"

"Intercept to the first in three minutes, late in boost phase. The solitary vertical hostile missile is still climbing, about half way through boost phase."

The phone chirped.

"XO," he said.

"Sir, it's Wilson again. I told fleet command about our surfaced submarine. They said they're on a legit joint navy operation. There's an *Ohio* class SSGN—the *Georgia*—out there overseeing it. I've set you up on a secure satellite communication with their captain.

"Patch me through."

"This is Lieutenant Commander Robert Stephenson, Executive Officer, USS *Bainbridge*. Come in, *Georgia*. Over."

"Roger, *Bainbridge*. This is Commander Michael Davis, USS *Georgia*. I'm at periscope depth commanding an operation to retake the Israeli submarine that just launched weapons. I assume you've been hit. Over."

"*Georgia, Bainbridge*, affirmative. We took two Harpoons. Starboard side of engine room is out. Bridge is out. Captain is dead. Best speed is twenty-two knots. Evading a torpedo on recommendation of new commander of *Leviathan*. Over."

"*Bainbridge, Georgia*, I confirm the torpedo. It's in your wake. If best speed is twenty-two knots, recommend you prepare to abandon ship. We can monitor the torpedo and give you warning before impact. Over."

Stephenson took a breath and realized that a nightmare unfolded around him.

"*Georgia, Bainbridge*, the *Leviathan's* commander gave me a course. Says he has a plan. Over."

"*Bainbridge, Georgia*, he's a brilliant commander. Trust him, but be ready to abandon ship. I'll listen on HF voice, and if I hear bad advice, I'll contact you. Over."

"*Georgia, Bainbridge*, I'll keep the line open. Out."

Stephenson hung up, ordered his watch officer to steer the recommended course, and then spoke into his microphone.

"*Leviathan*, I've confirmed who you are," he said. "What's your name?"

"Renard."

"Renard, I appreciate your assistance. We're on a non-secure channel. I won't give you my name."

"May I call you Captain?"

"Yes."

"I noticed that you're turning, Captain. I thank you for trusting me."

"What about my torpedo decoy?"

"Useless against a wake homer."

"I thought so," Stephenson said. "Tell me why I've changed course."

"Gladly," Renard said. "It's quite an impressive reason. I'm afraid that I've trained my protégé too well.

CHAPTER 22

"We're broached. Speed is falling off," Henri said.

"Raising the periscope," Jake said. "Come help me line up for HF voice."

Jake placed his orbital socket to the *Mercer's* rising eyepiece and felt Henri's presence on the elevated conning platform. Through the optics, he saw plumes of smoke. Letting his eye settle on the horizon, dozens of dissipating whitish contrails provided evidence of a destroyer's furious self-defense.

"Lined up," Henri said.

Jake took the microphone from him.

"Damaged naval unit, this is broached French submarine to your southeast. Over."

"*Mercer*, this is damaged naval unit. Renard explained your identity and intent with me. Please verify intent."

"I'm sprinting to you and ask that you sprint to me. There's a torpedo in your wake that I intend to absorb."

"Renard assured me that any tactic you might try to fool the weapon would fail. It will follow my wake until it finds a keel. One of our ships will be sunk."

"I know," Jake said.

"Then why are you doing this?"

"I don't know. Maybe because you have twenty times as many lives onboard."

"I'm also guiding anti-ballistic missiles against nuclear weapons that were shot at America. You're doing this for possibly millions of people."

"Good to know, but I really have no intention of dying," Jake said. "Sprint to me, maneuver around me before we collide, and toss me some life rafts as I pass. When I pass, I'll shut down my engines and drift in your wake until the torpedo hits. Nobody needs to be aboard when it happens."

"Done. We have the torpedo's data in our system from Renard's estimate. If you can sustain sixteen knots, this will work."

"We're making eighteen knots on the surface," Jake said. "We're still rising and slowing, but we can sustain at least seventeen."

"Good enough. I'll maneuver around you, drop rafts, and thank you when it's over."

Jake returned the microphone to its cradle.

"Have everyone put on life jackets," he said. "And blow our ballast tanks dry."

Henri nodded, walked to his control station, and flipped switches that unleashed high pressure air into the *Mercer's* ballast tanks. The imperceptible rising of the deck under Jake's feet extended his visual horizon. His eye followed billows of black from the sky to the masts of the *Bainbridge*. As a cresting swell lifted the Mercer, he caught a glimpse of the bridge.

"They took one in the bridge," he said. "It's gone. Just flames, smoke, and bent metal."

"How do you intend for us to evacuate?" Henri asked.

"Right after we pass them. We'll secure our screw as we pass. If we jump any sooner, we risk getting chopped by our screw or run over by the *Bainbridge*. Any later, and, well, you know the rest."

Renard never foresaw himself threatening a U.S. Navy SEAL, but he considered Gomez' present failure worth challenging.

"If you cannot line us up for secure communications with the *Georgia*, I will have no choice but to hail them on an open frequency."

Gomez responded while gazing at the keys he tapped on a satellite communications console.

"Don't blame me," he said. "You broke the communication wire to the *Georgia* when you surfaced us."

"Indeed I did," Renard said. "I did not foresee this scenario or consider that the wire would snap from the minisub when removed from its neutral buoyancy in water."

Gomez ignored Renard and spoke into a microphone.

"*Georgia*, this is *Leviathan*, over."

Renard heard footsteps. He turned and saw two SEALs escorting men with hands on their heads into the rear of the operations room. Smith exchanged brief words with one of his companions and moved beside Gomez.

"They surrendered," Smith said. "The ship has not been swept for other hijackers yet."

"Have them sweep from aft to forward and meet up with the team in the torpedo room," Gomez said. "Have our interpreter enter the *Leviathan* and question the prisoners while you guard them."

Smith moved away, and the Israeli systems expert stepped into his place.

"Let me try this," Marom said.

He held a communications manual in one hand while adjusting a transmission power knob with the other.

"I believe we were in a low power emissions control mode," he said. "Try it now."

"*Georgia*, this is *Leviathan*, over," Gomez said.

"*Leviathan*, this is *Georgia*. We hear you. Over."

"*Georgia*, *Leviathan*, give me the Israeli systems experts, over."

"*Leviathan*, *Georgia*, they're here. Over."

Renard watched Marom prop the communications manual on a console and withdraw the torpedo manual from under his arm. He cradled the manual in his palm and pressed his thumb into a page with drawings of a torpedo closing on a target while he held the microphone in his other hand.

He exchanged rapid words in Hebrew with his countrymen on the *Georgia*. One man, the apparent torpedo expert, dominated the conversation.

"He says that forty-eight knots is the torpedo's absolute speed, but with the zigzag, it's best modeled at forty-five knots," Marom said.

Renard darted to a tactical console and adjusted his estimate of the *Bainbridge's* fate.

"Yes," he said. "Now ask him about terminal homing."

Marom exchanged words in Hebrew.

"It will accelerate to terminal homing speed only upon successful return of its active seeker against the hull. In that case, the homing speed is sixty-five knots, and it is in a direct line. There's a final dive maneuver below the keel, and detonation occurs via the keel's disruption of a magnetic influence field."

"Is this zigzag from wake edge to wake edge or across a single edge of the wake?"

Marom again exchanged words with his countryman on the *Georgia* and lowered the microphone.

"A single edge," Marom said. "In our case, it would be the *Bainbridge's* starboard edge."

"Then if Jake gets there too soon," Renard said. "Jake will drift too far into the spreading wake, and the torpedo will pass him by."

"That's correct," Marom said.

"Damn!" Renard said. "I must speak to him."

Jake snapped his lifejacket buckles.

"Who isn't topside yet?" he asked.

"Just you, Claude, and me," Henri said.

"Head to the propulsion controls for Claude," Jake said. "I'll stay here and tell you when to cut the engines. Then you exit from the after hatch and jump."

Henri departed, leaving Jake alone in the operations room of the doomed *Scorpène* class submarine.

A familiar voice rang from a loudspeaker.

"Jake, it's Pierre. I must speak to you."

Jake reached upward and unclipped a microphone. He extended its pigtail cord and dragged it to the periscope. He placed his eye to the optics and saw the bow of the *Bainbridge* looming large in a scripted game of chicken.

"Pierre, it's Jake. Good to hear your voice, but I'm kind of busy now."

"Jake, you'll have to cut your engines soon or you'll overshoot the edge of the wake. The torpedo is a wake edge homing weapon. If you cut your engines after you pass the destroyer, you'll drift too far from the wake edge."

"Shit," Jake said. "This has to be tight."

"It will be," Renard said. "We have a precise solution on the weapon, and we know its characteristics. The destroyer also has a precise solution on you, and we know your deceleration characteristics."

"When do I cut my engines?" Jake asked.

"At eleven hundred yards from the destroyer."

"Does the destroyer know this?"

"Ask them. Have them coordinate. Good luck and remember to jump, my friend."

"Destroyer, this is French submarine, come in, over."

"French submarine, this is the destroyer. I heard your conversation and understand. I'll inform you when you're eleven hundred yards from me, over."

"Destroyer, this is French submarine. Remember to look out for my men in the water."

"French submarine, destroyer, consider it done. Out."

Jake counted down time in his mind while watching the *Bainbridge* approach through the periscope. White water washed over the destroyer's bow wake.

He teased his mind by trying to calculate eleven hundred yards from the destroyer's mast height and the trigonometry of the periscope cross hatches. Then he realized that no submariner needed to approach this close to a surface ship and awaited his queue.

"French submarine, destroyer. Mark eleven hundred yards. Cut your engines. Over."

"Destroyer, French submarine," Jake said. "Cutting engines. Out."

Jake reached for the communication circuit and flipped a switch to send his voice throughout the *Mercer*.

"Henri," he said. "Answer all stop and abandon ship."

The *Mercer's* rhythmic trembling ceased, and Henri's voice rang from the circuit.

"Answering all stop," he said. "I'll see you topside."

Jake marched forward to an open hatch and climbed into the sunlight. Wind whipped his cheeks as he took in the gravity of the wounded destroyer.

Its bridge seemed like a face blown off with the ship's self-made wind fanning the flames of unspent missile fuel. Jake noted that the bow pointed upward, indicating flooding in a low-riding stern, and the ship listed to its starboard side.

He turned and trotted by the *Mercer's* conning tower and saw his small crew topside. He closed in on Antoine Remy and Claude LaFontaine.

"Jump. Now!" he said.

"We were to wait until passing the destroyer," Remy said, yelling over the *Mercer's* self-made wind.

"Plan changed. The screw is stopped. Jump!"

Remy stepped away, ran three steps, and leapt into the swells. LaFontaine followed.

Jake walked aft, sweeping his arm and inciting men to join their colleagues in the water. He noted that Henri policed them, smacking a few hesitant stragglers in the back.

Near the stern, Jake stood with Henri. He glanced over his shoulder at the destroyer he estimated to be four hundred yards away.

"Ready?" he asked.

"Jake," Henri said. "I can't swim."

Jake placed his hand on Henri's shoulder and looked into his eyes.

"I understand," he said.

While Henri struggled for courage and a response, Jake slipped his hand to his elbow, lowered his weight, and stepped between the Frenchman's legs. He yanked his arm and pulled Henri's torso over his shoulders.

Jake stood with Henri draped like a doll across his neck, and staggered toward the water. He leaned and leapt, and he heard Henri spitting curses as gravity drew them into the swells.

Cool water enveloped him, and Jake released Henri. Swimming to the surface, he turned and kicked toward the silvery hair bobbing above the orange vest. He extended his arms, grabbed Henri, and kicked behind him.

He pulled to Henri's backside and drew his arm across the Frenchman's chest. Leaning back, he drew Henri over him and held him. Jake craned his neck for breath as he held Henri steady.

"Not so bad?" Jake asked.

"I would appreciate if you stay with me," Henri said.

"The vest will keep you afloat. But yes, I'll stay."

Stephenson returned the phone to its cradle and hailed his watch officer.

"The chief engineer has enough volunteers to maintain propulsion and steerage," he said. "Do we have an officer stationed for conning the ship?"

"Yes, sir. The operations officer is on the weather decks with visual on the submarine."

"Deck Division and life rafts for the submarine's survivors?"

"Stationed port side on the fantail."

"What about the evacuation?"

"All hands are stationed to abandon ship on the sound of the ship's whistle."

Stephenson doubted he could get the full crew off if he gave the order to evacuate, but he wanted the option to give them a chance. He surveyed the *Bainbridge's* emptying combat information center and spoke to his watch officer.

"Get everyone who's remaining into seats, including yourself," he said. "Tear the cushions off vacant seats, double up on seating cushions, and strap in. If we take a torpedo, that should help with the shock wave."

The watch officer had two sailors carry out the seating orders.

"Where are our anti-ballistic birds?" Stephenson asked.

"Ninety seconds from first kill. Our birds will catch the hostiles before they exit the atmosphere."

"If we're still here to guide them. Torpedo impact time?"

"Fifty-five seconds, sir. We have visual on it now."

"The torpedo's hump on the surface?" Stephenson asked.

"Yes, sir."

"Who?"

"Weapons officer, sir. He's on the fantail with Deck Division."

Stephenson raised his phone.

"Silence on the line. This is the executive officer. Weapons officer, come in."

"Weapons officer here, sir."

"Do you see the torpedo?"

"Yes, sir. Riding our wake."

"When the submarine passes us, inform me immediately if you see the torpedo pass by the submarine."

"Yes, sir. Inform you immediately if the torpedo passes by the submarine. Aye, sir."

The deck heeled as the *Bainbridge* turned.

"Submarine passing close aboard to starboard, sir," the watch officer said.

"Very well. Get ready for the longest twenty seconds of your life."

Stephenson glared at a display that showed the interplay of the *Bainbridge*, the French submarine, and the torpedo.

"Third stage rocket motor ignition, first bird," the watch officer said, slicing a heavy haze of silence that enveloped the room.

The chair nudged Stephenson forward as he heard the deep and pulsating explosion. He wondered if the torpedo had cracked the *Bainbridge* in half but the relief in the watch officer's face revealed the truth.

"From the weapons officer," he said. "The torpedo hit the French submarine."

"Very well."

"We'll celebrate later. We still have the hostiles."

"First bird engages first hostile in ten seconds."

Stephenson released the death grip on his chair and walked with the watch officer to a vacant monitor.

One by one he watched a radar-fed update of the *Bainbridge's* anti-ballistic missiles employing their kinetic warheads into the bodies of weapons that were arcing toward the outer reaches of the earth's atmosphere en route to American soil. One by one, *Bainbridge* birds intercepted and destroyed their targets.

"I underestimated Raytheon," he said. "They built us twelve missiles that just batted a thousand."

"There's still three flying, sir."

"Then I hope that the Army Patriots can handle them."

*   *   *

Jake kicked his legs, dragging Henri toward the direction in which he saw a life raft roll off the destroyer. He mistimed a swell, swallowed a mouthful of salty water, and coughed.

"You're sure you can't swim?"

"Yes, and I feel bad enough about it without you having to question it."

"Don't worry," Jake said. "The worst of it is over. I'll have us to a life raft, soon."

"Perhaps there's no need," Henri said. "I see their helicopter approaching."

Jake released Henri to his bobbing, turned, and rested his arms while watching the helicopter. He thought he noticed the pilot maneuvering sideways but then grew concerned as the aircraft continued through a slow circle and seemed to be losing altitude.

The helicopter rotor decelerated and bent upwards as the craft fell from view.

"Dear god," Henri said.

"Shit, Henri. Did he just lose power?"

"I fear so."

"Many men have died today," Jake said. "And there's nothing we can do about it but survive. Let's keep swimming."

Renard exchanged handshakes with Marom and Gomez in celebration of saving the *Bainbridge*.

"Let's coordinate with the *Bainbridge* for picking up the survivors," Gomez said.

"An excellent idea," Renard said.

He walked to the high frequency voice transceiver unit and grabbed its microphone.

"Destroyer this is *Leviathan*, do you need assistance in rescuing survivors?"

Renard heard no response.

"Destroyer, *Leviathan*, come in please."

"I don't hear even a static hiss," Gomez said.

"It's at full power," Marom said. "Something is wrong with our equipment."

"Well then, let us speak with the *Georgia* and have them contact the *Bainbridge* on our behalf."

Gomez nodded.

"*Georgia, Leviathan*, come in, over."

The hard glare overtook the SEAL's face.

"Georgia, Leviathan, come in, over."

"Perhaps there's a platform jamming our communications," Renard said.

"Not our secure satellite linkup with the *Georgia*," Gomez said. "It's possible, but not likely."

"Then what are we up against?" Renard asked.

"I don't know," Gomez said. "Head to the bridge and see what you can see."

Binoculars hanging from his neck, Renard climbed up the inner ladder of the *Leviathan's* conning tower and pushed open a grate. Lifting himself, he wiggled through the opening and straddled it.

He scanned his horizon and saw the *Bainbridge*, still burning, sliding through the water near the *Mercer's* survivors. Two life rafts were open. Raising his scan to the sky, he saw the arcs of missile contrails billowing into unrecognizable wisps.

Content that no new visible intruders approached, he looked to the *Bainbridge* for possible clues for the *Leviathan's* communication woes. He saw men in life jackets marching from the weather decks into the ship while others reached with pole arm hooks for life rafts.

Then, as he scanned the masts, he noticed a curiosity. None of the *Bainbridge's* surface or navigation radars were rotating. He slid through the opening and descended the ladder. As he moved within the conning tower, he realized another omission. The *Bainbridge's* helicopter was gone.

In the operations room, he huddled with his companions.

"The *Bainbridge* is picking up survivors," he said. "However, it's not rotating any of its surface search or navigation radars, and its helicopter is missing."

"Maybe some sort of electronic attack?" Marom asked.

"Let us find out," Renard said. "I will take a handheld bridge to bridge radio up the conning tower, and you will take one up our forward hatch. If we can communicate, that will tell us something."

Renard climbed to the bridge and spoke into the radio.

"I hear you loud and clear," Marom said.

Renard's heart sank.

"I believe I have a theory."

He dialed up maximum power on the radio.

"Destroyer, this is *Leviathan*, please come in," he said. "Destroyer, this is *Leviathan*, please come in."

"*Leviathan*, this is the destroyer to your east. Over."

"I had been speaking to your executive officer—your acting commanding officer—on high frequency voice, but it's no longer available."

"This is the operations officer. We've lost all our radar systems. Even the SPY-1 system is down. We've also lost communications with the outside world. Hold on, the executive officer is coming."

"Renard, this is Lieutenant Commander Robert Stephenson, acting commanding officer of the USS *Bainbridge*."

"Nice to know your name."

"The rules of communication just changed. We've been hit by an EMP attack."

"Dear god. It is as I feared. How? Who?"

"Exo-atmospheric detonation."

"That means..."

"The United States is at risk of catastrophic failure of all electronic systems. Everything that isn't hardened or shielded by metal or water just fried."

"Your helicopter."

"Yes."

"I just brought up a secure data link online and found a working frequency with fleet command. The entire northeastern seaboard is out, and it could be worse. There were fifteen ballistic missiles launched over the continental United States, and one straight up over water to the north. I could only take out twelve of the fifteen. The other three hit their targets but didn't explode."

"Decoys?"

"Probably. I think most of the fifteen were decoys and I took out the live ones. Looks like the solitary one was the high altitude detonation."

"Above the atmosphere," Renard said. "Raining down gamma rays from the ionosphere, destroying everything electronic in its path."

"I think it covered a big area. Depends on the nuclear yield."

"Are you heading back to port?"

"I recommend that you do," Stephenson said. "But not me. I've got other plans.

"Before you go," Renard said. "Can we arrange for me to have the survivors? You could likely do without the passengers, and I would like my crew back."

"Done."

"Can you tell me where you are going?"

"I'm bringing back my systems with spare parts and going hunting," Stephenson said. "I have a score to settle with a launch vessel to the north that just pissed me off."

CHAPTER 23

Six months later, Jake scratched his neck where his overgrown hair tickled it as a CIA intern escorted him deep into the facility at Langley. A door opened, and he saw a thin smile spread across the fair skinned face of CIA officer, Olivia McDonald. A dark suit muted her athletic curves, and she tied her hair in a long braid.

She invited him into a room that smelled stale and reflected bright, sterile lighting. As Olivia closed the door with a click, Jake glanced at absorbent, egg carton foam-like walls.

Olivia extended her hand. He accepted.

"Not even a hug?" he asked.

"I don't think we should. Maybe after some time."

"You dating anyone?"

"Yeah. A naval intelligence officer. He's a good man. You'd like him."

He expected a different answer.

"Even in this mess?"

"Things are starting to clear up. The riots are over, and power's back in most major cities."

"The news has been constant but of questionable reliability in France."

"It's been of questionable reliability here, too. Eastern Canada through Maryland was a warzone, and military and police forces barely kept the peace. If this attack had reached beyond the coastal states, we might be living in anarchy."

"Was that the intent of the other fifteen missiles?"

"Two of them. At least that's what we think their intent was, based upon their flight paths. They were going to detonate over Kansas and Kentucky and probably take out most if not all of the country's electronic systems."

"That was close," Jake said. "Imagine if they had access to more nuclear warheads. Then the other thirteen wouldn't have been decoys."

"You saved the country when you saved the *Bainbridge*."

Jake sighed.

"But I can't go home. I'm supposed to be lying at the bottom of the ocean on a Trident missile submarine. I'll pay for that the rest of my life, won't I?"

"Time heals everything, but you can't go back yet."

"Can I at least see my brother?"

She led him through the door into the larger room where he had last seen Nick Slate. Wearing loose fitting garments of hemp sat his older sibling

"Nick!"

Jake ran to him and embraced him.

"Wow, Jake, it's great to see you. You seem a lot happier than the last time we met."

"I think I appreciate family better. Too bad Joey couldn't make it."

"Give him time. He'll come around."

Jake snorted.

"You're always the optimist," he said, "except with your omen of death. You had me scared out there."

Jake felt Nick clasp his palms over his hand as he bowed his head.

"Again, Nick?"

"Quiet, please," Nick said.

After several moments, Nick raised his gaze.

"You're still in danger," he said.

"What?" Jake asked. "After what I've been through?"

"No, it's not that. It never was. There was too much in your destiny that was screening me from the truth, but I see it now. The death I saw was a risk to a friend. You're in danger of losing a friend."

Jake yanked his hand back.

"I hate when you do this."

"It's what I do."

"Who is it then?"

"Pierre."

Jake called his friend, Grant Mercer.

"Hey buddy," Jake said. "Where are you?"

"Chicago," Mercer said. "Back home, so to speak."

"Uh, what about the security deposit you laid down on that submarine I wrecked?"

"Rickets helped me get that back. After the full spectrum of this attack became clear, he was able to reimburse me from legit defense funds. Plus I'm making a chunk on biodiesel sales from my South American interests to people in need in America. The crisis turned out to be an opportunity for me."

"That's a real relief."

"After what you did, you didn't have to worry about it. Hey, are you coming my way any time soon? I'd love to see you."

"I'm not sure what the CIA rules are on that," Jake said. "I'll have to check. They're trusting me to run around on my own now, with my alias, but I have to check in like I'm on parole. We'll work something out, even if you have to meet me in France."

"You're sure you want to do this?" Jake asked.

"Indeed," Renard said. "Are you?"

"No. But if you will, I will."

"Very well, then. Shall we?"

Deep in an underground floor of a federal building, a guard escorted him and Renard down a long corridor of cells holding federal prisoners behind clear plastic walls.

Toward the end of the hallway, the guard stopped.

"This is the one you want. Just walk back to the guard post when you're done with him. There aren't any special rules beyond the ones you've been given."

Jake recognized a handsome man of tall, lean build from photographs he'd seen in multiple news sources. Hana al-Salem sat in an armchair reading the New York Times.

He folded the paper upon seeing his visitors and walked to the glass.

"You're reading rubbish," Renard said.

"I agree," Salem said. "I read this waste of murdered trees as an exercise in appreciating the worthy news sources I have access to."

"You're fortunate that you have any privileges."

"Hardly. Do you not realize that I am a living martyr? I may spend the rest of my days in captivity, but if any harm comes to me, people from more than one nation will rise in response. And your liberal-appeasing justice system is more concerned about my rights than my punishment. The same is true for my surviving crewmates."

"It sickens me," Renard said.

"I have been inundated with visitors of all types," Salem said. "But I am grateful for each new face, even those who judge me harshly. Will you be so kind as to identify yourselves?"

"I took the *Leviathan* back from you," Renard said.

"And I stopped you from taking out the *Bainbridge*," Jake said.

Salem's eyes glared.

"I am honored," he said. "And admittedly caught off guard. Do you realize what you've both done?"

"We defeated you," Renard said.

"Maybe," Salem said. "Or perhaps you perfected my attack. Had you failed, two weapons would have crippled the entire continent, but in retrospect, such an outcome may have been excessive. The single weapon that was impossible to stop by its distance from your defense systems provided just enough of a glancing blow to matter."

"What?" Jake asked.

"I apologize if you came here to gloat," Salem said. "But I assumed that men of your quality are above that. I assume that you are here to understand the intent and mindset of a likeminded adversary."

"You have no right to assume anything," Renard said.

Jake put his arm around Renard and whispered.

"No, Pierre. He's right. I couldn't put words to it until he said it, but he's right."

"Jake, no. I..."

"What?"

"Very well," Renard said. "If I'm honest with myself, I may have come here to gloat. This is my capstone operation, and I wanted to complete it by confronting my adversary with victory already decided. Don't let him alter the outcome with his tongue."

"He gave you a purpose. If you want to learn more about what makes you tick and drives you, you need to learn what makes him tick. Go with it."

"Damn you," Renard said. "So be it."

"What drove you to this?" Jake asked.

"I had been arranging the taking of the *Leviathan* for its own sake," Salem said, "to turn its weapons against targets of my choosing."

"Tel Aviv?" Renard asked.

"Yes. But when I was introduced to a communications channel to the Iranians, I had to combine the *Leviathan* operation with the Iranian electromagnetic pulse attack capability. The inspiration was divine. My purpose was clear."

"Go on," Jake said. "Your purpose. What was it?"

"I did this as an enlightenment and an awakening," Salem said. "I did it for the sake of humanity."

"You bastard!" Renard said. "How do you awaken people by driving them to starvation and killing?"

"I regret that I had to take the lives of warriors, but the thousands who died..."

"Thirteen thousand," Renard said. "You killed thirteen thousand people at last count."

Jake felt Renard's frustration rising.

"I am given both credit and blame for this, but it is undeserved. That people chose to kill each other for food, that people chose to ignore neighbors in need, that so-called countrymen raped, beat, and stole from each other is the result of me having done no more than turned the mirror upon yourselves."

"You failed to mention that people banded together," Jake said. "There were plenty of accounts of people helping each other. Even vigilante militias to protect neighbors."

"And nobody took keener note of this than I," Salem said. "America has individuals of merit. But the net result of its populace in mass is telling. You are not yet capable of sustaining yourselves when driven to rely upon your senses of community and personal reliability. The truth is ugly, but now thanks to me, exposed."

"I give little credit to a man who exposes a problem without offering a solution," Renard said.

"The solution is self-evident," Salem said. "By having exposed it, I have shown the solution. It is a change at the personal and cultural level."

"So you think you're a hero?" Renard asked.

Salem waved his palm dismissively.

"I am called this by many, but a hero's title is undeserved and irrelevant. I saw a problem, developed a resolution, and displayed the courage to see it through. I fulfilled my destiny."

"You're a madman," Renard said. "How hypocritical of you to waste an economist's insight on mass destruction and think you accomplished something righteous."

"You two strike me as noble men and worthy adversaries. We are more alike than you care to realize."

"I dislike his perspective," Renard said. "It's time to leave."

"Farewell, gentlemen," Salem said. "I will always welcome your company."

Jake let Renard take a few steps as he glanced at the prisoner. For a moment, he remembered having seen the world from a perspective more harsh and jaded than Salem's.

He looked away and followed Renard.

"Do you want to talk about him?" he asked.

"Not at the moment," Renard said.

"Then what?"

"You pick a topic. Just get my mind off that rat."

"Nick said you were in danger."

Renard stopped.

"Did he?"

"Yeah, Pierre. That's the omen he threw at me before we went out with the *Mercer*. He just gave me an update."

Renard inhaled and sighed.

"I was trying to spare you the burden of knowing. I was diagnosed with lung cancer prior to our operation with the *Mercer*," Renard said. "But in the six months since our return, it seems to have reversed course."

"Why didn't you tell me?"

"I wasn't sure I wanted to fight it."

"That's why you were on and off with the cigarettes."

"I'm off now. For good. Our work on the *Mercer* reminded me that I will always be able to find a purpose."

"Good, Pierre. Because you're the best friend I've ever had. I don't know what I would do without you."

"That is one reason I am determined to survive.

"Have you undergone any treatment?" he asked.

"One round of chemotherapy. That's all."

"How well has it reversed course?"

Renard smiled.

"I think I just may pull through."

Jake called the CIA officer that had replaced Olivia as his watchdog and told the young man he was driving to Charlotte, North Carolina.

He entered a familiar suite of the Westin Charlotte Hotel and leapt onto the plush king sized bed's satin sheets. Alone, he called his brother.

"Hi, Nick," he said. "How are you?"

"Fine."

"Do you have any sense about Pierre?" Jake asked.

"You know," Nick said, "I had a dream about him last night. I felt a sense of enlightenment. I can't be sure, but something important might have happened for him."

"If I tell you what I think it might be, will it ruin your radar?"

"It might. Don't tell me. I just think something turned around for him."

"Like a few months ago, perhaps?"

"No," Nick said. "No, it was recent. Within days."

"His life's been pretty uneventful recently."

"Were you with him recently?"

"Yeah. Yesterday."

"Something you said to him mattered."

"Oh."

Jake sat up on the bed.

"Look, Nick. I've been thinking. I would like you to spend some time with me."

"You mean like living together?"

"Yeah, like that. Only I'm not sure where."

"That's a tough one," Nick said. "I have friends and clients here, and you have limits on where you can live."

"I just want us to consider the concept. I bet we can make something work."

"Well, where are you going to be in the next few weeks?" Nick asked.

"That depends," Jake said, "on what happens in the next few hours."

Jake withdrew a wrinkled business card from an old travel bag and went online to map the address. He dressed in his best Armani sport coat and slacks but left his long hair shaggy.

On the curb, he had a doorman hail him a cab. He expected to feel nervous on the ride but felt calm as the taxi dropped him off at a hair salon.

It was Saturday, and the salon was busy.

A woman wearing a sleek black stylist's smock with voluptuous and pronounced curves tended to a patron at her chair. Her straight dark hair reached shoulder length, and her swarthy arms moved with graceful purpose around the head of her customer.

A receptionist stopped him.

"Who's your appointment with?" she asked.

"Linda. Please let her know I'm here."

"Your name please?"

"Uh, Jacob Jones."

The receptionist angled between stylists and reached the Iraqi-American chambermaid that Jake had met long ago. Linda looked up from her chair and recognized him. She followed the receptionist back to the storefront.

"Mister Jones," she said. "It's good to see you again. You look familiar? Where did we meet?"

"At your other job. Maybe eight or nine months ago."

"Well, I'm glad you're here. Did you want to schedule an appointment? I'm unfortunately booked today."

Jake reached into his breast pocket for a money clip and pulled out hundred dollar bills. He pinched two of them between his fingers and brandished them.

"I really, really want to see you now."

Linda's eyes lit up.

"That's a lot for a cutting a man's hair."

"You're taking my beard off, too. Remember how you said the mountain man thing doesn't work? I want you to take me back to normal."

"I'm glad the mountain man thing isn't normal. I don't like it."

"It's not me."

"Okay, I'll have someone finish up a client I'm working on now. I can move my schedule and get you in my chair in fifteen minutes."

"Good, and if you like what you see when you're done with me, you're going to have to join me for dinner."

"My kids."

"I'll pay for a babysitter."

"I can't ask you to."

Jake reached again for the money clip and showed her ten more hundred dollar bills.

"I'm filthy rich, but I would give away half of it for a woman as beautiful and strong as you to listen to my story and care."

She blushed and her tone became soft. The pupils of her brown eyes opened and invited his gaze. He sensed a connection.

"I think that will be possible," she said. "And for less than half your fortune."

He reached for his eyes, scratched out his brown contact lenses, and tossed them to the garbage.

"Blue eyes!" she said. "Beautiful."

"Thanks," he said. "And I can't wait to tell you why I no longer give a damn about this annoying mountain man look while you rid me of it."

"Great. That sounds like fun. Take a seat Mister Jones, and I'll get you in my chair as soon as I can."

"That's not my name," he said. "That's what I wrote on the hotel ledger and what I just told your receptionist, but it's a lie, like my contacts, beard, and hair."

"This is getting interesting. What's your real name?"

"My name," he said. "My name is Jake Slate."

THE END

About the Author

After his graduation from the Naval Academy in 1991, John Monteith's career in the U.S. Navy included service aboard a nuclear ballistic missile submarine, and a tour as a top-rated instructor of combat tactics at the U.S. Naval Submarine School. Since his transition to civilian life, he has continued to pursue his interest in cutting-edge technology. He currently lives in the Detroit area, where he works in engineering management when he's not busy cranking out high-tech naval action thrillers.

Novels by John Monteith include ROGUE AVENGER, ROGUE BETRAYER, and ROGUE CRUSADER.

Also From Stealth Books...

JEFF EDWARDS

**brings you more white-hot naval action
from the pages of**

the Sea Warrior Files...

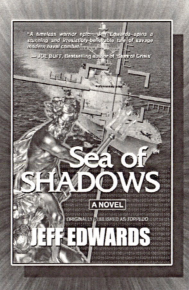

SEA OF SHADOWS

The only way to survive is to change the rules...

www.StealthBooks.Com

232-7661

Jim Clyspenger

Vic Sister of
Guith?

CPSIA information can be obtained at www.ICGtesting.com
Printed in the USA
LVOW122136270912

300675LV00001B/160/P